BABY STEPS

BABY STEPS

HONEYMOON SERIES, BOOK 5

LILY ZANTE

AUTHOR'S NOTE

'*Baby Steps*' is the fifth and final book in the '*Honeymoon Series*'.

I have also written a spin-off series called the '*Italian Summer Series*' which tells the stories of some of the minor characters who first appeared in the '*Honeymoon Series*'.

The timelines of both series are connected and you can find the recommended reading order here.

Honeymoon Series:

Honeymoon for One
Honeymoon for Three
Honeymoon Blues
Honeymoon Bliss
Baby Steps
Honeymoon Series (Books 1-3)

Italian Summer Series:

(A spin-off from the Honeymoon Series)

It Takes Two
All That Glitters
Fool's Gold
Roman Encounter
November Sun
New Beginnings
Italian Summer Series (Books 1-4)

CHAPTER ONE

"Don't tell me there *might* be a problem," Nico snapped as he sat in his study, silently cursing to himself.

He'd sneaked a call to his project manager, Bruno, while Elisabetta was sleeping. "Tell me you can do it, and then get it done." He coughed, and then instinctively touched the side of his chest where the tube had been inserted. He was on the mend now and back to normal, but it had been a long six weeks since his car accident.

And he was still *pissed*.

Pissed that the Cazale Ravenna, his new spa hotel, still wasn't open for business, pissed because every moment it remained closed, it sucked up money, pissed because he needed to get back into the swing of things and it was impossible to concentrate on his work, to have conference calls, or business calls while everyone else was at home; his wife, his daughter, his mother-in-law and his housekeeper.

Now, only two days into the New Year, he was more desperate than ever to get back to the Casa Adriana, the main family hotel and his main place of business.

"All I'm saying is that we're on a tight deadline as it is,

especially if you still want to open next month. We've still got to re-paper, re-paint and re-plaster all the affected walls."

"We *will* open next month."

"We don't even have a date for the next inspection, Nico. Those people take their time."

"I don't care how difficult it is," Nico replied through gritted teeth. "I just want it done. Use your contact." Bruno's friend in the health and safety department was the one who'd alerted them to why the hotel might have failed its safety check. Armando Vieri—his malicious ex-girlfriend's new lover and a politician old enough to be her father—had meddled in things which were none of his business. Nico was sure of it, though he didn't have the hard proof to back up his assumption.

"Hear me out," Bruno insisted. "You don't want to mess up again." There was a slight pause before he back tracked. "Not that you messed up—"

"I didn't mess up." It wasn't illegal to have old wiring. Nico had been told by his architects and builders that it was fine, but in hindsight, he should have had all bases covered. His father would have. But Edmondo wasn't here now and this project, this supposed new offering in the Cazale chain of hotels, was something he had a lot riding on.

His reputation for one thing. People were watching him, the press and business people. Nico was certain they were all waiting for him to fall flat on his face and because of that he was more determined than ever to prove them wrong.

A lot had happened this year; meeting Ava, falling in love, his father's death, his marriage and the subsequent birth of their daughter. Thankfully Elisabetta's arrival had taken his mind off what had happened and distracted him from the pain and inconvenience of his injuries. He'd nearly missed her birth because as he'd raced to the hospital upon learning that Ava had gone into labor.

The car accident—completely his fault—could have been fatal and he might never have seen Elisabetta.

All this he blamed on Silvia and Vieri. He had tried to put on a brave face about it but his resentment towards those vipers simmered not too far below the surface.

"The inspectors will be stricter this time around," Bruno warned, interrupting his train of thought. Nico pursed his lips tighter together. Forced to agree, he grunted. "Yes." Bruno had a point. "Which is why you must ensure it's done properly."

Nico lowered his head, contemplating events. Bruno was damn good at his job and more importantly, he wasn't a 'yes' man. Nico didn't need any more of those around. He wanted results and he wanted people who could do the job and Bruno was the right man for it.

"Do your best," said Nico, knowing that his irritation was misdirected. It wasn't only the delay in the hotel's opening that annoyed him. He hated not being able to do things at full capacity. He wasn't used to being incapacitated. He was used to rushing around, being capable, having a body that was in peak fitness and while his recovery had been good, resting at home when so much needed to be done, had made him a brooding menace.

For the first two weeks he'd been too weak and incapacitated to ponder on the recent turn of events. He'd had trouble breathing but at least he was alive. Elisabetta's arrival had helped but those early weeks had been a blur.

Elsa, his mother-in-law had arrived soon after and had been a huge help to them both and yet he wasn't the only one who was trying to get back to normal. Ava was also recovering from the birth which hadn't been easy.

Their first Christmas together as a married couple had

been quiet and they'd ushered in the New Year without any fanfare. But now that the holiday period was almost over, he felt the pressure starting to build up again. Each day the Cazale Ravenna remained closed, it was costing him money.

He found himself caught up in the same vicious circle thinking the same vicious thoughts until Elisabetta's soft cries caught his attention.

"Is that Elisabetta?" Bruno asked.

Nico exhaled slowly, a softness melting his tense body. "Yes." It was his beautiful little girl.

"She's loud," said Bruno, laughing.

"She has a pair of lungs on her that would put me to shame," Nico said as the baby's cries grew louder.

Bruno chuckled.

"She can be a handful, sometimes, but she's a beautiful handful." These random bouts of crying that she would suddenly break into—Ava said it was 'colic'—these were hard to deal with. But for the most part, he had enjoyed being at home; though the resentment he felt towards what had happened tainted his enjoyment of being a new father.

He stepped out of his study and into the large hallway entrance, cocking his head towards the direction of the kitchen. During the day, Ava was usually downstairs and they would set the Moses basket in the part of the dining room that connected to the kitchen. Ava often set up her laptop on the large kitchen table.

His irritation rose with the pitch of Elisabetta's howls. *Where was Ava?* He hoped she wasn't back on her computer in her study upstairs, sneaking a look at her emails. There was no need for her to work and he couldn't understand why she insisted on it.

He flexed his fingers. He couldn't think amidst this noise and this, mixed in with him being cooped up at home for so long had made him jittery. Impatient. Frustrated. He walked into the dining room and Elisabetta's cries amplified.

"It sounds like you need to go," Bruno offered. "We can talk about this tomorrow."

Nico shook his head. How was he supposed to get his business back in order when he couldn't even think in peace? "We need to discuss this properly," he said, making a decision there and then. "I'll come by on Monday."

"Already?" Bruno sounded surprised. "Shouldn't you be resting?"

"Any more rest will kill me." Just then, Elisabetta's cries turned into a whimper.

"Don't put yourself through the headache, Nico. I've got everything under control."

"I'm sure you have."

"I can keep you updated."

"I know," replied Nico. "But I'll be over all the same." He wasn't surprised that his project manager didn't sound keen for him to show up on site. They'd had over a month without him and he was anxious to see for himself how they were getting on. The cellphone recordings of the work in progress that Bruno often sent him, and the daily updates didn't give Nico peace of mind.

"You're the boss," said Bruno as Nico wandered into the kitchen.

"And don't you forget it. I'll see you on Monday." He hung up and stared at Ava. She was sitting at the kitchen table with the laptop in front of her and the baby at her breast.

CHAPTER TWO

"That's better, isn't it?" Ava cooed softly. She looked up to find Nico watching her. "She needs feeding every two hours."

"She does." A half-smile settled on his face as he looked out of the kitchen window.

Did the sight of her breastfeeding put him off that much?

She couldn't dispute that he was attentive and caring but she was still silently disappointed.

She had expected more.

She had expected him to have been more hands on, warmer and more considerate. She had tried to be the same for him. Outwardly nothing had changed much, but she sensed a subtle shift in him which was getting harder to blame on his accident and business problems.

"She was crying for a while," he said. "Where were you?"

"In the shower." *Where were you?* "Helena was here when I left. She's probably sorting out the laundry." Having their housekeeper around, as well as her mother meant more eyes and ears on the baby.

"I was on a call with Bruno," he explained.

"More updates?" He was always on the phone to Gina or Bruno; most of the time it didn't feel as though he was really here for her.

"You know how it is," said Nico. Yes, she knew exactly how it was. He was here in body but he might as well have been at work for the amount of time he spent brooding and mulling over business matters. "I'll need to go to Ravenna on Monday."

"Don't you think you're taking too much on?" But even as she posed the question she knew it was futile to ask this of a man who always took too much on. The fact that he was recovering from his accident hadn't seemed to slow him down in any way. "I mean you're still not—"

"I need to go in, Ava. I can't sit around waiting for the business to collapse."

"Nico," she murmured softly, sensing his resentment and trying to make him see that things weren't as dire as he thought. "Your business isn't about to collapse. You need to get well first."

"I *am* well." He tapped his fingers on the worktop. She didn't understand why he couldn't take this time off and spend it with them without worrying about his hotel. Too much had happened in the last few months and while she understood his anger and frustration, she had expected that the arrival of their first child would have made him realize that there was much to be thankful for.

She'd hoped to have a wonderful Christmas and New Year and while it had been different, having a new baby and being in a different country, the festive season hadn't quite lived up to her expectations. Her husband didn't make a good patient and his obvious frustration which stemmed from work matters made him moody.

He wasn't the same Nico she knew, the man she had

fallen in love with. These days he seemed more of a desperate man constrained by the limitations of his healing body and eager for the hotel to be operational as soon as possible.

It was as if he couldn't make allowances for his recovery, nor see the point of slowing down and obeying the doctor's orders.

In the days after they'd come home from the hospital, he had been a walking, barely talking, simmering well of resentment. She understood that the root of his anger had been his former girlfriend, Silvia Azzarone, and her new lover, the ageing dinosaur of a politician, Armando Vieri. Nico blamed them for meddling in his affairs, for somehow influencing the decisions of the safety department and of having a hand in failing the safety check on his soon-to-be-opened spa hotel.

She didn't know what to believe and many times she feared that her husband was becoming obsessed by his ambitious grand plans.

What she resented the most was that he seemed to take out his frustrations on her. She didn't like this side to him, and it unnerved her, as a new mother who was herself frazzled and overwhelmed by the demands of a new baby. She, too, was busy with her online business. Sales had exploded and she could no more shut down her business than Nico could walk away from his hotel problems, but she didn't let her business pressures determine her moods.

"Can't you take it easy for one more week?" she pleaded. "Work part-time hours again, if only for this week." That's all she was asking. He'd been going into work for one to two days each week before Christmas, but he also spent most of the time conducting business from home.

Like her, he never switched off completely. He usually

spent the mornings in his ground floor study, while she brought her laptop into the kitchen and flitted around, tending to the baby while keeping an eye on things. But in the afternoons, once the US office opened, she moved her laptop to her own study upstairs and tried to work there, stealing pockets of time while Elisabetta napped.

"I can't sit around any longer, Ava. I have a business to run and I can't leave it all to Gina. We open next month and I can't have another delay. I can't. I *need* to be there."

Elsa kept telling her that a lack of sleep and tiredness from tending to a new baby would be difficult, that it would bring out the worst in her if she wasn't careful and that it would cloud her judgment, but Nico's sour moods were beginning to wear her down. She tried to remember her mom's advice, but it wasn't always easy, especially when her husband always seemed more concerned about his business than his wife and child.

"Sit around?" Her indignation flared. "You say it as if it were a prison sentence, spending time at home with me and the baby."

"That's not what I meant." He took a step towards her as she switched her baby to the other breast.

He cleared his throat and turned his head away. "You're busy. I'll let you feed her first." Once more she felt as if the sight of her feeding Elisabetta repulsed him and the thought upset her even more. "Do you want to do the next feed?" she offered. "I expressed some milk earlier." She wanted to see if he would turn and look at her again but he continued to stare at the floor instead.

"Okay." But his voice was flat, and she feared that he had no interest. It left her feeling even more disillusioned. What had she been hoping for? That there would be lots of time for them to talk and grow closer? That they would spend their days counting their blessings and being thankful for this beautiful new chapter in their life? Here she was, a frumpy woman in a loose-fitting maternity top and she felt increasingly insecure, unsure and unattractive. Once more she came back to the thing that gnawed at her the most whenever she felt low; she'd only known Nico a year and in that year they'd already had more life changes than most people experienced in five. She'd known Connor for years before he'd shown his true colors.

Could it be that she was seeing Nico's true colors now? Worse, had she made the same mistake again?

Her mother had been right. Her tiredness and constant fretting over Elisabetta kept her nerves frayed. She didn't allow herself to rest either and whenever the baby slept, she used that time to work. But she had to put on a brave face, needing to show her mother and Nico that it was easy to juggle the baby with her business; to do otherwise would be to fail. She sensed that both her mother and Nico disapproved of her constant attention to the business.

She stared down at Elisabetta's mass of dark hair and touched it softly. Her baby made sucking noises, and Ava felt the heaviness in her breasts slowly drain away. Nico rubbed his brow and made to walk away. "I need to get back into it. I wish you would understand."

"I'm trying to."

"Maybe later, when it's all running smoothly. When Elisabetta's a little older maybe we can take some time away for a family vacation."

"Maybe," she said, watching him walk away. He'd dismissed her concerns easily and wasn't interested in slowing down.

He'd taken too much on. Not only did he now have full

responsibility for the string of hotels his father had left him, but this new venture of his—the spa hotel—consumed all his time and energy.

Something new, he said. Something different. Something his father hadn't tried before. She was all too aware of her husband's high ambitions and his raging desire to prove that he could run his father's empire as well as his father had, but he had nothing to prove to anyone.

Though Edmondo had passed on many months ago, it seemed as if Nico's grief and anger for his father's sudden and unexpected death still festered. She knew that Nico wouldn't rest until he'd turned the spa hotel into a resounding success.

Lately, they just seemed to rub one another the wrong way. It was just as well that Nico's home was huge; this beautiful, sprawling and elegant mansion, set in acres of greenery boasted a magnificent avenue of cypress trees and fountains and statues. Sometimes it was a relief to take the baby out in the stroller and walk around the grounds in order to distance herself from her husband's moody temperament. It meant that even when the two of them were at home, they could easily spend the whole day without seeing one another.

"There you are." Elsa took one look at her and walked over to the sink where she filled up a tall glass with water. "I've told you that when you're feeding, you need to drink and you need to drink a lot."

"She was crying," Ava explained, "and I rushed out of the shower."

"Where was Nico?" Elsa took a seat across the large rectangular wooden table.

"On the phone."

"I was outside, sitting under the cherry tree," Elsa explained.

"Were you lost in your thoughts again, Mom?"

"I was thinking happy thoughts. Don't you start worrying about me. I'm fine."

But Ava *did* worry. It hadn't even been a year yet since Nico's father had passed away and she knew that even though her mom tried hard to put a mask over her feelings, she was still coming to terms with his death.

Their's had been the start of a beautiful friendship and sometimes Ava wondered if there might have been the seeds of something more. Her mother never disclosed anything but that wistful look on her face whenever there was talk about Edmondo said more than a thousand words ever could.

Edmondo's death had left a huge gaping hole, not only in her and Nico's lives, and Elisabetta's—who would never know a grandfather—but it had also touched Elsa's life. Ava was ever mindful that while her mother liked to visit Verona, her time here was now embroidered with threads of regret, of memories that she grasped at, and of a man and a friendship that were no more.

"Happy thinking is good, Mom, but if you feel sad, you have to let yourself *feel* it."

"I do, honey." Her mother patted her hand. "I don't need you to see it, not with so much on your plate, and anyway, that man doesn't let me stay sad for too long." Ava had a sense of foreboding at the idea of her mom having conversations with an imaginary Edmondo.

"That new gardener is making more mess in those gardens than anything else."

"He's not so new, Mom, and I'm pretty sure he knows what he's doing."

"He likes to think he does."

"Since when did you take up gardening?" Ava asked, astonished.

"I know enough to know when he's making a mess."

Ava winced. Her mother seemed to be more than a little attached to the gardens at the Casa Adriana these days and she behaved as if they were hers. Nico found it amusing and had told Ava to let her mom be. "It reminds her of my father," Nico told her once when she mentioned it to him. "If she finds any comfort in that place, you should leave her be. I doubt that Salvatore is offended by it."

"Nico's thinking of going back to work full-time next week," Ava announced.

"So soon?"

"That's what I told him, but you know how he is. He's more obsessed than ever with getting the hotel open. He seems to have taken this obsession to another level."

"He's been away from it for a long time, Ava. It can't be easy for him."

"It's not easy watching him getting so uptight about it either. I thought he might have enjoyed this time with us, with me and Elisabetta. I thought this was what he wanted."

"It *is*," her mother replied, leaning forward and smiling at the baby who was now starting to doze off. Babies had such a simple and untroubled life; feeding, sleeping and pooping. Ava wished her life could be that simple. "It doesn't feel that way," she grumbled.

"You don't see the way he looks at you."

"With disgust."

"Nonsense." Elsa looked up at her. "With pride."

"Pride?" Ava didn't seem convinced.

"That man needs you right now, honey, even if he's not showing you in a way that is obvious."

"Sometimes I just can't tell." Ava wasn't convinced and instead she looked down again at the bundle of softness that was snuggled up to her chest. She loved the way her baby held on to her finger, as if she was holding onto it for dear life. At times Ava found herself surprised that she was a mother—that she'd done it, reached this milestone in her life—that she now had a baby who depended on her.

Her whole world had stopped the moment Elisabetta had been born and Ava's life now revolved solely around her baby. It was frightening and uplifting all at the same time. Of course, it also meant that she didn't have as much time, or mental and emotional energy for Nico. Maybe that was why she felt a little distanced from him.

"He's put a lot into that building—his heart and soul from the sounds of it and he wants it to work out. And now with all this trouble surrounding it, he can't rest until it does. You're no different, honey. You two are more alike than you know. You have sleepless nights when your shipments don't reach Denver in time."

Ava shrugged. She knew it was the truth. And yet ...

"I imagine he's losing more than money," said Elsa. "His reputation, and what others might think."

Her mother was right. Wrapped up in his grand plans for the Cazale Ravenna were Nico's ambitions. It wasn't only that he'd wanted to prove himself to Edmondo, he also wanted to show the world. He wanted to prove that he had moved on from his playboy days. That he wasn't just a rich kid who got lucky when he inherited his father's wealth.

"I can't wait for it to be open and done with." Ava wiped Elisabetta's mouth. "One more month," she said, placing her hand under the baby's chin and rubbing her back.

"It's not too long to wait. Here, let me have her." Elsa got up and reached for the baby. "Let Grandma do this. It's the one thing I can help with." Ava carefully handed the baby over and adjusted her own clothing.

"Now that I've got her," said Elsa. "Why don't you go and take a nap?"

Ava headed towards the door.

Take a nap? Not a chance. She had a mountain of emails from Rona and Kim to deal with.

CHAPTER THREE

I t felt like home.

The next day Nico walked across the black and white checked marble floor of the lobby at the Casa Adriana and felt the tension slip away the moment he'd stepped inside. Over by the reception desk Gina was talking to the new receptionist. She smiled at him warmly as he approached. "Happy New Year, Nico."

"Happy New Year," replied Nico, acknowledging both women. "I need a few moments of your time, when you're free."

"I'm free now," she said, and excused herself from the receptionist. She followed him into his office. "What are you doing here?"

"Getting ready for my return."

"Shouldn't you still take it easy?"

"No," he replied, emphatically. "I've had enough time off."

"I could have sworn you had another two weeks off."

"Working a few days here and there isn't going to solve our problems or make us money." He'd come to work for a few days here and there in December. Once to welcome the new members of his management team, and then he'd worked one or two days in the weeks leading up to Christmas. His driver had taken him to Ravenna a month ago, because he was anxious to check up on the spa hotel but between these scattered visits, he'd barely been here. He knew there would be many things to oversee on his return. "Things are starting to pile up and working from home is getting harder."

"It must be difficult pulling yourself away from that beautiful little baby of yours," Gina said.

"Yes," he replied, smiling. "But I have too much to do, and I need to get on with it."

Gina's eyebrows shot upwards. "You don't look completely well, Nico. Besides, I've got everything under control."

"I know. I have faith in you." He clasped his hands together. He couldn't run this place without Gina. She was the lynchpin of the company and always had been. They spoke every day, often several times during the day, and she kept him updated with how things were getting on here at the Casa Adriana, their main hotel, as well as the other sister hotels around Italy.

He'd been hoping to alleviate some of her workload because she'd been doing more than her fair share of work for a long time. As it was, she'd already helped the new members of their management team to settle in.

"This place only runs because of you." It was the one thing he always said to her.

"We both know that's not really true," she replied, dismissing his words easily, the way she always did. "You look thinner," she commented, examining him carefully. "I can save you the time and tell you that everything is running smoothly."

"I'm sure it is. How are Ines and Demetrio getting on?"

"They're settling in fine. Ines is amazing. She has some smart ideas and she's done very well to get up to speed with the sales campaigns you and that ad agency were working on."

"That's good to hear."

"She's been working through the media packages and press releases, and she has ideas for the website and the social media campaigns, but she needs guidance. You'll need to sit down with her at some stage, when you're well enough."

He'd been lucky to get Ines. She had previous experience of working with branding and advertising for luxury hotels and he had the feeling she would do well here. He needed someone to take control of the marketing because he could no longer do everything.

"I *am* well enough."

"Don't push yourself too hard, Nico. You don't look one hundred percent as it is. But enough talk about work." She sat up in her chair, excitement spreading across her face. "Tell me about Elisabetta and Ava. How are they?"

Nico couldn't help but smile each time he thought of them. "They're doing well. Ava's finding it difficult but that's because Elisabetta seems to want to feed every few hours. I didn't know babies could get so hungry."

Gina shrugged. "I don't have any experience with babies."

"Ava's doing a wonderful job but I know she's not sleeping much."

"It can't be easy."

"It isn't. I want to help, but I end up getting in the way. I've offered to wake up and do the 2am feed, but Ava won't let me."

Gina nodded. "That's because she wants you to get well first."

"I suppose it is." Most of this last month had passed by so

fast that most things were still a blur to him. He knew Ava was struggling but he felt helpless most of the time. The baby seemed to cry whenever he held her and it seemed that only Ava's magic touch, usually her breast, helped soothe her. One of his friends, a father of twins, had told him this was natural and to be expected, and this advice had made Nico feel a little better.

"I don't know how she does it," Gina commented. "Keeping an eye on her business at the same time as looking after a newborn."

He rubbed his jaw. "She doesn't need to do both, but I can't stop her from working on her store."

"You're both as bad as each other."

His wife was spreading herself too thin, trying to keep up with work and look after the baby. Ava thought he didn't notice when she—after feeding the baby—would be on her computer. A few times he'd gotten out of bed to find her hunched over the keyboard at 3am or some other ridiculous hour. She didn't need to work. He had more than enough to take care of them, to give her a fabulous life. She could easily become a lady of leisure but it wasn't her plan and she was stubborn and continued to burn the candle at both ends on more than one occasion.

"You can no more expect her to give up her store than she can demand you give up the hotels, Nico."

He shook his head, not wanting to admit to the truth that Gina spoke. But she was right. He and Ava were both as bad as one another and this added more fire to their disagreements. Neither of them wanted to back down, each believing that they were right.

They hadn't made love since the birth either, and he didn't want to put any pressure on her, but he missed the intimacy. Yet as time went on, and the more he saw Elisabetta laying claim to the breasts which he'd often feasted on, it made him back away. He loved his wife but something had changed and it was far easier to dwell on the hotels that needed his attention than to work out what was going on in his relationship with his wife.

"Did the sleepers fit?" Gina wanted to know.

"Sleepers?"

"The Christmas present I gave her? The soft yellow one with carrots and the blue one with—"

"Bananas," he said. "Oh, thanks. Yes, they fit. We can never have enough, the rate at which she goes through them."

"Good."

He tapped his fingers on the desk. "How's Demetrio getting on with the upgrade project?" Nico had delivered the piece of work Demetrio was to work on—an upgrade of the software and hardware at each hotel.

"Fine, I think," Gina replied, coughing lightly.

"You think?" Nico asked, curiously. This was nothing like Gina. She was usually on top of everything and would know— like the back of her hand—where everyone was and what they were doing. "He's not keeping you informed?"

"He's getting on with it as far as I can tell."

Nico wasn't sure what to make of this. From his resume and past credentials, the guy seemed like the perfect candidate and was well placed to carry out this project himself. That was what Nico wanted to test. The work he'd asked him to do didn't exactly fit what would usually be expected for the role of Chief Technical officer but Nico needed to see how Demetrio would cope and whether he could get his hands dirty. Above all, Nico wanted to see if the man could deliver a project by being in the trenches. In time, he'd get to manage his own team, but these were early days for the new team and Nico needed workers more than he needed managers. He and Gina had been wearing too many hats.

"He's got a computer studies degree from one of the best colleges in Italy," Nico remarked.

"And he won't let you forget it, either," Gina remarked, testily.

He grinned. "If there's anyone who can put him in his place, I'm sure you will." With this new team working together, he and Gina could concentrate on other things instead of being responsible for everything. He could concentrate his efforts completely on the spa hotel and right now, with all that had happened, this was the main priority. He needed to get the Cazale Ravenna operational, and he had his sights set on bigger things. He had plans to buy more hotels.

"You don't find this isolating?" he asked, waving his hand around her office. He'd had two of the utility rooms converted into two offices; a smaller one for Gina and the second, a larger one, for Ines and Demetrio to share.

"Isolation isn't necessarily a bad thing and I like having my own office."

"Me too," he agreed. "And the best thing about it is not having any baby interruptions." He got up. "I'll show my face and get re-acquainted with our new team members."

"Is the re-wiring done yet?" Gina asked. "At the Cazale Ravenna?"

"Almost." That was one of the things he would get to find out for sure with his planned visit.

"I forgot to tell you," said Gina. "Silvia came in a few weeks ago."

He scowled at the mention of her name. "Here?"

Gina nodded. "Yes."

"What for?" He was secretly relieved he hadn't been here to see his scheming ex.

"Afternoon tea, that's what she said."

He felt a tightness in his eyes. "Was she alone, or did she have that scumbag with her?"

"She was with a girlfriend. It looked like a casual visit but she did ask one of the receptionists if you were around."

"I wish that interfering little gold digger would leave me in peace."

CHAPTER FOUR

"They were a great discovery," Kim told her. "Our customers love the d'Este cribs, Ava. You've found a real winner there."

It was great news. "Excellent!" she cried. "That's exactly what we need." A hot product selling like crazy. The last shipment she'd sent out had been for two thousand cribs and it had arrived in Denver the week before Christmas. Having the new warehouse in the US was a godsend and it meant that she could keep her inventory well stocked now that they had a proper holding area for it. "Have we shipped any of these out yet?"

"No," replied Kim. "We've still got some from the last shipment. It won't be long though."

"These are a winner," declared Ava as she examined the dried-up patch of milk on her shoulder. She'd been looking at her online data late last night after she'd fed the baby at 2am. Her visitor figures were through the roof and her sales were amazing.

So what if she was sitting in her study in a pair of sweats and a dirty baggy sweatshirt and hadn't run a brush through her hair? Who could say she wasn't making it work? She was dealing with motherhood and running a flourishing business and it had all happened in the space of a year.

The sudden reminder of the passage of time jolted her. It had been around this time last year that Connor had told her he no longer wanted to marry her; that he didn't love her and in doing so had set off a chain of events which had led her to where she was now.

She was so much happier. *Wasn't she?*

"We have another delivery arriving," said Kim. "Gotta go."

"'Bye."

Ava hung up and then her hand hovered over her cell phone as she considered calling Nico. It was early evening and she'd expected him to have arrived back home by now. She should have called him to make sure he'd reached Ravenna safely—there was no reason to suspect otherwise, and he wasn't driving himself there. Yet her hand lingered. She'd been busy with the baby, and her work. He was being driven to Ravenna and had no baby to look after. He could have called her if he really wanted to.

He's fine, she told herself. *And this will pass.* This feeling of disconnect that had slowly seeped into their life, along with Nico's accident, and the hotel setbacks, and Elisabetta's drawn out birth.

This wasn't how things used to be.

They hadn't made love since then and the distance between them wasn't only in their physical expression. Emotionally, they seemed to have drifted apart. At night, while they lay in bed, they talked and snuggled but whenever Nico turned to kiss her or initiated anything, which hadn't been often, she told him she was tired.

She wasn't lying either. On more than a few occasions

he'd slept on his side turned away from her and she was often in and out of bed, feeding the baby, or tending to her. When she returned to bed, the only thing Ava craved was to lie down and sleep.

Sex was the last thing on her mind. And yet she wanted to have Nico's big, strong arms around her while they lay in bed. She missed snuggling up against his chest but hadn't attempted to in case he wanted more. Giving birth had turned her insides to mush, or so it had felt like that for days after. She'd been afraid to go to the bathroom for fear of everything '*down there*' falling out. Sex, most definitely was the last thing on her mind.

She was about to go back upstairs when she heard the doorbell, then Helena's voice and a voice that sounded like Andrea's.

What was she doing here?

For a second she was surprised, wondering if she'd missed a meeting or had forgotten something.

"She's in the kitchen," Helena announced, just as Ava walked out into the hallway. Her face broke out into a smile at the sight of her friend.

"Andrea!" They hugged and Ava was the first to draw away quickly, feeling messy in her milk-stained clothes. "Well, this is a nice surprise," she cried. "I'm happy to see you, but did I miss something? A meeting or—?"

"This isn't a business call," Andrea replied. "Is this a bad time?" The top-to-toe glance her friend gave her didn't go unnoticed by Ava, and she immediately regretted not having brushed her hair properly and having tied it up into a messy ponytail. Normally she would have made *some* effort, but Nico was out for the day and she'd been more concerned with getting as much work done as possible away from his disapproving eyes.

"Are you kidding? It's never a bad time where you're concerned. I'm so happy to see you." And she was, despite her own pitiful appearance.

"I was hoping you'd say that," replied Andrea, happily. Ava smoothed down her hair and noted Andrea's camel colored cashmere coat and stylish handbag. She stood with her arms wrapped around herself, in a comfort pose, and felt the soft rolls around her waist, vowing to get back into running when she had more time. She didn't relish living in sweats and loose clothing forever. Not as the wife of Nico Cazale. She smiled and sucked in her breath, squeezing her stomach against her spine.

"Can I see the baby?"

"Sure." Ava looked around then pointed upstairs. "My mom was feeding her." She led the way upstairs to the nursery and opened the door to find her mom sitting in the glider with a sleeping angel in her arms. Ava's heart melted, the way it always did when she saw her daughter. She had never known this pull—this invisible, tight cord, a connection she had never felt before. Nothing in her life up to now had made her feel this protective and vulnerable at the same time. Elsa opened her eyes and smiled acknowledging them as Andrea mouthed a quiet 'hello' in return.

"She almost always falls asleep during a feeding," Ava whispered.

"She's adorable," cried Andrea, her face glowing as she stared at Elsa and the baby.

"She's not so adorable when she's crying continuously and can't be stopped."

"She's beautiful and she looks like you and Nico."

"I would hope so," Ava replied, grinning at the odd comment which so many people often made. Who else did they expect a baby to look like if not its parents?

"She's grown so much since we last saw her." Andrea and her business partner, Leo, had visited them at home a few days before Christmas. She and Nico would never forget the support that these two friends had given to her and Nico while they'd both been in hospital—Nico from his accident and Ava giving birth. It had been the most worrisome of times and the happiest.

"Could I hold her?"

"You could," Ava replied, with slight hesitation, "but maybe another time. I don't want to risk waking her." She now understood why Rona had always longed for the times when her daughter, Tori, had gone down for a nap. Only a mother knew the sheer bliss of that window of quiet time when a child was asleep. "Let's have some coffee and then we can see if she wakes up."

"I'll bring her down if she wakes up," said Elsa.

"Shall I put her in her crib. Mom?"

"Let me hold her for a while," Elsa replied, and she looked as if she didn't want to move from the glider. "Go and enjoy a good catch up with Andrea. You've been longing for some adult company." Her mother and friend smiled at one another.

"You're not in a rush are you?" Ava asked as they walked down the stairs. She was glad to have some company for a change other than her mom or the baby, or Nico to talk to. Apart from a few walks outside with the baby in a stroller, she didn't venture out daily and now, after many weeks, she was beginning to suffer from the effects of minimal interaction with the outside world.

"No," Andrea replied, slipping off her coat when they were in the kitchen. Ava couldn't help but stare at Andrea's super slim figure. She was dressed in loose fitting, wide legged Palazzo pants and a black satin blouse which hung loose and shimmering from her thin frame. She looked as if she'd fallen off the pages of a women's magazine. Ava sneaked another stare at her. "I love your outfit," she said, clearly envious.

"Thanks."

"Coffee?"

Andrea nodded.

"You're looking insanely chic for the warehouse," Ava commented as she got out the cups.

"What warehouse?" wailed Andrea.

"Sorry," replied Ava. Ever since the fire that had completely burnt down Andrea's warehouse, she and Leo had been forced to move to two smaller adjacent units around the corner from their previous location. "We're still in the two warehouses for now."

Ava looked up. "But you'll get compensation, won't you? For the fire?"

"You know what it's like, so much red tape and paperwork. We'll get the money eventually." Andrea leaned against the wall with her arms folded. "I had a meeting with Dino earlier."

Dino Massari was the smooth-talking owner of the company which made the cribs that were her best sellers. Ava's lips curled upwards into a smile. "You did, huh?" No wonder Andrea looked so gorgeous. She took the cups over to the table.

"Thanks." Andrea wrapped her fingers around the hot cup and took a sip.

"What did Mr. Massari have to say?"

"We were discussing your ever-increasing sales volume."

"Those cribs are hot sellers. I had a huge order arrive in Denver before Christmas and I won't be surprised if I have to place another one soon."

Andrea's brown eyes widened. "Really?"

"I expect them to continue to sell. We haven't actually dipped into the new shipment yet, but we'll start to in a few weeks' time—or so Kim leads me to believe." She sipped her coffee. "So, you met with him to discuss my order sizes?"

"I have to meet with my suppliers from time to time to ensure that everything is running smoothly."

"I'm glad you do." Ava shuddered to think what a problem with suppliers would mean for her. "And you dressed like *that* for the meeting?"

Was it a meeting or was it something else?

"Like what?" Andrea laughed weakly. "What's wrong with this?"

"Nothing at all." Ava smiled mischievously. "I'm sure Dino like it very much."

"Stop that! You're looking at me as if I turned up in a short skirt that barely covered my butt."

"You still haven't answered my question."

"What?"

"Is there something you want to share with me?" Ava asked, grinning.

Andrea breathed out loudly, as if she had no choice but to own up. "If you must know, Dino asked me to dinner but I had to rush back."

"Rush back for what?"

Andrea shrugged. "Oh ... you know, uh ..." She seemed to be struggling for words. "I wanted to see you. There." She nodded her head as if to convince herself.

"You avoided dinner with *him* to have a cup of coffee with *me*?" Ava snorted. She didn't buy that for a minute. "Clearly he's interested." But Andrea shook her head quickly.

"Aren't you interested? I mean, you're single again and—"

"And I'd like to stay that way."

"It has its virtues," Ava remarked. She'd tried both—being

single and being with someone and being in a relationship with a man who loved you was definitely the more appealing of all the possible statuses, even if she and Nico were going through a rough patch right now.

"I don't have time for a man in my life."

Ava nodded and smiled, not wanting to probe or offer too much advice unless Andrea asked for it. She cupped her hands around her coffee cup and took comfort in the warmth. She missed this—girl talk with a good friend. Ever since she'd moved to Verona, she had missed female company but because she'd been so busy here and had so much going on in her life—and because she'd fallen in love with Nico—she hadn't noticed it too much.

Until now.

Now that Nico was busy, and she was stuck at home, it dawned on her that she needed friends. Or even one close friend with whom she could confide in. It wasn't the same telling her mom everything that was troubling her or niggling at her. Sometimes she just wanted to have a conversation with a like-minded friend who understood her and knew where she was coming from.

Andrea was that person.

"With all this worry over your business," said Ava. "It must be a huge help having Leo around?"

"He's pretty clued into things," Andrea agreed. "And yes, I didn't realize how much easier things would be when you don't have to take on the responsibility of a business alone. It's much easier when you can share the troubles and the good times with a business partner."

It had been interesting to see Leo and Andrea together and Ava felt sure that there was more going on between the two of them than Andrea liked to let on, and so she didn't say anything, preferring to wait until her friend said something first.

"We should go out one evening," Andrea suggested.

"Go out?" Andrea might as well have asked her to fly to the moon. "That's not really an option for me at the moment."

"Your mom is here helping out and you use Lizzi sometimes, don't you?"

"She's gone back to college," replied Ava. Lizzi, the gardener's granddaughter had been a huge help for the few weeks after Elisabetta's birth. She'd kept an eye on emails and inventory in the early days when Ava had been too sore to do much of anything and recovering from giving birth.

"But your mom's here now and I'm sure Nico would love to have Elisabetta all to himself one evening while you go out. You need to get out more."

"Do I look that bad?" Ava asked, frowning. It was bad enough that she felt frumpy in her loose clothes.

"No," said Andrea. "You look mommy-ish."

"*Mommy-ish?*" Ava was disheartened to hear these words. Mommy-ish wasn't a something she aspired to look like. She wanted to look like Angelina Jolie and 'Mommy-ish' wasn't a term that came to mind with *her*. Even after giving birth to twins the woman still looked fabulous.

But Andrea was right. Ava looked down at her baggy top. Even the nursing bras she wore gave no real support and her body was loose and flabby all over. No wonder her own husband didn't try too hard to seduce her. Back in the day, sinking into bed with Nico at the end of a tiring day meant the start of other, fun activities.

Life couldn't already be going downhill now, could it?

She had yet to turn thirty.

Andrea's cheeks colored slightly. "It means you look like a real mom, putting your baby first." Her friend was doing her best to dig herself out of the hole. "But you look as if you could do with a night out."

Ava forced a smile. "I don't even know what that means anymore."

"Then let's set a date and go out and have a nice meal and catch up." But Ava couldn't conceive of getting dressed and leaving Elisabetta for a few hours. Apart from the guilt she would feel for leaving her baby at home, even if Elsa or Nico were around to look after her, she didn't like the idea of being away from her daughter. "Give me a few weeks."

Or a few months. By then, she expected this feeling of not wanting to do much, not even wanting to leave the house, to have passed. "Maybe we could go out, the four of us?"

"The *four* of us?" Andrea didn't look too excited about that proposal.

"Why not?"

"You do know that Leo and I aren't together?" Andrea asked.

"I know that. I know you're only business partners. You've drilled that into my head many times." Ava chuckled. "I'm not about to forget that anytime soon."

But maybe getting Nico out of the house might do him some good. She couldn't imagine her and Nico going for a romantic meal alone—not any time soon but maybe they both needed to go out with another couple and who better than Leo and Andrea?

CHAPTER FIVE

He'd brought along some documents to read through on the car journey to Ravenna but he was unable to concentrate and instead found himself staring out of the car window.

But this didn't help much either and only made him feel more drowsy instead. He hadn't slept too well because Elisabetta woke throughout the night and each time she stirred, or Ava got up to feed her, it also woke him up.

As hard as it was on him, it was obviously much harder on Ava and he wished she would let him take the early morning feed. But she was adamant that he needed his rest. She was good like that, but he was already up and his sleep had been broken, so he might as well have made himself useful. But it was no use arguing the point with Ava.

She wanted to move Elisabetta into the nursery next door when she was a year old, but Nico had half a mind to suggest they do it when she was maybe six months old. He understood Ava's concern to have the baby by her side and with her being so little, he didn't want her anywhere but in the same room. But he couldn't survive a year of broken sleep.

He needed to be sharper and he needed to get back into the game. He needed to get the Cazale empire flourishing and growing year after year. The media were already dismissing him as a lightweight and the playboy image was a hard one to lose.

For now, his focus was on fixing the problems. Then he would feel better about the business and himself. It hadn't been a year since Edmondo had died and already Nico had big ideas about expansion. He had his eyes on a few more plots of land in Sicily and Sardinia, and even the Amalfi coast. He wanted to build hotels throughout Italy, setting them up in areas that visitors flocked to the most; beautiful, scenic areas in picturesque settings.

He wasn't sure Ravenna was exactly a highly sought after destination yet, it wasn't one of the prettiest parts of his country, but he was determined to turn the Cazale Ravenna into a highly desirable destination for rest and recuperation.

The car pulled up outside the newly refurbished Cazale Ravenna Spa Center and Hotel, more commonly referred to as the Cazale Ravenna. The spa center was a completely new building which had been built alongside the existing and newly improved hotel and the two were connected by a glass foot tunnel. A huge forecourt in front of the main hotel spilled out and encompassed the area along the tunnel which was decked with a pond, benches and greenery. He'd tried to recreate a part of Montagnano, the beloved village he grew up in. There was a lot of land even after the spa center had been built and Nico had more grand plans, but he kept these things under wraps for now. There was no point in talking about anything else until the hotel opened. He was counting on the grand event taking place around the end of February.

Right now, it looked lifeless, even though the buildings were ready, and the grounds were well maintained. There were a few vans and workmen scattered around, due to the re-wiring project but these should not have been here. What should have been here were guests with beaming smiles, coming and going.

"You've got two hours to do what you want," Nico told his driver, "I'll call you if I finish sooner." He got out and walked slowly towards the mobile unit that served as the headquarters for Bruno and his team. His project manager had already seen the car pull up and he was now walking towards him.

"Ciao." Bruno reached out his hand, and Nico shook it with less vigor than usual. "You can't keep away, can you, Nico? Can I get you a coffee?"

"No," Nico replied, but instead of heading into the trailer, he turned to his project manager. "I want to see how the rewiring's coming along."

"Already? Don't you want to—"

"No," Nico replied. "I'd rather see the work."

"This way," Bruno replied, obviously well used to his boss's temperament.

"What's the latest update?" Nico asked and listened as he followed Bruno as they made their way to the staff quarters.

Bruno told him and Nico questioned everything, the budget, the projected finish date, the expected delays, and the expected date of the second safety check. Bruno had answers for everything. This time, Nico wanted to leave no stone unturned. The hotel *had* to open on time, no delays, no interruptions, no nasty surprises.

No interfering politician creeping out from the corners, on the pretense of lobbying for workers' rights. He was overly obsessed by the need to ensure that he had all corners covered. "We have to hit the February date," he said quietly to himself. Their publicity drive and marketing campaigns had already had to be delayed once.

"Are you sure you're going to be ready for February?" It sounded as if Bruno thought this might be a problem.

"We have to be."

'You must expect to be surprised and outsmarted at every turn,' his father had once told him, 'and it is your duty to make sure you come out winning.'

Edmondo had told him that he'd never been fond of giving an exact date for hotel openings, preferring instead to start quietly and let customers come slowly. But his father's hotels had opened decades ago and back then word of mouth recommendations spread slowly. Business was slower. Things took time. That had been the way Edmondo Cazale had always operated, but in this new world, this smaller, more connected world where word of mouth and reputation weren't as dependent on footfall but on social media reach, things could go spectacularly well, or die an embarrassing death in front of a global audience.

Once the Cazale Ravenna was open, he'd have to sit down with Ines and begin an aggressive marketing plan for the other hotels for he had as good as forgotten about them.

"The work will be finished by the end of this month, Nico, and hopefully we'll have the safety inspection soon after. I've already submitted our application but even so, expecting to open a few weeks after might be wishful thinking."

"Maybe so," replied Nico slowly. "But losing money each day is crippling me."

"We were unlucky. I have a friend who worked on a similar project and he told me that their building got inspected and passed the same day. We could have done without Armando Vieri sticking his nose in where it's not warranted."

"He's an interfering son-of-a-bitch." Nico hadn't had a

peep out of the man or Silvia since that day. But he kept an eye on the man's dealings, or as much as he was able to from reading about him in the papers and online. Vieri had done the damage and had moved onto other matters.

"Politicians," Bruno spat out the word in disgust. "Did you know he's screwing around with a blond almost half his age?"

Nico didn't answer but leaned against the wall and coughed.

"You shouldn't be here," warned Bruno. "It's a health hazard."

And for once, Nico agreed with him.

CHAPTER SIX

E lisabetta had fallen asleep as usual after her 10pm feed and Ava hoped she would stay fast asleep until 2am, or longer.

An uninterrupted night's sleep was something that Ava craved, though tonight she had other things on her mind.

Tonight, she was hoping to woo her husband back.

She'd showered and donned what she hoped was sexy but not too revealing—a midnight blue satin baby doll slip; something she hadn't bothered to wear for months. She surveyed her reflection warily. Andrea's visit last week had been the wake-up call she'd needed. Her friend looked so glamorous in such a simple but striking outfit that Ava decided to make more of an effort herself. She was always on call for her baby, and for Nico, and for her business but she had to make time for herself, too. This was something her mother had often told her but she now saw the truth for herself. Unless she made the time, the whole day would be swallowed up in taking care of everything, and everyone else.

This evening, Ava had done just that. After putting the baby to bed, she'd taken her time having a long bath, shaving her legs and underarms, and using a face masque. She'd pampered herself for the purpose of enticing Nico. The poor man's romantic attempts had been rebuffed so many times that he'd given up trying and she wondered if sexual frustration added to their current problems. It was time to get the intimacy back, now that she felt fully recovered from giving birth.

Primped and preened and shaven, with silky skin moisturized by Kukui oil and shea butter, she sashayed into their bedroom smelling like a summer bouquet. She clambered into bed from Nico's side, since the crib was lined up flush with her side of the bed.

"You're still reading?" She was pleased that he was still awake. A part of her was a little anxious, too, because it would be difficult to pull him away from his paperwork. Once, it would have been easy to command his attention, no matter what work he brought home but those days seemed to be in the past.

"I was reading through the marketing plan Ines has been working on." His head was still lowered, his mind still on his work.

"Ines?" Ava crawled seductively like a lioness, onto her side of the bed. Her heart hammered high up in her chest and she felt nervous again, like a virgin. Nico looked up momentarily, and if she was hoping he'd noticed her sexy lingerie, she was mistaken. "The new marketing manager," he replied, and immediately turned his attention to the paperwork again. "Didn't I mention her?"

"You did," she said, settling under the duvet. He continued to read but Ava wasn't going to back down so easily. She sidled closer to him. Even now, dressed down in bed, he was a handsome sight. In the past he used to wear boxers and not much else apart from an inviting look. That time seemed distant now, as if it belonged to a different man and woman. Now he wore a loose t-shirt. Tonight she hoped to change the way things had become.

"What's she like, this Ines?" Ava asked, resting her chin on Nico's shoulder and letting her breasts brush against his biceps. She ran her fingers slowly over his arm and trailed them gently down to his forearm.

"She's...she's..." He turned to look at her, a film of confusion coming over him for a moment. "She seems good at what she does and she has a lot of interesting—" He seemed to have lost his train of thought.

"She has a lot of interesting what?" Ava purred, as she continued to stroke his forearm, knowing how much he liked it.

"Ideas. She has lots of interesting ideas and Gina likes her."

"Then she obviously has something going for her." Ava dropped a kiss on his shoulder. It felt strange at first, making this move after such a long time but the old familiarity quickly returned and her heart began to gallop as lazy waves of desire rolled through her. Her senses slowly reawakened as she kissed his shoulder a second time, then trailed her lips softly down his bicep.

He made a noise, a low rumble deep in his throat, and shifted back against the headrest, throwing his paperwork onto the floor. She moved back with him, then felt his hand brush her cheek before he cupped it. It was all the reassurance she needed. In one fell swoop she straddled him, pushing his head back against the headboard and drawing courage from the hungry look he gave her. "The paperwork can wait, can't it?" she murmured, the flat of her hand resting firmly against his chest.

"Yes." He took her hand and kissed her fingers, making

her smile. The Nico she loved was slowly coming back to her. "Sit up," she ordered, overcome by a rush of bravado. He did as commanded and she lifted his t-shirt from the bottom and tried to roll it up and over him. He pulled it off himself, revealing his wide and finely sculpted chest. His stomach wasn't as flat as normal, on account of his exercise regime falling to the wayside, but still, he was a fine specimen of a man, and he was *hers*, and in *her* bed. She swallowed, the hairs along her arms and the back of her neck prickling with the excitement of being this close to her half naked husband.

"I like this," he said, his voice husky and low, his eyes glittering as his gaze traveled slowly along the length of her chemise. It wasn't revealing; there was no see-through lace to tease, but it had a plunging neckline and two spaghetti straps that begged to be pulled down.

"You like this better than my maternity wear?" She asked, teasing.

He growled, unable to utter a coherent word. "Sexy as hell," she thought he said, and she leaned in to kiss him because that mouth of his was calling her. They kissed softly at first. Lips softly touching lips, to gauge a feeling, a reaction, to experience and feel the thrill but it didn't take long for him to get excited and his hands soon claimed her body, exploring feverishly over her back and sides before they settled in front. One hand caressed her stomach, just below her navel, while the other palmed her breast. With his thumb he stroked it, fast and rhythmically, soon teasing it to a hard peak and she couldn't help but let out a moan.

It had been too long since she had felt *this*; a throbbing between her legs and prickles of heat spreading across her stomach and chest. He kissed and breathed into her mouth as his hand cupped her breast again, kneading, and pulling, and tweaking and then he pulled her body closer to him so that her breasts fell against his hard-as-rock chest. Heat in her body slowly spread from her stomach to the tips of her toes and she felt his hardness through her panties. She melted into his mouth, tasting and sucking his tongue, biting his lower lip.

She had missed him, in her bed, in her arms, in her thoughts.

His hand slipped to her shoulder and he pulled her barely-there straps down so that the flimsy satin fell and revealed her nakedness. The look in his eyes was desperate and hungry and as his lips parted, she arched her back, anticipating the feel of his mouth on her. But in the next moment, the familiar sensation of release—and the sudden gush of milk from her breasts—made her gasp in shock.

Nico's eyes and mouth opened wide together. She thought she heard him chuckle. "You're leaking!" Her milk shot out onto his face and she clasped her hands over her chest and scrambled off the bed, embarrassed and humiliated as she rushed to the master bath.

"Ava!" He called after her but she locked herself away in the safety of the room. Milk squirted out full speed until she quickly pulled her old nursing bra out of the laundry basket and grabbed two nursing pads from the cabinet, stuffing them into her bra to absorb the flow.

So much for a night of seduction.

"Ava." Nico's voice was soft when he knocked on the door a second time. "I'll be out in a while," she replied, but she had no intention of showing her face anytime soon. Shaking with humiliation, she waited it out and stared at the flimsy baby doll slip that lay in a crumpled heap in the basket.

She had to face him at some point, and after a good while, she crept out, only to find Nico sitting on the edge of the bed waiting for her.

"Sorry," she said, feeling sheepish, and embarrassed, as

she glanced at the cot, hoping that Elisabetta would wake up and provide a welcome distraction.

"Sorry, for what?" His voice was a whisper. He took her in his arms but she squirmed, trying to move out of his hold. He held her even tighter. "Don't be embarrassed." He kissed her nose. "I'm sure this happens to many women." She could only whimper in response and turned to stare at her baby. "Hey," he said softly, moving her face so that she couldn't look at anything else but his face. "Don't be embarrassed. We can try again. We can try now."

But her libido had vanished.

"Or we can wait," he said, when she didn't answer. "I didn't mean to laugh, Ava." He still hadn't let her go.

"I know." But he had laughed and the situation had been humiliating enough, even if he hadn't.

"Come and lie down with me," he urged, tugging at her wrist.

"I..." She hesitated, not wanting to lie down with him or to talk about it. "I need to check some emails."

"Now?"

"Now."

He let go of her wrist that very instant.

CHAPTER SEVEN

Nico sat back in his chair in the conference room and observed his new team. He observed how good it made him feel to know that he finally had a team at all.

Four minds were better than two and discussing their ideas and obstacles during these meetings took a load off him.

It was only now that he was able to delegate so many of his tasks to others that he realized how much he'd taken on. When his father had been alive, Nico had barely noticed it. A few years ago when he'd decided to finally heed his father's words and to follow in the family business, he had started off by helping Edmondo but he hadn't noticed the vast breadth of what was involved in running a chain of hotels. Now that he had sole responsibility for the business, it was plain to see that it was too much for one person, or two, with Gina, to take on and run successfully.

He often caught himself thinking of what Edmondo would have made of all this; of the progress he'd made in trying to honor his father's legacy. In April it would be a year since his father's death, yet Nico felt his presence by his side every day. It spurred him to do better and to make his mark and he was only sorry that Edmondo wouldn't be around to see it.

"If you have any questions or concerns, you know where to find me," Nico said, closing the meeting. Ines and Gina were deep in conversation as they left the room but Demetrio hovered around the door waiting for Nico. "Make sure you order all the hardware you need," Nico told him as they walked down the hallway towards the main reception area. "Gina can sign off on the invoices if I'm not around."

"I'm looking forward to visiting the other hotels," Demetrio announced. "I'm proud to be a part of this business."

"Why's that?" Nico wondered what sort of smooth answer Demetrio would have.

"It's small enough that I can make a difference and large enough to matter."

"Are you saying small things don't count?"

"I'm saying it's good to get noticed. The Cazale hotels aren't as well-known as they could be, but some of my friends have heard of them. It was an eye-opener for me and when I told them I was the Chief Technical Officer for the chain, they were really impressed."

Nico cleared his throat. "But you do understand that in this early stage, where you don't have a team, that you're going to have to do that grunt work yourself?" Nico wondered if that might cause a problem.

"Yeah, of course. I get that. We're only going to grow. It's great that I'm here from the start."

Nico considered what he said. "Well, no. Not exactly. The hotels have been running a long time. Over twenty years, but we're taking them to another phase now."

"That's what I'm excited of being a part of."

"We're expanding, as you know."

"I know. There's an interesting article about you in The Verona Times."

"Oh?" Nico didn't give many interviews, but there had been a recent flurry after Edmondo's death and people were watching him.

"It was a few months ago," Demetrio said. "Obviously, expansion is the right move for you. You can't trade on your father's legacy forever."

"I'm glad you agree."

"And I'm certain that all of your efforts into the Cazale Ravenna will pay off."

"They will," Nico replied, drily. He turned his head, and thought he'd heard the sound of a child gurgling. And then he saw them. Ava was near the reception desk, watching proudly while Gina and Ines gushed over Elisabetta.

"Could I run some things about the upgrade project by you?" Demetrio asked.

"What things?"

"The timescales."

"What about them?"

"Gina has me down to spend four days at each site but I think it's going to take five or six. I'm certain that her estimation is off."

Nico turned his heard towards Demetrio. "Then revise your plan and discuss it with Gina. You don't need a meeting with me for that."

"I don't think she's technically minded enough."

His words startled Nico. "She doesn't need to be an IT expert to make estimations. She's basing it on how long its taken before." Nico narrowed his eyes at Demetrio. "I'm focusing my efforts on the Cazale Ravenna and Gina is your first line of support for any issues."

"I'll speak to Gina," said Demetrio. Then, "Is that your wife and daughter?"

"It is." Nico walked towards them, leaving Demetrio behind. "I didn't know you were coming here today." He was so happy to see his wife and dropped a light kiss on her cheek.

"I wasn't planning to," Ava replied. Things between them were almost back to normal again after that night. Almost. And 'normal' was still being fine with one another, but without any sex. Not even kissing. Nico brushed it off with the notion that being parents required an adjustment. This was temporary, and they would figure out a way back to their relationship

"She's *adorable!*" shrieked Gina, cradling the baby in her arms. "Look at her. She's grown *so* much."

Ava laughed. "You haven't seen her in a while."

"Not since before Christmas. Do they grow so quickly?"

"Yes, and no. She's all dressed up in layers and coat."

"How old is she?"

"Nearly two months," Nico replied. Two months which had whizzed by as if they'd been a couple of weeks. His friend had told him that it seemed as if time had sped up ever since he'd had children and Nico now understood what he meant. He couldn't wait for Elisabetta to be walking and talking and needing him as much as she currently seemed to need her mother.

"I think she likes me." Gina's face was a picture of happiness and Elisabetta seemed content to be the object of everyone's admiration.

"Ava," said Nico, placing a hand across her lower back. "You haven't met the newest additions to our management team." Nico introduced her. "This is Ines our marketing manager and this is Demetrio." He purposely left out the job title since Demetrio already seemed so hung up on it.

"It's wonderful to meet you both at last." Ava warmly shook hands with them both. "Nico has told me so much about you."

"Could I hold her a little longer?" Gina asked.

"You can hold her for as long as you want," Ava said.

"I'm going to sit down by the sofas. I won't be far." Gina walked away hugging the baby.

Nico reached out for Ava's hand. "This is a nice surprise." He wondered how she'd found the time to get away from her computer.

"I wanted to get out," replied Ava. "I feel cooped up in the house all day." He'd experienced the same thing during his time off. "You need to get out more."

"That's what Andrea said. She wanted the two of us—me and her—to out one evening."

"Why don't you? I'll look after Elisabetta." But, just as he thought she might, Ava made a face as if this was a concern. "I don't want to leave her yet, she's so young."

"I'll be able to cope."

"It's not you I'm worried about." She smiled and laid a hand on his arm even though he didn't find her remark calming.

"I *am* her father," said Nico, defensively. "I'm pretty sure I can look after her."

"I know you can. It's me." She raised her hand to his face for one tender moment. Maybe what they both needed was a short trip somewhere where they could rediscover their passion and romance. He took her hand and started to lead her towards the conservatory. "Where are you going?" she asked, glancing over her shoulder at Gina and the baby.

"To sit in here and have a cup of coffee with my wife, or we could go for a walk in the gardens. Elisabetta is in good hands; I trust her with Gina, don't you?"

"Yes, but—" She still didn't look too certain. He stopped and let go of her hand.

"But what?" Annoyance crept into Nico's voice.

"I came in to grab a few files as well as to see how I could rearrange my office."

"For what?"

"I'm thinking of working from here, maybe, for one or two days a week."

"Already?"

"Not right now," she said, hastily. "But hopefully next month when Elisabetta's three months' old. I'll have weaned her off the breast by then."

She looked away quickly but all he could think was that it was too soon for her to be heading back to work. It wasn't ideal anyway. She already spent too much time on her computer at home, liaising with Kim and Rona in Denver. She had never really let go of her work, apart from the days surrounding Elisabetta's birth. Apart from that, she had been juggling time between Elisabetta and her business. No wonder she had no time for him. "Next month? What about Elisabetta?"

"I'd bring her in with me."

He could feel the muscles along his jaw tightening. "Here? While you work? You might as well work from home."

"Or I could get a babysitter to look after her around the Casa Adriana while I work for a few hours."

"Have you thought this through properly?"

"I know I don't want to spend a year at home."

"But you have Kim and Rona handling things in Denver," he said. "I don't understand why you still need to be so hands on, especially at a time like now—when our baby is so young, and you need to rest."

She gave him a cutting stare. "And you have Bruno and

his workmen dealing with the Cazale Ravenna, Nico." Her voice took on that edge he'd come to know. "But that doesn't stop you from calling him three or four times during the day."

Had she been counting? "I call him a few times," Nico replied defensively.

"But you went to Ravenna earlier this week to find out how things were."

"Because I hadn't been in nearly a month."

"But if Bruno is handling things for you why do you need to be there?"

His body tensed as he tried to formulate a reply. His wife seemed determined to say her piece but he didn't want to get into a disagreement over work. Now that she was here he wanted to avoid things turning bitter, the way most of their conversations seemed to end, these days.

"And why are you here now?" she asked. "Why don't you let Gina and Demetrio and Ines take care of things?"

She was going in for the kill. "They do," he replied, looking around to make sure that Ines and Demetrio had left. "But I'm better now and I need to get on with things."

"You never really stopped, Nico. Even when you were at home unable to move around properly, you still had the phone stuck to your ear. We're not so different after all." She walked over to Gina and left him standing alone, pondering about what had just happened.

He pressed his lips together and was left feeling as if she'd pummeled into him without taking a breath. Whether it was being cooped up at home or a mixture of tiredness and lack of sleep, his wife was mad about something. Nico followed her towards the sofas.

"I could hold her all day," he heard Gina say as she handed the baby back to Ava.

"You're welcome to," Ava replied as Elisabetta waved her arms around in delight.

"Why don't you come over one day?" Nico asked, joining them. Maybe having company visit her would be good for Ava, especially if she didn't seem took keen to go out. Maybe it was time he got some friends over for dinner to spend time with them? A plan began to hatch in his mind. Why not invite Leo and Andrea at the same time?

"Why don't you come over for dinner one evening? We could ask Leo and Andrea over, too, couldn't we?" He sought Ava's approval for his suggestion.

"Er—yes," she replied, hugging the baby to her shoulder.

"I don't know. You both seem so busy right now—" Gina began.

"But we have lots of help," he said, thinking of Elsa and Helena. "The extra company would be good, wouldn't it?" Nico asked, looking at Ava again as he attempted to gauge her reaction.

"Uh—yes, he's right. We don't get out much," Ava said.

"It would be lovely," Gina concurred.

"We'll arrange a date," said Ava. "I'll find out when Andrea's free."

"And Leo," added Nico.

"They're not together."

"It doesn't matter. He was there with me at the hospital, they both were. It's the least we can do."

Ava shrugged.

"Let me know," said Gina, giving Ava a quick kiss on her cheek. She touched the baby's hand and rushed off.

Left alone, Nico looked at his watch. "How about we go to lunch?"

"My mom and I are going to Gioberti's."

"You are?" he asked, disappointed.

She nodded as she laid the baby back in the stroller. "Now that I'm out of the house, I want to make the most of my day."

He didn't like Gioberti. "Why don't you go someplace else?"

"Because Gioberti's has the best gamberoni."

He gave her a tight smile. "There are other restaurants in Verona. Better ones."

"But we're going to Gioberti's. You can join us if you want."

He shook his head. "You go ahead." He looked around. "Where's your mom?"

"In the gardens. She wanted to see Salvatore about something."

CHAPTER EIGHT

Elisabetta still woke up at night every three hours for a feeding. The one time Ava had mentioned this to her mother, Elsa had laughed. "You think your baby cares how much sleep you get?"

How did working women do this? The ones who commuted and left their babies with babysitters? If she and Connor had married, would this have been her life? Her previous job as a freelance copywriter might have sustained her, but for how long? And if she had married Connor, then she would never have come to Italy or found these products, and maybe her side hobby—which was what her online store had been back then—might have trickled to a slow death.

She doubted whether Connor would have been happy enough for her to be a stay-at-home mom and whether he would have taken on the responsibility of being the breadwinner. He had certainly surprised her when he'd asked her for a loan. It was still eating away at the back of her mind, one of those things that she preferred not to think about, and which was so low on her list of priorities. She also felt guilty for not having told Nico. It never seemed to be the right time and she knew her husband didn't like any mention of Connor. Her ex had said he'd pay her back but so far he hadn't paid a dime. She feared that Connor would hope that she would forget. He had sent them a Christmas card, but he hadn't even acknowledged Elisabetta's birth and she knew that Rona had made it a point to let him know.

She secured the diaper across Elisabetta's stomach and then bent down and blew a raspberry on her stomach. The baby laughed, and kicked her arms and legs, so Ava did it again. She stared down at her daughter, her face glowing with love as she held out her index fingers and watched as Elisabetta clasped her tiny hands around them.

Ah, the joys of being a mother.

The love she felt towards this tiny bundle was overwhelming and Ava wondered what it would be like to give Elisabetta a brother or sister.

Already?

She shook her head. "Your Papa would say yes in an instant," she said, using the same word that Nico had used to address his own father. She already knew that Nico wanted more babies. He'd agree to it now if he could. She felt sure he'd want her pregnant all the time, but she had other plans. She wasn't set up to be a trophy wife or a baby making machine. She was an independent woman, a businesswoman and entrepreneur, as well as a mother. She'd make it work. She would, with or without Nico's support.

A second baby would come when the time was right for her. She had much to do before then, as well as slipping in a visit to Denver sometime towards the end of the year when Elisabetta would turn one.

As much as Ava was looking forward to having friends over for dinner, she was also dreading it. She struggled especially with the structure of her day what with Elisabetta's on-demand feeding and random evenings where her colic acted up. It helped that Helena was cooking the meal, but even then Ava wasn't in the mood to entertain anyone and by the time Friday arrived, she wished Nico hadn't organized it.

She blew another raspberry on Elisabetta's peachy soft feet then looked up when her cell phone buzzed in the back pocket of her jeans. She grabbed it, stroking Elisabetta's foot as she answered it.

"Kim?" She instinctively felt uneasy because Kim only called when it was something important or if there was a problem.

"I don't want to alarm you but—" It wasn't the best way to begin a sentence, especially when Ava was already stressed about her guests turning up for dinner.

"What is it?" asked Ava, feeling alarmed already.

"We might have a problem with the cribs."

"What kind of problem?" Her breath stuck in her throat.

"I'm not entirely sure yet but we've had several reports from people saying that these weren't what they'd ordered."

"What do you mean?" Her insides churned as if she'd done a 360-degree loop on a roller coaster ride. "Did you double check the orders and the catalog numbers?"

"Yup."

"And you've checked the items in our warehouse?"

"Yes. It looks fine to me."

"We need more information from the customer."

"I had an email a few days ago and then someone called this morning. The lady sounded pretty angry. She said something about it not being a static crib."

"We only sell static cribs."

"I know. I checked their orders with our catalog."

Ava rubbed her forehead. It didn't make sense. There had been recent shipments in November and December but this was the first time they'd had any problems. "Do you know which shipment these cribs are from?"

"I can double check but I'm pretty certain. Wait—I can check now."

Ava waited with bated breath, letting go of Elisabetta's foot. "Kim?" She picked up Elisabetta and laid her on her shoulder as she paced around the room.

"I'm double-checking." As always, Ava was glad that she was dealing with Kim and not her sister Rona. "Yup. The ones we're getting the complaints about are from the December shipment."

"How many cribs have we sold and dispatched?"

"Around two hundred but, again, I'd need to check."

"Don't send any more out," Ava warned as Elisabetta nuzzled her nose into her shoulder, often a signal that she was ready to sleep.

"I won't. Let me look into it here and I'll get back to you."

"Ava!" Her mother's voice sounded from the distance.

"I'm up here, Mom!"

"Leave it to me," Kim said, "I'll call you later."

"Okay." Ava hung up.

"Your guests are here," Elsa announced, walking into the nursery and casting a disapproving at Ava. "You're not even dressed and Andrea and Leo are already here."

"They are?"

Was it already 8 o'clock?

"They are."

"And Nico?" Ava asked, handing Elisabetta over to her mother.

"He's not here yet."

Where was he? This whole thing had been his idea. The thought of her guests unattended downstairs made her even more tense.

"You need to get dressed, honey, and get downstairs quickly."

Ava wiped her hand across her face. She was torn between calling Nico and asking him where the hell he was and rushing to take a shower. Where had the time flown? Elsa coo-ed and aaah-ed and showered the baby with her own Grandma brand of loving while Ava decided what to do.

"Ava, your guests are waiting."

"But I need to take a shower." She reeked of thrown up baby milk and other baby smells.

"I thought that's what you were doing. You were up here long enough." Elsa fixed her with a stare that saw right through her. "Were you on your computer again?"

"Please, Mom." Ava grabbed the dress she'd laid out on her bed, then she changed her mind. At the last minute she opted for comfort instead. Rushing to her closet she picked out a pair of elasticized trousers and a loose top.

"Why don't you take Elisabetta downstairs, while she's playing happily," Ava suggested. She could quickly get ready while her guests fawned over Elisabetta. Silently, she prayed that Nico would be here soon.

Or else.

CHAPTER NINE

"I volunteer to babysit whenever you want me to," Andrea announced, as Elsa left the room with the baby.

"I'll bear that in mind," Ava replied, taking in Andrea's warm brown wraparound dress. It was plain yet stylish and the way it hugged her super slim body, it was difficult not to stare. Even Leo's gaze drifted a few times, Ava noted. She suddenly felt drab and dowdy in her middle-aged outfit and she wished she'd worn her dress instead and looked as if she'd made an effort.

Nico still hadn't arrived.

Typical.

Ava filled up their wine glasses and wished that she could drink some wine too. One more month of breastfeeding and she'd be able to. "To friends," she said, clinking glasses with them. "Nico and I wanted to take you out for a meal but we don't get to go out as much as we used to."

"Feeding on demand can't be easy," Andrea agreed, speaking as if she knew all about breastfeeding.

"And Nico has a lot going on at the moment," Leo remarked. "Andrea said he'd returned to work full-time."

"He never really went part-time," Ava replied. "Even when he was at home he was constantly calling Bruno or Gina for updates."

"Just like you," Andrea said.

"Just like me, I suppose," Ava agreed, reluctantly. They sat back down on the sofas. "I know he's under a lot of pressure."

"It can't be easy, following in Edmondo Cazale's footsteps," Leo remarked.

Ava sighed. "It isn't. This isn't a good time for him, and I know he has a lot riding on this hotel."

Andrea made a sad face. "You poor things. You've both had an awful time of things lately. Maybe we should have invited you over."

Ava shook her head, looking horrified. "That would have been difficult," she said, sipping her lemonade. "I'd have had to bring diapers, and a change of clothes for her, and then walk around with her on my arm. She's not used to new environments. They always freak her out and she'd likely be unsettled." As if on cue, Elisabetta let out an ear-piercing shriek from the other room.

Andrea sat forward. "What was that?"

Ava didn't flinch. "She has colic. At least, I'm told it's colic —this episodic crying for no reason. It happens most evenings."

Andrea looked shocked. "Aren't you going to see to her?"

"My mom or Nico will beat me to it." Ava cocked her ear towards the door and waited.

"Isn't there something you can give her?"

"We've tried all sorts of things," Ava replied. "Nothing really seems to work."

"Still, it must be such a help to have your mom over."

"It is." Ava stared nervously in the direction of the door

when the noise didn't die down. They smiled at one another politely. "Please excuse me a moment." She got up to go and tend to her but as she stepped out into the hallway, the cries stopped. The front door opened and Nico walked in, making an apologetic face. "Sorry," he whispered, putting down his briefcase. He walked up to her and kissed her on the cheek. "What's the matter?"

"Elisabetta is acting up."

"I'll see to her."

"Mom's got her." She folded her arms, and in a lowered voice asked, "Why are you so late?"

"I'm sorry. I was caught up in paperwork which needed to be done in order to get the second inspection—"

She waved her hand not needing his drawn out explanation right now. "Leo and Andrea are here but we're still waiting for Gina."

"She canceled at the last minute and sends her apologies," said Nico, speaking in a hushed tone as he started to go upstairs. "She said something about her mother not being well."

"That's a shame."

"Aren't you getting ready?" Nico asked.

"I *am* ready," she replied in a flat voice, suddenly feeling like a sack of potatoes. "Try to hurry up."

"I'll be down in five." He rushed upstairs and she returned to the living room with a fake smile plastered on her face. "Nico's here. He won't be long." She tried to sound light and breezy but just at that moment, the baby started to cry again. Ava closed her eyes and winced. "Trust her to be fussy today," she said, hovering by the door and as she listened out for her daughter's shrieks.

"Go and see to her," Andrea urged. "Don't worry about us." But as she was about to, the Elisabetta's cries silenced.

"Nico's probably got her," Ava replied. "She's the first thing he wants to see as soon as he gets in."

Sure enough the silence continued. As much as she had been looking forward to having her friends over for dinner, the novelty was beginning to wear thin. They hadn't even had appetizers yet and already her nerves were frayed.

CHAPTER TEN

The look on his wife's face said it all.

Nico raced upstairs and wondered why he'd suggested this dinner in the first place. He could have done without the extra headache tonight especially after the shitty day he'd had; it had been another day full of paperwork and meetings.

The good news however was that work on the Cazale Ravenna was now complete. The staff quarters had been rewired as expected and all that remained was for the safety inspectors to make their final visit. As yet there was no date for this but Bruno appeared confident that it would soon be forthcoming.

Nico walked into the nursery to find Elsa fussing over the baby. "It's that time of the day again," she said, hugging the baby to her chest. Nico looked at his daughter's tightly clenched little fists, and her tiny red face with tears streaming down her cheeks and was helpless to do anything. It killed him, especially because he could see she was in such great pain. "Let me have her," he said, and held out his arms to take her from Elsa. He hugged the baby to his chest and kissed her head softly and for a few moments, she quieted down. He pressed his lips to her hair and inhaled her clean cotton and baby scent. "Papa missed you, bambina," he murmured softly.

It didn't matter what type of bad day he had at work, coming home to Elisabetta made everything worthwhile. It was *her* future he was securing, and he was working hard to hand down a legacy greater than the one Edmondo had left him.

Carefully supporting her head and neck, he cuddled her in his arms so that she was snug against his chest. He sat down slowly in the glider, placing his feet on the ottoman, and breathed out slowly, reflecting on how much this little one depended on him. It was a feeling that frightened him and yet gave him the courage to move forward with his dreams.

"You have the magic touch," said Elsa.

"She loves her Papa."

"Of course she does," agreed Elsa. "You look as if you've had a hard day, Nico."

Yes." He didn't want to talk about it.

"You mustn't overwork yourself," Elsa cautioned. "Are you really ready to go back full-time?"

"I don't have a choice."

"You always have a choice."

He didn't agree. "Some things can't wait." He pinched the bony surface above the corners of his eyes. When he pressed down, he could feel a dull pain along his eye socket, as if tension had curled and woven its way around his body and had taken up home right there, in that one space.

He heard Elsa sigh and was glad when she didn't push that line of questioning. "Your guests arrived a short while ago and Ava's been waiting for you to get home." If that wasn't a hint to get himself downstairs, he didn't know what was and yet he didn't want to get up, nor give Elisabetta up or move from this place of comfort.

"I hate to do this to you, Nico, but Ava hasn't had an easy day either and you need to go down and take care of your guests."

Her words did the trick. With a measured push he slowly raised himself to standing and begrudgingly handed his daughter back to his mother-in-law. At once Elisabetta began to cry, something which made him feel a little happy—not the sound of her tears, but the idea that his daughter didn't want to leave his arms. Often, it seemed to be the case that Elisabetta only found solace when she was with her mother.

"There, there," crooned Elsa, bouncing around the room with her granddaughter and in time Elisabetta stopped crying. Nico stood by the door watching, not wanting to leave the nursery.

"Nico?"

"I'm going."

He walked into the living room not more than fifteen minutes later and greeted his guests while avoiding meeting Ava's gaze. "I'm sorry I was so late." He picked up the bottle of wine and refilled Leo and Andrea's wine glasses. He saw that Ava still had an almost full glass of lemonade. Filling his own glass up, he took a seat next to his wife and explained the reason for his lateness. "I got caught up talking to Bruno."

"Is the rewiring complete?" Leo wanted to know.

"All done. Cheers," he said, proposing a toast. "To good friends, and a good year for us all." They clinked glasses and muttered the same.

"It's all done?" Andrea asked, sitting back and crossing her long legs.

"It's all done." Nico wondered why Ava hadn't dressed up. He'd been hoping this would have been an evening for her to unwind and make an effort but perhaps, as usual, he'd overlooked things. He had completely forgotten that Elisabetta could be difficult to manage in the evenings.

"So, you'll open on time?" Ava asked.

He winced. "I hope so. We've got to go through the safety inspection again, and this time we should pass it with flying colors."

"I'm sure you can't wait," Leo commented. "The delay must be costing a fair amount as well as messing with your advertising campaign."

"It is." But Nico wasn't in the mood to contemplate the negatives again. He'd spent the whole day crunching the figures again and it looked bad.

"At least you're back to your usual self," Andrea commented.

"I ought to be." He made an effort to laugh. "I've had two months of rest."

"Rest?" Leo questioned. "Is it possible with a baby at home?"

"But what perfect timing," Andrea said, "to be at home with Ava and the baby over the Christmas break." Nico turned to his wife and nodded, wondering if she would see it that same way. "It's been a good time to be off," he agreed. "It would have been even better if I had chosen to take that much time off voluntarily and not forced to because of my injuries."

For a moment they all fell silent.

"Did you ever hear from that politician?" Leo asked. Nico shook his head. He hadn't heard anything from Vieri or Silvia. He hadn't expected to, either. He shrugged. "That man is the last person I want to see. He's done enough damage and it's in his own interest to stay away from me."

Ava squeezed his thigh. "It will be alright," she told him,

bringing a smile to his lips. She obviously wasn't that mad at him.

"And what about the two of you?" Nico asked. "How are things at the warehouse?"

Andrea spoke up. "Booming on account of your wife."

"Would that be due to the cribs?" Nico asked.

"It certainly is. The d'Este cribs are a hit in the US." She turned to Ava. "I spoke to Dino and I'm meeting him next Thursday."

"You are?" Leo asked, as if this was news to him. "But we've got a meeting with the insurance people on that day."

"You don't need me there. You can take of it," Andrea replied. Ava and Nico looked at one another, sensing a point of disagreement between the two of them.

"Dino has some new products which I wanted to look at," continued Andrea.

"Excuse me," said Ava, getting up. "I need to check if the appetizers are ready." But as she walked towards the door Elisabetta's cries started up again.

"I'll go," said Nico, getting up.

"No, I'll go," said Ava, "I have to see how Helena's getting on with the entrée. The appetizers should be ready."

"I can go, Ava." He could see how tired Ava was.

"I've got this." There was an edge to her voice that had slowly crept in. Nico smiled at his guests when she left the room.

The rest of the evening progressed with some awkwardness. It wasn't the type of relaxed affair that Nico had anticipated, but it could have been worse under the circumstances.

Ava was in and out of the room, and even though he offered to take over, she declined, mainly because the baby acted up more than ever as the evening wore on. They were halfway through their main course when Elisabetta's cries rang out again. Andrea looked up at them as Ava left the room.

"Sorry," said Nico, apologizing for what must have been the fifth or sixth time. "Some evenings can turn out like this."

"Is she like this every evening?" Andrea asked, her face a picture of disbelief.

"We have a few good days, or rather, Ava does." Now he felt guilty that she had to take so much on. "We have good days when she doesn't seem to suffer from bouts of colic at all."

They ate in silence and this time, Ava was gone for much longer. Nico was half tempted to go upstairs and check on her but knew that it would only make her more angry. Also, it wouldn't do to neglect their guests. He could already tell from their faces that they seemed uncomfortable.

Ava didn't come down after that and Leo and Andrea left soon after dinner, not even waiting to have dessert. From the looks on their faces, they seemed relieved to leave.

By the time Nico went upstairs, the baby was sleeping peacefully in the crib and Ava was in the bathroom. He quickly got changed and slunk in between the sheets by the time she came out. "That didn't go too well, did it?" he asked.

Ava shrugged.

"I shouldn't have organized dinner just yet. I'm sorry."

She glanced at him. "Why did you?"

"Because I thought it might be good to have friends over. You said you were cooped up in the house and that you needed to get out and about. I was trying to do something nice for you."

"It's too soon to be having company over and Elisabetta's colic isn't helping." She climbed into bed alongside him.

"I was only trying to help." He leaned over and kissed her

on the cheek and when she didn't say anything, or rebuff his advances, he kissed her on the mouth; a chaste, barely-there kiss. He waited for her to say something but she didn't. "Why didn't you wear a dress?" He'd seen it laid out on the bed.

"I hadn't shaved my legs." She paused, before adding. "Why? Did I look frumpy next to Andrea?" He examined her face when she asked this, unsure what it was she was getting at. She couldn't still be hung up over that fact that he and Andrea had dated before. *Could she?*

"You never look frumpy to me," he said and attempted another kiss but she turned to her side and reached for her eReader. "Are you going to read now?"

"Yes."

He trailed his fingers along her thigh.

"Don't." She opened her eReader.

"Don't?"

"Not tonight, please, Nico. I'm tired."

Tired and yet she still had time to read. He turned his back on her and closed his eyes.

CHAPTER ELEVEN

Ava lay in bed staring at the ceiling, then turned to her side to watch Nico sleeping peacefully.

She was tempted to reach out and touch his lips but feared waking him up. He roused easily these days, and having Elisabetta's crib next to their bed didn't help. But still, she liked this quiet time in the morning to contemplate.

The duvet reached up to Nico's shoulders and she bit her lip, her fingers fluttering as they traced gently across his chest. If he awoke now, he'd stare at her with his first-thing-in-the-morning look, an invitation for something more, and she would allow herself to melt, and to give in.

Or would she?

Or Elisabetta would wake up and that would be the end of that.

She moved her hand away. It would be far better to get out of bed and check for further updates from Kim. There had been nothing more since Friday night, and nothing yesterday. Weekends were slow and Kim and Rona weren't going to spend their time working. Running her store never felt like work to Ava; she never kept track of the hours she spent on her business but she understood that it wasn't the same for her employees.

She lay on her back and stared at the ceiling, thinking. If she got her work out of the way in the morning, maybe they could take Elisabetta out for a long walk in the afternoon.

"Hey." Nico's hand skirted across her waist just as his voice shook her thoughts. She turned to see him propped up on his elbow, gazing at her with that mischievous smile that hinted at other things.

"Good morning,"

"It could be," he replied, moving his hand slowly across her stomach and keeping it there. If she wasn't careful, that smile of his would ensnare her and her plans to check her emails would disappear.

His fingers slipped beneath her nightshirt and when he caressed her soft fleshy stomach, she sucked in hard, trying to make it flat. He moved his hand further down, his fingers skating over her panties before moving down to stroke her thighs. His feather-light touches slowly awakened every cell in her body. Warmth spread along her stomach and breasts and he rolled on top of her, supporting his weight with his elbows. He was hard again, hard below, and hard here, where she splayed her hand across his chest, feeling his heartbeat. She felt like liquid jelly lying beneath him. "Don't kiss me," she shrieked, as he dipped his head down, as if he were about to do that very thing.

"Okay ... I could go and brush my teeth, but I don't want to take a risk and wake her up." They glanced over at their daughter lying fast asleep in the crib. "And staying here feels kind of good." He tugged at her panties, trying to roll them down with one hand and she giggled, a little louder than she had intended.

They hushed and froze, staring at the crib with bated

breath, waiting to see if Elisabetta would rouse. After a few silent seconds, Nico's gaze returned to Ava's face. She smiled and snuggled down further into the mattress, touching his chest, feeling his coarse hair between her fingers. He reached down lower feeling, stroking, probing and she mewled in response, parting her legs wider because it felt *soooo* good, when he touched her there.

"Let me kiss you," he begged.

"No!" She squirmed, suppressing a giggle as she turned her head to the side. She squeezed his buttocks, wishing he would hurry up and take her. The time for slow foreplay was gone. Urgency called.

"Then I want to..." he dipped his head and laid it against her breasts. She felt *completely* unsexy, wearing her maternity bra with those pads she'd inserted. "Don't take it off," she warned.

His puppy dog eyes drooped with disappointment, but not for long as he started to leave a trail of kisses along her jaw, all the way to below her ear. His lips were soft and tender and they tickled. She giggled, kicking the crib by accident.

Elisabetta stirred.

They froze and stopped breathing and the red-hot heat that had been curling around in her body, screeched to a halt. Elisabetta shifted again, her lips wavered, even though her eyes were closed. And then she started to bawl. Loudly.

Ava closed her eyes in disbelief. Lust wilted away and frustration took its place. "Now look what you've done," she whispered, annoyed. *Why hadn't he just hurried up and thrust into her?*

"*You* kicked it," replied Nico, sounding just as deflated.

"You made me!"

They both lay on their backs for a few seconds, contemplating the lost opportunity until Nico reached across the crib and turned on the musical mobile which hung above Elisabetta's head. The baby suddenly quieted, absorbed by the brightly colored animals slowly spinning around in mid-air. "We could still..." he said, snuggling up to her again.

"Not with her looking!" She was shocked by his suggestion. His raging hard-on had clearly turned him insane.

"She's looking at the mobile," Nico insisted. "She won't know what we're doing." Speechless, Ava stared at her husband in disbelief. "Come on," he begged, his fingers poised on the round curve of her hip. "You know you want to."

"We can't have sex with our daughter lying next to us." Irritated, frustrated and unsatisfied beyond belief, she climbed out of bed, dumbfounded by her husband's suggestion.

"What are you doing?" Nico sat up in bed, wearing a scowl. Bare-chested and ready for her, he wore nothing more than an invitation to make her come. She knew it would be a sin to walk away and the heat between her legs confused her further.

Until Elisabetta gurgled again. With her mind now made up, Ava rolled her panties back on and lifted the baby, placing her on the bed between them. They fawned over her and in response, Elisabetta waved her arms up and down excitedly.

"We could move the crib into the nursery," he suggested. "She'd only be a stone's throw away and we can have the door open. At least it would give us some privacy."

"Not until she's a year old. We agreed," Ava reminded him and she got up and started to walk away.

"Where are you going?"

"I need to check a few things." Kim might have emailed her during the night.

She wasn't the only one who was left feeling irritated and unsatisfied.

The rest of the morning didn't go too well for Nico either. He'd been on a call for a long time and had a face like thunder when he finished, retiring into his study later. At times like this Ava knew better than to question him and so she let him do as he pleased. The Sunday afternoon she'd planned with only the three of them, soon fell to the wayside.

There had been no emails from Kim overnight, but she was eager for an update and wanted to find out more. She'd held off calling Kim until Elisabetta was having a nap but it seemed that her child was refusing to take a nap today.

Ava tried to sneak into the study a few times when the baby was asleep but after a short while, Elisabetta would stir again. In the end, fed up with the constant scurrying back and forth, Ava picked her up and held her in her arms while she called Kim.

"Do you know how many we shipped out?" Nervousness chewed the insides of her stomach. She sat upright in her chair, clutching the phone with one hand and bouncing the baby on her knee trying to calm her.

"Two hundred and fifteen."

"From the new shipment?"

"From the new shipment," Kim confirmed.

"Any more complaints?" Ava was anxious to find out.

"No more than the ones I told you about a few days ago. I'll check the stock properly tomorrow when I get to work," Kim promised. "I didn't get a chance to go to the warehouse over the weekend."

"Don't worry," Ava replied, just as Elisabetta started to cry. She quickly put the baby to her breast.

"Some orders came through yesterday and I expect a similar amount today, but I'm going to hold off sending them out. We need to find out more from the unhappy customers, but I'm wary of calling them over the weekend."

Ava relaxed into her chair. Kim was a godsend and a woman after her own heart. The two of them thought alike. "It's probably best if you call them tomorrow, and we'll speak later," said Ava. Just as she hung up, the study door opened and Nico walked in, catching her by surprise so that she dropped her cell phone. He picked it up and gave her a derisory glance while the baby suckled at her breast. She felt uncomfortable, and exposed, and wished he would leave. But he didn't. He just stood there.

"Is it necessary to feed Elisabetta in front of the computer? Can't your work wait, Ava?"

He was telling her? This man who stayed up late and constantly worried and harangued Bruno? He was one to talk. "Something urgent came up," she answered, her voice icy. "I needed to deal with it just the way you take care of urgent things with your business, Nico. You always lock yourself away in your study."

"But you've got Elisabetta in your arms," he countered. "What if she fell?"

"I'm not about to drop my baby." Ava could feel her cheeks heating.

"But you dropped your cell phone," he cried. "You should see yourself, Ava. You're working too hard."

"I'm taking care of my business." She wished she had one of her cotton cloths to cover herself up with. For some reason she felt naked in front of him, and at a disadvantage.

"You should be taking care of your baby."

She threw her head back and gave him a hard stare. *Did he really mean that?*

"I'm sorry," he said. "I didn't mean it like that. I know you're a fantastic mother, and you take great care of

Elisabetta, but you have the worry and stress of the store on your shoulders. All I'm saying is that if you slow things down, enough so that Kim and Rona can take care of it without much input from you, you'll always be able to carry on later."

"When later?"

He shrugged. "I don't know, Ava. Whenever the children won't be so demanding. All I'm saying is why can't you take some proper time off? People take maternity leave, don't they? We have it here as well."

She seethed inwardly, not sure whether he was being facetious or condescending. "I *am* taking maternity leave, Nico. I'm taking three months off."

"Except that you're still working."

"I'm doing a little, just as you are and you didn't even let yourself get better."

"But I *am* better."

"Why is it so different for you?" she asked, covering up and sitting Elisabetta up in order to burp her. "Why can't you see that this is important to me?"

"And your baby isn't?"

She scowled at him. "You're not doing this to me. You're not going to make me feel guilty."

"I'm not trying to make you feel guilty. I'm trying to make you see that it's too early yet. That you can't do everything at the same speed you did before the baby. You have to take it slow, Ava."

"I can't take it slow." She couldn't. Not with these recent rumblings of potential problems with her stock. The d'Este cribs were her bestselling products and she didn't want to think what it might mean if there was a fault with them. Nico placed his hands on her shoulders and started to massage them.

"What if I drop the baby now?" she asked.

He immediately stopped. "I don't want to have an argument with you over this."

She turned to him. "This is my career Nico. You knew that when we met. This is a part of my life, another part of me. I was never going to be a woman who attended charity events and dined with the likes of Silvia."

He made a face and she realized she'd used the wrong example. He hated Silvia as much as she now did.

His about turn was the thing that hurt her the most. He'd supported her business when he'd first met her. He'd believed in her and her dream of making this store a success, and he had helped her by introducing her to Andrea. He'd given her the encouragement that Connor never had.

And now he was asking her to walk away from her responsibility for a while and to enjoy motherhood by turning a blind eye to her business? She couldn't turn off her ambition just like that.

"Don't you want to spend more time with Elisabetta?"

"Don't you think I spend enough time with her?" She lifted her baby up and kissed her on the forehead, feeling a sense of pity for her daughter who had no idea that her parents were arguing over.

Elisabetta let out a little burst of wind and Ava stopped rubbing her back. She got up, putting her baby to her shoulder. "I worked hard to get this business up and running, Nico. I didn't have it handed to me. I worked for it." She realized her mistake as soon as she'd it.

"That's what you think, too, is it?" he snarled, his temper flaring. She knew instantly she'd hit a nerve. The papers were constantly deriding him, claiming him to be nothing more than a playboy, and a wannabe businessman who would never take over from his father. She'd effectively said the same to him just now and she might as well have slapped him for it was easy to see the hurt in his eyes.

She wanted to rest her hand on him, to tell him she hadn't meant that, but it was too late. Nico walked away.

Her words had cut deeper than she had intended.

CHAPTER TWELVE

He drove into work the next day on a crisp Monday morning but try as he did he couldn't shake off Ava's words. It was bad enough that the papers were constantly on his back but he didn't expect it from his wife.

When he'd parked in the Casa Adriana parking lot, he sat back and stared at the interior of his car. He missed his old convertible which had had been written off when he'd crashed it. He didn't care for the latest or the most expensive model. All he wanted were the broken in seats of his old car and his old CD collection. The collection had all the songs that were tied to memories from the past and which had now been ruined in the accident. He hadn't even gotten around to replacing it yet.

Things sucked and on a bleak Monday morning—on the trails of a tense weekend with his wife—they seemed to suck even more. He felt a sense of lethargy about his daily routine and he couldn't pin down what it was that bothered him exactly—the spa hotel, the safety inspection or Ava and her business.

But there was no point sitting here thinking about it. That

wouldn't solve a thing and his hotels wouldn't run by themselves.

He entered the lobby, nodded at the receptionist as he walked past, then made his way over to Gina's office. The door to her office was slightly ajar and when he knocked on it, it opened further. Gina sat at her desk, her face set into a half-scowl. She obviously hadn't heard him knock. He knocked again and stepped inside anyway. "Why so glum?"

"Monday morning. You know how those are."

"I do." He closed the door behind him and sat down.

"Demetrio has proposed new timings for the upgrade project," Gina announced.

"He finally spoke to you about it."

"He spoke to *you* about it?"

"He mentioned something, and I told him to talk to you," said Nico. Gina pursed her lips together but said nothing more. "He thinks he needs a few more days per site," Nico explained. "So I suggest you give him a few more. He's new and therefore needs more time to familiarize himself with our networks and processes."

"But the contractors we used before did it in three days. I don't see why he needs—"

He sensed that something was a foot here and wondered why their personalities clashed. "I would let him have the extra days he needs, Gina. Let him ease into the job. You know our business inside out and he's only learning about it."

"It's his job title that he has a problem with," sniffed Gina. "He doesn't want to get his hands dirty.

"That may be," Nico agreed. He needed more time to see how the man performed. "On another note, what happened to you on Friday night? We were looking forward to seeing you." The expression on Gina's face changed in an instant. She shook it off with a shrug. "My mom wasn't feeling too good."

Nico waited for more and when Gina wasn't forthcoming, he asked. "And how is she now?"

"Much better."

Not ever having had an insight into her family life, not even sure of her status, he pressed further. "What was wrong with her?"

"She had an upset stomach. I'm sorry I missed dinner. I'd been looking forward to it, especially to seeing Elisabetta again and Ava."

"You're welcome to come any time," he told her, scratching the back of his neck and wondering why he knew nothing about her personal life or circumstances, and she knew everything about his.

CHAPTER THIRTEEN

She preferred it now that Nico was back at work full-time. It was in such contrast to how she'd felt after the accident on hearing that he would have to take time off work and recover at home.

Maybe the problem wasn't with them but in the circumstances around them. He had much to deal with. It seemed that each phone call to Bruno only dampened Nico's mood further. Maybe if they'd managed to have sex, their frustrations would have been easier to deal with. But Ava had a feeling that things weren't as simple as that.

Who could she talk this out with? Rona wasn't around and Andrea didn't have her problem. And Gina, the only other person she got along with well enough to trust, wasn't exactly forthcoming about her own private life. The last thing Ava wanted was to burden her with her own set of problems.

Without her mom and Nico around, the house was relatively empty for a change. Helena was around, somewhere, or on one of the other floors. She was always busy cleaning or cooking or ironing. Elsa had gone to the Casa Adriana before noon, saying that she needed to spend time in the gardens there. Ava was certain that her mother was secretly keeping an eye on Salvatore because she didn't trust him with her beloved lemon trees. The idea of her mother watching over the gardener made Ava smile.

Alone in the huge house with its acres of grounds, she felt truly alone and cut-off from the rest of the world. There were no other houses in sight around them. Maybe once the baby was older she would join some toddler groups, but not until Elisabetta was walking. There was no point in going to a group when her baby only wanted milk and to poop. She would also need to learn to speak in Italian. She would feel so left out if Elisabetta and Nico spoke in Italian and she couldn't understand a word they were saying.

When her cell phone rang, she leapt to answer it, more out of a feeling to hear the voice at the other end.

"Bad news." Kim didn't mince her words.

Ava's heart dropped. "Tell me."

"A customer has reported that her baby fell out of the crib and suffered a nasty bump to the head as well as bruising along his arms."

Ava collapsed into her swivel chair. "Babies can't fall out of our cribs."

"They can out of these new ones."

"What?" Ava got up and began to pace around the room. "What do you mean?" Dino had assured her that all the cribs manufactured by his company underwent rigorous testing.

"The cribs in the December shipment aren't static. They're drop-side cribs. I unpacked a box to check."

"There has to be a mistake," said Ava, her hand flying to her temple. "We're not supposed to sell drop-side cribs in the US. They're banned." Her voice turned flat and monotone, but deep down her insides churned.

What the hell was Dino playing at?

"I think I know what the problem is," said Kim. "In fact, I'm certain of it. The order numbers are crazily similar. I had it scribbled down somewhere, but I need to check online to confirm. I have a feeling that the number on the boxes in our warehouse isn't the same order number we requested."

Ava's heartbeat started to race. "Please let me know as soon as you find out."

"Sure."

"How old is the child?" Ava asked.

"He's ten months old, and his parents are as mad as hell." Kim's words clanked like a heavy chain around her ankles. Oh, dear god. A child had been hurt and it was all her fault. Ava flopped back into her swivel chair, making it bounce with the pressure. "How is he now? Is he okay?"

"He's fine. I heard a baby in the background and I assumed it was him, because she said she only had one child, and then she gave me the whole story of how her and her husband had been trying for ages and how finally, after so many years, they had him, and her parents brought them the crib as a present. But, yeah," Kim paused to take a breath. "I think the kid's fine."

"It's still bad," said Ava. "This is really, *really* bad." She pictured broken arms and legs, and worse for children who were still using the cribs. "We need to call in all cribs we've shipped out."

Before another child got injured. She wanted to dive down a dark rabbit hole and disappear. She could see lawsuits flying towards her, and businesses folding, not only hers, but Dino's and Andrea's, too.

"Yeah," said Kim, sounding dismayed. "You should have heard the father. He was raging."

"I'm sorry you had to deal with that." But Ava was already worried. Who would call next? How many more children were at risk of injury? "The three of us will need to have a conference call later." She'd need to speak to Rona and Kim at the same time to save explaining everything twice. But they would have to let all the customers know that there had been a problem and then begin the process of arranging for these cribs to be sent back. "I'll send out an alert on our homepage and a newsletter, and a PR release letting our customers know about the problem."

This was bad bad bad.

"At least we have all the contact details for our customers," Kim reminded her. "It's not an impossible task."

"No, it's not. We'll have to act quickly." Ava mentally recounted all the things she had to do, feeling the pressure of the ticking time bomb she was racing against in order to prevent one more child from getting injured. "I need you and Rona to work around the clock and make sure every single crib owner is notified of the problems."

Kim yawned. "I will."

"Get some rest first," said Ava. It was past midnight in Denver. "Go to sleep and we'll talk tomorrow."

"I will." Kim hung up and Ava fell back into the chair and held her face in her hands. A baby had hit its head but what if it had been worse? It was almost too frightening to contemplate. She suddenly wished she hadn't worked with babies. Why not sell candles, or packaging?

Or envelopes?

Why had she settled on children's products where there was so much that could go wrong?

There was nothing to do but meet with Andrea immediately. But just as she began to dial Andrea's number, Andrea called her.

"You have to recall your cribs," Andrea said, in place of 'hello'.

She knew. "I did. I mean, we're in the process of doing that."

"Dino called to say that there's been a terrible mistake. Your order was mixed up with one of the European orders and you ended up with—"

"Drops-side cribs."

"Not exactly," said Andrea.

"No?"

"Dino's company make drop-sides for the European market but these have immobilizers for those parents who want to fit them."

She'd seen these immobilizer kits before, they came in various shapes and sized but mainly involved for a few extra brackets to be screwed onto the crib. It was fiddly to do and extra work and it was far easier to just buy fixed side cribs. She didn't understand why Dino sold them but it would explain why some of her customers had complained and some hadn't. It could explain how the drop-side opened and the ten-month-old fell out; it seemed probable that those parents hadn't fitted the immobilizer. But then again, whose fault was this? Those parents certainly hadn't expected to receive a drop-side crib in the first place.

"How the hell did Dino's company make a big mistake like that?" Ava was dumbfounded.

"He's not happy," confirmed Andrea.

"I'm not happy either," retorted Ava, "I have a customer whose baby son fell out and banged his head."

Andrea let out a loud whooshing sound, like the sound of a balloon deflating. "Are you serious? That's terrible. Poor boy. Do you think his parents will sue?"

"I have no idea."

"Doesn't everyone sue in the US? For everything and anything?"

Ava groaned. "I don't expect the parents to be silent and do nothing. Thank goodness it wasn't worse."

She'd never contemplated the idea that any harm might come from what she sold but thinking about it now, selling goods for young babies and children was a risky venture. She didn't want to live with the guilt of a child getting injured because of something his parents had bought from her store, because of an error at Dino's end. Right now, she was the face of that order. People would blame her, not Dino. "We need to meet with Dino," said Ava, starting to recognize that she needed to set things into motion.

"That's why I called you," said Andrea. "He's coming to see me and we'll discuss how we're going to deal with this. It affects all of us, even if the fault lies at Dino's end."

"I'll be at yours by noon," Ava said and it was only when she had hung that she realized that her mother wasn't around to look after Elisabetta. She walked into her bedroom where her daughter lay peacefully asleep having her mid-morning nap. Smiling, despite the dire news about the cribs, Ava knew she had no choice but to leave Elisabetta at the Casa Adriana with Nico. But first she would call and forewarn him. He answered on the first ring.

"Can you look after Elisabetta today?"

"I'm at work, Ava." His voice sounded strained even if his words were gentle. "Why?"

She told him what had happened.

"Poor boy," Nico commiserated.

"I'm going to call his parents and make sure everything's alright."

"You're going to call your customer and apologize?"

"Yes."

"Don't," Nico cautioned.

"Why not? I can't just ignore the problem and hope it goes away."

"They'll sue you."

"They're probably going to sue me whether I call them or not. They might go after Dino, but they bought the product from me. It's good customer relations to call them back."

"Shouldn't Dino be calling them?"

"They bought the crib from *me,* Nico..." Ava shook her head. Time was running out, and she hadn't called him to seek his counsel. "I have to go to Montova. I'm meeting with Dino and Andrea in the next hour and I need you to look after Elisabetta. My mom's not here. She told me she was going to the gardens at the Casa Adriana so she'll be around to help look after the baby, if you need her to."

"Do you have to go today?"

"Didn't you hear what I said?" she exclaimed. "Yes, I have to go today." She never questioned him when he went to meetings, or asked him where he went, or how he conducted his business and she couldn't see why he was being this way with her now. "I'll be there shortly."

"But I have a heavy day of meetings—"

"And so do I." *Did he expect her to forget about her business because his was so much more important?* "I'm leaving Elisabetta with you, Nico. But if you're going to resist and complain, then I can take her to Montova with me." As if he would ever take Elisabetta to the spa hotel for one of his meetings.

"Leave her here," he said, not sounding too excited about the matter. She didn't care and hung up, slamming the phone down hard. She understood his stresses and the demands of his business, but why was it so difficult for him to understand hers?

CHAPTER FOURTEEN

Elisabetta was in a happy mood by the time Ava reached the Casa Adriana. She wheeled the baby into the hotel and carried the diaper bag and all the other million things Nico might need. She'd packed three changes of clothes and five diapers, just to be on the safe side and hoped that her mother would pick up her cell phone message soon.

As soon as she walked in, Gina rushed up to her. She could see Nico standing in the lobby talking to someone. He hadn't yet seen her. "I get to look after this one today?" Gina cried happily, bending over and whispering sweet nothings to an entranced Elisabetta.

"I'm sorry, it was all last minute. My mom was supposed to be here by now. Have you seen her?"

Gina shook her head.

"Strange," said Ava. "She should be here soon. I've left a message on her cell phone."

"May I?" Gina held out her arms eagerly, and Ava handed her baby over just as Nico walked up and kissed her on the cheek.

"I have to go," she said. "There's milk and diapers and changes of clothes."

"When will you be back?" he asked.

"I don't know."

"Don't worry," Gina said, hugging the baby to her chest. "We can manage."

Ava gave Nico a pointed stare. "My mom should turn up at some point. I hope it doesn't get too much for you." He was about to answer but she had no intention of hearing what he had to say and, after kissing Elisabetta a few times and fawning and fussing over her, she left.

She was fuming as she left the Casa Adriana. It was always so different when Nico had business to take care of.

She resolved that one of the first things she would do once the crib problem had been resolved was find a good nanny. She felt uneasy about the idea of leaving a stranger to look after her child while she was working, but she hoped that when she found the right person, her concerns would melt away.

In the past she had always relied on a driver to take her to Montova but as she got into the car today, with these angry thoughts swirling around in her mind, she suddenly felt brave for driving all the way herself. This little slice of independence, leaving the baby behind and going to a meeting, gave her a sense of freedom that she hadn't felt in months.

Next up on her list would be to start learning the language, then finding a nanny. She was feeling better already and despite the nature of this visit, it still felt freeing to be out of the house.

As she drove, the concerns of the morning occupied her thoughts. This recent crib problem was cause for concern and served to remind her that she needed to be over-zealous in the new products she took on. D'Este was relatively new to her. She didn't know Dino that well and she didn't know much about the company's history, how long they'd been in business, or what their past track record was like. She'd only sought them out because she'd liked their cribs. Maybe she'd been unlucky and this was simply a case of something going freakishly wrong? But the consequences could be huge—for all of them, her, Andrea and Dino.

She arrived at Montova just over an hour later and out of habit, made her way to Andrea's old warehouse, having completely forgotten about the fire which had burned down Andrea's warehouse.

Shock rolled over her as she stood in front of the charred building. A man walking past told her that Andrea had moved around the corner. Ava thanked him and made her way to the new units.

Unsure which door to go through, she was about to try the first one when it opened and Leo stepped outside.

"Ava." He reached forward and shook her hand. "Come in. I'm going to get coffee. How do you like yours?"

"White and no sugar, please."

"I won't be long."

She walked inside and saw Andrea with a man she presumed to be Dino, sitting at a table at the far end. Andrea got up as soon as she saw her and kissed her on the cheek. "This is perfect timing."

"I came as fast as I could."

"This," said Andrea, waving her hand at the man who was sitting down and looking over some papers, "is Dino Massari."

"Hello," he said, getting up and shaking her hand. "We finally meet."

"Nice to meet you," Ava replied. They exchanged pleasantries and sat around the table waiting for Leo. A short while later, Leo returned with a cardboard drink carrier holding four cups. "Coffee," he said, "and now we can officially begin."

Dino glanced at his watch. "I'd like to go first. I need to leave in an hour." And without waiting for their response, he opened the discussion, explaining how his company manufactured two types of cribs, static once specifically for the US market where drop-side cribs were banned, and the other types for Europe and the rest of the world. "But we have a range of drop-side cribs and most of these come with immobilizers which we provide."

"A what?" asked Andrea. "That sounds like a part from an automobile."

"It's a device that secures a drop-side and turns it into a fixed crib," Ava explained. "Fixed or static, it's the same thing."

"And so," continued Dino, "I believe there's been a mix-up with the order numbers and the wrong order has gone out to Denver."

"It's a pretty large order," Ava retorted. "Don't you have checks in place for when you ship out products? I mean, two thousand cribs isn't a small number to get wrong."

"Of course we have checks in place," he replied, testily. "But we're not infallible. My staff are humans and they do make the occasional mistake."

She waited for the apology and when none came, asked him, "How stringent is your testing process?"

"Extremely stringent, feel free to visit the factory and see for yourself. But the problem isn't with the product, it is simply that the wrong order went out."

"And like I said, it's a pretty big order." She was getting worked up, and she knew she was goading him but something about his smug and arrogant manner, and the way he wasn't backing down and acknowledging his mistake, and the fact that he hadn't yet apologized, riled her.

"You've already stated that twice." His eyes were hard as he answered her.

"Look, Mr. Massari." Ava fixed her pincer gaze on him. "I have a customer whose ten-month-old son fell out and suffered a nasty bump on the head, and bruising along his body. We're lucky it wasn't worse."

"Have you verified this claim?"

She stared at him in disbelief. "Verified?" *No, of course she hadn't. How could she?* It hadn't even occurred to her not to believe the customer. "My staff in the US have taken a few calls during the weekend about the cribs not being what they ordered and so if a customer calls and tells me that her child was injured as a direct result of using a crib I sold them, I'm not going to ask they if they could verify their claim." She struggled to stop herself from pointing a physical finger at him. "It's not how our customer service works."

"But you need to be certain," Dino replied, rolling up his sleeves. "Some customers can be like parasites once they hear of a fault. You're going to get a lot of crazies calling you and threatening to sue. Your main market is the US, isn't it?" he asked, glaring at her.

"For now," she replied as calmly as she could. She wasn't going to let this Neanderthal bully her.

"Then expect a string of lawsuits coming your way."

"Not *my* way, Mr. Massari. I didn't manufacture the cribs, *you* did, and you'll be held accountable." She hadn't meant to go in fighting, but the man had already pushed her buttons.

"We need to calm down," said Leo, with a light-hearted

chuckle. "This isn't going to help us resolve the problem. We're all at risk of getting sued, even though we didn't manufacture the cribs, and the fault was not ours." He turned to Ava, "You probably know this already but federal liability laws in the US hold the manufacturer, distributor and seller responsible. The whole chain of command is responsible—and that means we all have a lot at stake here."

Ava blinked. She hadn't been completely sure until just now. Her heart clanged against her ribcage as possible ramifications of Dino's order mix-up hit home. Andrea sighed. "We need to ensure that this doesn't happen again and getting angry and pointing fingers isn't the way forward."

"I'm not pointing fingers," replied Ava. "I'm just laying the responsibility where it is due but," her voice turned firmer, "it's clear that we have a problem, and we need to fix it as soon as possible."

A hush fell over them and for a while nobody spoke. Ava flipped off the lid to her coffee cup and took a sip.

"But if the drop-sides have been shipped with immobilizers, then why not use them? Wouldn't that fix the problem?" Andrea asked.

"It's not fixing the problem because those cribs aren't what the customers ordered. Drop-sides are banned and those with immobilizers aren't encouraged," said Ava. "I certainly don't want to sell them because I'm all for safety, especially when it comes to cribs. We're going to recall all of them and you're going to have to pay for the shipping back to Italy." And she would have to find a way of making it up to her customers.

"I can arrange for their original orders to go out," Dino replied. "Since it was my fault, I'll absorb the shipping costs for the replacements."

Ava pushed back. "But my customers might not want that, in which case I'll have to give them a credit note."

New parents especially, didn't have time to mess around waiting for replacement orders. Unfortunately, fixing this problem wasn't going to be as simple as Dino seemed to make out. Sitting across the table from him, it was difficult to avoid looking at the hardened expression on his face. He was clearly displeased and rightly so, but this wasn't her fault and she wasn't going to pay for it. It was bad enough that she had put her customers' children at risk and she was probably going to incur a lot of bad publicity over a problem that wasn't of her making.

"You'll need to ensure that a problem of this magnitude doesn't occur again," Leo said, addressing Dino.

"I'm aware of that. You people seem to think that I'm not doing a thing. Trust me, the order number problem has never happened before and it won't happen again."

"And how exactly are you going to enforce that?" Ava demanded. Just then an email from Kim arrived. *Did that girl never sleep?* Ava read the email and understood exactly what had happened. "Do you even know what the order numbers in question were?" she asked Dino, raising an eyebrow, and anticipating his reply.

Dino Massari appeared to play it cool. "I don't have it at hand but then I'm not a database and I don't store all the order numbers in my head."

"Then let me tell you." She opened Kim's email. "The order number for the drop-side cribs is DE6789 and the order number for the fixed or static cribs, the ones my company sells, is DE6879."

A hush fell over the table as they all digested the news. "I can see how an error might have occurred, but I don't understand why you didn't put checks in place to ensure this never happened." If it were her, she would have used completely different numbers to avoid a problem like this from occurring in the first place.

Dino gave her a look that could have cut her in two. "There will be a complete audit of this, you can rest assured."

Ava sighed. "I'll have my support reps call around to have the two hundred and fifteen cribs recalled back to my Denver warehouse."

"That's a good start," said Andrea. The tension was heavy, the atmosphere, strained.

"I know what I have to do, Andrea," Dino replied. "But we all need to keep our heads calm over this."

"It's easy to say but you're not the one who's dealing with people," Leo chimed in, and Ava was grateful for someone taking her side. At last, someone who understood. "You're not the one who is dealing with angry parents. I can imagine that the situation takes on a different kind of urgency when real people are involved."

"We're all real people," Dino shot back. He pinched himself. "See, that hurts. Therefore I'm real."

Ava rolled her eyes when Leo glanced at her. She simmered in silence, tolerating the patronizing a-hole who sat opposite her. "We need to work together, and lose the negativity," Leo said.

Dino huffed out an exasperated breath. "I don't doubt that. This has serious consequences for my business, and you have my word that I'll put things straight."

Based on what Leo had told them, Ava now knew for certain that it would have serious ramifications for her own business, especially if those parents threatened to sue. More complaints would crawl out of the woodwork, more reports of children being hurt. It was imperative to warn all the parents of the order mix-up and to recall the cribs she'd sold.

She'd also have to get in touch with the CPSC. The Consumer Product Safety Commission would have to be notified and it would be better if she was seen to be proactive in correcting this mistake. She had to prove to them that this had been a genuine error at the manufacturing end. And she had to start praying that no child would be injured. Because drop-side cribs were banned in the US, her store never ever sold any of these items. Dino's order number mix-up could be their million-dollar mistake.

This had the potential to bankrupt her and to finish off the business she had worked so hard to build.

Her heart sank lower until it fell into the base of her stomach. She slumped back, feeling suddenly powerless, as if she had no control over her body, as if her skeleton had melted and dissolved inside her.

Maybe it was time to suck it up and do the one thing she'd been putting off; calling Connor and getting his advice. He was a corporate lawyer but he would mostly likely know someone who could advise her.

"I'll need to look through your catalogs to find alternatives," said Ava, and she couldn't stop herself from adding, "Because I'll need something other than d'Este cribs." She saw the vein in Dino's neck and noted that he remained silent.

Leo looked around. "We'll find you some more catalogs. Unfortunately, our stuff is all over the place."

"Do you think you might need to go to Denver?" Andrea asked.

Ava was certain she would. "I have to go over at some point." It was difficult to run an international business with only her at the helm. But with this sudden problem that could prove disastrous, it might be better for her to go now. At least in this way she'd be seen to be proactive and if she acted fast to reclaim the faulty cribs, then it might be enough to help save all their businesses—hoping and praying that nobody sued.

The more she thought about it, the more it seemed likely that she'd have to return to Denver sooner than she had planned.

CHAPTER FIFTEEN

"I've got you, yes I do," Nico babbled away, chattering in baby talk as he changed Elisabetta's diaper.

The stationery, paper weight and paperwork on his desk had been moved to the side to make way for this delicate procedure. Lying among it was the local paper. This morning's edition had been particularly hard to stomach and in light of the delay at the Cazale Ravenna, the media had gone to town, calling him the playboy who couldn't live up to his father's reputation. He'd read the entire article and had tried to bury it deep inside his soul.

He continued to fasten the fresh new diaper and made faces as Elisabetta gurgled back at him. "Papa's got you, princess," he said, slipping her legs back into her sleeper and doing the buttons up. So far it hadn't been too bad. He'd fed her, and then she'd fallen asleep, and he'd been able to get on with his work.

He didn't know what the fuss was about; he didn't understand Ava's complaints about spending the day looking after the baby and struggling to do her work. It didn't seem that much of a chore, and he'd been looking after her for two hours.

Bruno still hadn't heard back from the safety department but his men were doing the last of the finishing touches. They had to re-paper and re-plaster the walls and the ceilings that had had to be stripped to replace the cables. It was the only thing that stopped Nico from getting on the phone and yelling at someone from the safety department. He wanted to ensure that Bruno's men had finished completely.

He could hardly believe that the spa hotel was finally, nearly, almost there.

"Come in," he said, when he heard at knock at the door. Ines poked her head in and her face grew curious to see him. He was supposed to be meeting with her now to go over the advertising campaign but it didn't look as if it was going to happen.

"You brought your daughter in today," gushed Ines, walking into his office with a smile when she saw Elisabetta. The look on her face turned all soft and gooey—just like it did when most people first saw his daughter

"Hey, you," Ines cooed, softly. Elisabetta suddenly perked up and waved her arm around excitedly, and then in the next moment her lower lip began to tremble and she started to cry. Ines looked horrified. "What did I do?"

"I'm not sure." Nico picked up his daughter and put her to his shoulder. "She might have thought you were my wife." With her shoulder-length, sandy brown hair she looked nothing like Ava, but perhaps to a baby...

"Or maybe she's figured that she hasn't seen her mother," said Ines, trying unsuccessfully to soothe the baby down but Elisabetta's cries only grew louder.

"Could you—" He was about to hand the baby to Ines,

because he wanted to wash his hands, but knew he couldn't hand her over when she was crying. "Hey, hey princess." He tried to calm her but his words only seemed to make things worse.

"I'm sorry, I've frightened her." Ines backed away. "Is there anything I can do?"

Nico shook his head as he laid his crying daughter into the baby stroller. "We'll have to postpone the meeting to tomorrow.

"Tomorrow is good." Ines gravitated towards the door. "Are you leaving?"

"Yes. I'd better. I can't get anything else done here." He struggled to get all of the baby's scattered belongings into the bag. Ines held the door open for him and by now Elisabetta was howling as he pushed the stroller out into the lobby. An alarmed group of guests looked up. Nico smiled at them politely.

"We're going home," he told Ines. It would be easier to take Elisabetta home and to feed her there. There was no way he was going to be able to concentrate or o get any work done here with this much noise.

A few minutes after he'd driven off, Elisabetta's cries trailed into silence. He let out a deep breath. He glanced at her over his shoulder and saw that she was wide awake, but seemed content, whether it was the car motion, or the noise of it, or a combination of the two, it didn't matter. She was quiet. It was good to know about such an effective silencing technique. Pleased with himself, he spoke in silly baby language as he drove and when Ava called him, it instantly went to the car's loudspeaker.

"Hey." His wife sounded exuberant.

Behind him, Elisabetta gurgled, probably at hearing the sound of her mother's voice.

"Hey, baby. Hey, Elisabetta," Ava chirped back. "Where are you?"

"In the car."

"Oh," she sounded surprised. "How come?"

"We're going for a drive." Nico didn't need to confess to his wife that he had accepted defeat and was going home early.

"Is everything okay? Did my mom show up?" Ava wanted to know.

"Everything's fine but I haven't seen Elsa." He hadn't even thought to venture out into the gardens to check.

"That's strange."

"It's fine, really." He was eager to prove that he had everything under control.

"How are you coping?"

"Great," he replied. "We're having fun, aren't you, princess?" He glanced over his shoulder again.

"Good," said Ava. "Because Andrea and I are going for a late lunch. I'll be back later."

Later? Nico's body tensed.

"Unless you need me to come back now." Ava's voice carried the implication that he couldn't manage by himself.

"I've got her," he said, hastily.

"But didn't you have a day of meetings?"

"It's all taken care of." He wanted to ask how her meeting had gone. It couldn't have been too bad if she had nothing better to do than to go to lunch with Andrea. He glanced at the clock on the dashboard. It was three o'clock. And it was only then that he remembered he hadn't had lunch.

"You go to lunch with Andrea," he urged, "and don't worry about us."

"Okay, if you're sure."

"I'm sure."

"'Bye baby Lisabetta." Ava blew loud kisses. "I'll see you later."

"See you later." He ended the call feeling a little anxious. "Mommy's going out to dinner," he said, looking at his daughter through the rear-view mirror. "It's just you and me, princess." But with her mother's voice no longer to be heard, Elisabetta dissolved into howls of tears once more.

And Nico's jaw tensed up.

The next few hours were like Groundhog Day. He fed her, then burped her, then changed her, then tried to get her to nap, and when that failed he tried to read to her, or play with her, or rock her. And then he fed her, and burped her, and changed her again, and once more tried to get her to nap.

It still didn't work.

For some reason his daughter was fighting her sleep, but she was tired, he could see it in her eyes. When she continued to wail for more than ten minutes and he couldn't calm her down, he got in his car and drove around.

She was asleep within minutes.

Feeling completely worn out himself, he carried her gently back to the bedroom and, exhausted himself, he lay down with her.

When he next came to, it was to the sound of Elisabetta crying on the bed beside him. Nico opened his eyes and turned over. He'd propped pillows up on the other side of her to stop her from falling. It was past six in the evening.

Where had the time gone?

He'd had some paperwork and emails to catch up on but it had been impossible to get anything done with Elisabetta around.

How did Ava manage?

He wondered if having breasts might have helped his

cause, because nothing he tried seemed to work. "Hey," he crooned, holding his daughter against his shoulder. She continued to cry. Then he hugged her against his chest, then rocked her but nothing seemed to help. "Does your diaper need changing?"

Was that it? How much pee could a baby do? He ran his hands over her bottom to check but her diaper wasn't bloated or soggy. He bent his head down and sniffed but he couldn't smell a number two either.

"Hey, Elisabetta," he rasped, his voice almost faint. "Shush, Mommy's going to be here soon." But of course his words had no effect. "Milk. Do you want some more milk?" Maybe she wanted more milk. He'd tried all the other options. He opened his bedroom door just as Elsa knocked.

"That's where you were hiding!" she exclaimed, her eyes shining as soon as she saw her granddaughter. Nico could almost have kissed her when he saw the bottle of milk in her hands. "I heard her crying, so I got her milk ready. Shall I take her?" Elsa offered.

Nico didn't need to be asked again. He couldn't hand the baby over fast enough.

"I'll feed her in the nursery," said Elsa, and entered from the main door.

Nico followed. "When did you come home?" he asked, watching Elsa ease into the glider slowly. "About an hour ago. My phone battery died along the way and I didn't notice until later and that's why I didn't get Ava's messages or I'd have turned up sooner."

"She was hoping you'd be at the Casa Adriana."

"I was, much later. Salvatore went to the nursery to look at some things for the gardens and I went along with him."

Nico nodded, understanding.

"But we didn't get back until late afternoon, and that's when Gina told me you'd gone home. I came as soon as I heard."

"You didn't have to do that." But all the same, he was relieved that she had. He wasn't sure how much more of Elisabetta's crying he could have taken. The baby hadn't been like that when he'd been at home convalescing.

Of course she hadn't—Ava had been here. Perhaps all his daughter wanted was her mother. He leaned against the door with his hands in his pockets and watched Elsa throw an adoring look at her granddaughter whose tiny hands gripped the bottle as if she would never let it go.

"Ava's having dinner with Andrea," Elsa remarked, beaming at him as if this was good news.

"I know."

"It's good for her to be out and about. She needed a day to herself."

"I suppose she did."

"I was beginning to worry with her being at home all the time. It can't be easy, Nico, and it's not as if she has a lot of company and she's been so busy with her work."

"She doesn't have to work," he said it before he could stop himself, but he also knew that Elsa wasn't one to go running to her daughter and relay all that he'd said to her.

"She doesn't have to work, no," replied Elsa carefully, "and she's very lucky to have that choice, but she *wants* to work, and you're very lucky that she's that sort of woman, and not the type who wants everything handed to her on a silver platter." If that didn't put him in his place, he didn't know what would. Feeling sheepish, he straightened up. "That's not what I meant."

"I know, but you don't look happy, and I can't help but overhear the things you two bicker about. I don't want you to take it out on her when she gets back. Having a baby can put enormous pressure on a couple sometimes, and the two of you haven't had an easy time of things. Instead of taking it out on one another, maybe you both need to remember who you were when you first met."

He had to give it to her. Elsa had a way of putting him in his place and spelling things out for him and he didn't mind. Not the way she said it. He coughed lightly. "It's not that I've forgotten, Elsa," he said, trying to salvage his reputation. "It's that there are so many other urgent things that are screaming out for attention. It's easy to take things for granted, and it's easy to get irritable."

"That may be," replied Elsa stiffly. "But having a new baby isn't easy and, I know you might not want to hear this, but it gets harder as the children get older."

His heart sank. This afternoon had been nothing like he'd expected and now Elsa was telling him that it was going to get worse?

"But that stage doesn't last long either. In fact," she seemed to be talking more to herself than to him, "All the stages in our life are fleeting when you look back on them from where I'm standing. You should stop and take a moment to enjoy them, Nico, for they will soon be over."

He let the words sink in. "Is that how you feel?"

"My life has flown by so fast. Seeing you both with your baby, it reminds me of when my girls were that age, and if I let myself wallow in the memories too long, it doesn't seem as long ago as it really was."

He nodded.

"You wait until Elisabetta turns into a teenager." Elsa looked up at him. "They think they know everything then. They think they don't need you. Something for you to bear in mind."

He couldn't imagine a time when his own daughter would tell him she didn't need him and it wasn't something he wanted to think about.

"Why don't you go and do whatever it was you need to do," Elsa suggested. "I've got my granddaughter."

CHAPTER SIXTEEN

"That was delicious, and I got to eat without any interruptions."

"See what you'd have missed out on," said Andrea.

"I was anxious to get back home."

"You shouldn't worry about Elisabetta. Your mom is there, and you have the housekeeper."

"The housekeeper doesn't look after the baby and my mom, well..." Ava wiped her lips with her napkin. "My mom's been rather busy lately, and I'm not sure what with."

"Oh?" Andrea held the wine glass in her hands as if waiting for more gossip. "She's doing her own thing, and I suppose I must let her. I mean—" Ava wiped her mouth and laid down her napkin, "I want her to do her own thing, I don't want her to feel that she's bound to me, to us, in any way. She helps out a lot as it is, but today, of all days—I could have really done with her being around."

"You mean to say that Nico's looking after Elisabetta?"

"He sounded fine when I called him."

They giggled.

"It will be a good experience for him," said Ava. She

wanted him to know what a whole day with the baby could be like.

"I'm sure he's a really good father," said Andrea. "I mean," she sat upright, "I mean the way he was with Alessa on the few times I saw him with her. When he used to talk about her it often seemed that he cared more for that child than her own mother did."

"He did." Ava remembered the early days when she'd started to fall for Nico. Around that time, and before, there had been many rumors that Silvia Azzarone's child had been fathered by Nico. They'd had a short summer fling, and when the child was born people assumed it was Nico's. Silvia had never set the story straight and it took a paternity test for the truth to come out.

The child wasn't his.

"Silvia's a sly little snake, isn't she?" Andrea declared, before taking a sip of her wine. Ava nodded, agreeing. She felt nothing but contempt for the woman who seemed to have made it her life's work to cause problems for her and Nico. "She hates you," said Andrea, putting her wine glass down.

"I know she does. The sad thing is that we feel nothing but pity for her."

"Pity?" Andrea asked. "You don't hate her?"

"Hating would mean exerting too much of my energy. I *should* hate her, because she found a way to get to Nico, but hate is a strong emotion and I don't feel that much for her."

"You mean with the hotel inspection?"

"We think so but we can't prove it. All we have is the project manager's word to go on. He has a contact at the safety department. We don't actually have proper proof."

"He was trying to lobby for worker's rights wasn't he?" asked Andrea.

"He made a thinly veiled reference to businessmen who

forget they have a duty to do the right thing, and then he mentioned something about a new hotel opening and the owner, a multi-millionaire not re-wiring it properly—something along those lines." Ava's voice was weary as she recounted it. "He was smart, he mentioned no names but that's what he said. I've read the article in the paper."

"So how did what he said stop your hotel from opening?"

"It didn't. The health and safety department didn't pass it based on a few minor technicalities and somehow," she air-quoted the 'somehow', "the people we'd newly hired to work at the hotel, all of a sudden they started to grumble."

"It sounds like too much of a coincidence," remarked Andrea, making a face as if she'd smelled a skunk.

"He drove back later, soon after that meeting, and that's when he had the accident. I'd gone into labor and he was racing back to get to me."

Andrea squinted, as if recalling that time. "That's right," she said softly. "It all happened that day."

"And then I had the baby and we were both recovering, and here we are." Ava took a sip of her lemonade.

"I'm surprised Nico hasn't disputed it."

"What's the point?" Ava shrugged. "He's gone ahead and fixed it now, and he's desperate for it to open and start making money."

"He must hate the sight of those two."

"With a passion," said Ava. "I don't know what he'd do if he saw Silvia again. Every now and then we read things about her and Vieri in the local papers and it makes Nico's blood boil."

Andrea raised an eyebrow. "He gets around, that politician. He's always in the news for one thing or another. But I don't understand what she's doing with him. He must be old enough to be her father."

"Silvia is all about status and power," Ava retorted. "She doesn't care how old he is, or even what sort of a person he is, I'm not even sure they have that much in common. All she wants are connections."

"Thank goodness she didn't get her claws into Nico," said Andrea. She quickly added, "Not that he ever would have gone back to her. He knew what to avoid, and he knew a good thing when he found it."

Did he? Ava wondered, and forced a smile because there was nothing positive or truthful she could say in return. "I should get back." She glanced at her watch. It was past 6pm—not too late but late enough. She'd been away from Elisabetta for hours and she wasn't used to it.

"What's the rush?" asked Andrea. "Stay a little longer. We still need to have dessert and coffee."

Now *that* was a good idea. Besides, she'd called her mom a short while ago and everything seemed to be fine back home. She could stay for a little longer and be home in time to feed Elisabetta. No doubt her little one would be hungry, and Ava would need her to feed well, to relieve the ache in her breasts. She'd never gone this long before without feeding. "Dessert and coffee sound great."

So, they ordered coffee and spent some more time on idle chit-chat. "Interesting character, Dino," Ava mused.

"Interesting?"

"I expected to like him, based on what you'd told me about him."

Andrea's cheeks colored. "And you don't?"

"He's very defensive."

"And you're not?" Andrea asked. "I think you both got off on the wrong foot."

"You're getting defensive about him!" replied Ava, angling

her head. She ran her fingertip around the lip of her cup. "Are you sure there's nothing you want to tell me?"

"I have nothing to tell!" Andrea exclaimed, leaning back in her seat.

"He's good-looking."

"Who's looking?"

"Hard not to notice," continued Ava, watching her friend carefully. Andrea squeezed her eyes to slits and looked at her with suspicion. "You're married to the perfect man and you—"

"I'm not looking, but I can't deny it. If he wasn't so pig-headed I'd encourage you to flirt back."

"He's not flirting with me!"

"He's obviously taken with you, Andrea. You're blind to it." Ava sipped her coffee. "Which is why you can't see that Leo seems kind of taken with you."

"Leo is a colleague, a business partner. That's it." Andrea's voice was so firm that Ava held back from insisting. "I get that," she said. "You both seem to be pretty comfortable around one another."

"And so we should be." Andrea scratched the base of her neck. "He's my business partner and nothing more than that."

"Okay." Ava took the hint. She'd already sensed that Andrea didn't like to talk about her past, and so she didn't bring up the American who'd been her last boyfriend. She might not ever find out what had caused this sudden shift in Andrea to be done with men and romance, but Ava had a feeling that the American had a lot to do with it.

"I don't care what you think, Ava, whatever it is you and Nico are speculating about but it isn't what you think."

"Nico doesn't speculate on these things." Her husband didn't have time to talk about anything that wasn't to do with the hotel.

"Don't forget to take a look through those catalogs," said Andrea, changing the subject completely.

"I'll have a look and get these back to you as soon as I'm done." After the meeting, once Dino had left, Leo had dug up the supplier catalogues of some new manufacturers whom he and Andrea were looking to do business with. Even though the recent problem with the cribs was due to a mix-up with the orders numbers and nothing to do with a design fault, Ava was still hesitant about ordering from d'Este. Even though the d'Este static cribs were her bestsellers, she wasn't too keen on Dino Massari at the moment.

"Keep them," said Andrea. "I'll order some more."

"Thanks," said Ava. "And now," she looked around to catch the waiter's attention. "I need to pay and go."

"You're worried about Nico and the baby?"

"No. He'll cope, but I'm interested to find out how his day went."

About time too.

It would be good for him to find out what it was like being at home with a baby for longer than the few hours he spent with her each evening after a 'hard' day at work.

Andrea had been right all along. This was exactly what she'd needed, to get away for the day and to be back in the driver's seat again, to be in control, an independent and working woman, not only a mother.

CHAPTER SEVENTEEN

Ava was later than he'd expected when she finally returned home. Elisabetta lay on the bed beside him, happily gurgling away.

For once the colic hadn't reared its ugly head and the evening had been calmer for it. Nico lay propped up on his elbow, stroking Elisabetta's cheeks and lips and nose, and letting her tiny fingers try to grab his. He looked up when Ava walked into the bedroom. "You're back?" He'd meant to say 'hello' but the words tumbled right out of his mouth.

"Yes." She slid onto the bed, her attention solely on the baby. She lay on her stomach with her legs bent at the knees and her feet up in the air and peppered the baby's face with tiny kisses. All at once Elisabetta, on hearing her voice and smelling her scent, started to wave her arms and kick her legs with glee. "Mommy's back." Ava made all manner of noises, getting Elisabetta even more excited.

"Don't I get a welcome?" he asked.

A trace of a frown crossed her face; it was hard to miss. "Hi," she said, turning to him.

Now it was his turn to frown. "Hi? Just 'hi'? Don't I get a

kiss?" She looked good in that light grey skirt and jacket with a black satin blouse and her hair tied back in a beehive ponytail. She looked chic. In answer, she leaned forward and gave him a peck on the lips. It was better than nothing, even if he'd had to ask for it.

"How's she been?"

"Good. She's missed you," he told her, when she lay back down again and turned her attention back to the baby. "She acted up earlier."

"Was it colic?"

"No, it was all quiet on that front. She was hungry when she woke up earlier. She needed her milk right then and there."

Ava smiled. "She wants it instantly. I need to feed her," she said. "I'm almost at bursting point." She shrugged off her jacket.

"How did it go?" he asked, eyeing her in her sexy blouse.

"It's worse than I thought." Her face turned serious. And slowly it all came out; the order mix-up, the child being hurt and the potential threat of a lawsuit.

He sat up on the bed and rubbed his hand across his forehead. "I didn't know it was that bad. Why didn't you tell me?"

"I wasn't sure. I've been reading up about it, and it's all happened so quickly but Leo is right. We're all culpable, not just Dino. I need to go to Denver and fix what I can."

"How can you fix anything?" he asked, a little louder than he'd intended. *And what the hell did she need to go to Denver for?*

"My customers are in the US. I sell only to the US and I've sold over two hundred of these cribs there. *I* need to get over there and sort this mess out."

"When?"

"Soon." She took off her blouse and slid on her nightshirt.

Nico's stomach muscles tensed. He didn't like this plan of hers and wondered at the practicality of taking a baby with her. How much could she do with a baby to look after as well?

Ava picked the baby up and jiggled her around, cooing and grinning and rubbing her face against Elisabetta's while he sat on the bed processing this latest development. "What is it that you're most displeased about?" she asked, throwing him a stone-cold stare.

"It's ... just ... that ... Elisabetta's still so young."

"It's not my choice to go right now, but a baby's been injured and I have a lot of customers that I need to warn. The CPSC could have me over this."

"Shouldn't Andrea be doing something? And Leo?"

"They are," she replied, still looking at him coldly. "We all are. It affects all of us. We have to work together and Dino's looking at the processes in his factory. It's not a design fault but a stupid error that should have been picked up. Those cribs shouldn't have even left his warehouse and frankly I'm shocked that they did. Unfortunately, it's going to hit my business first because I'm the one who's selling these cribs. This cribs are banned in the US, Nico." Ava's voice rose, as if he wasn't quite getting it. "Maybe because they have immobilizers, the error didn't get picked up so easily, but I could be looking at more customer complaints, and possibly more children being harmed. I really want to get there as soon as I can so that I can do whatever it takes, even if all I do is help Kim and Rona make phone calls."

"I still don't understand why you have to be the one leading it."

"I'm not leading it. They're doing what they need to. I sold these through my website. The customers, the first person they'll sue is me. Not Andrea, not Leo, not Dino, but me." She hugged Elisabetta tighter. "I can't believe the way you're reacting." Her face contorted. "Is it too much to ask for a little sympathy? To get some reassuring words from you? All I wanted was for you to tell me it would be okay, and you can't even do that."

He jumped off the bed and strode towards her. "I—I just didn't understand it—" He reached out for her but she stepped back, flinching from his touch.

"Don't. It doesn't mean anything when you have to be told how to empathize."

He'd been trying to tread carefully, not wanting to get into an altercation with her again but it was too late. With the baby still in her arms, she asked him, "If one of your workers fell off the scaffolding and hurt themselves, do you expect me to believe that you wouldn't visit them? That you wouldn't run off to Ravenna so fast without giving it another thought?"

"That's different—"

"Why?"

With the raised voices, Elisabetta began to whimper. "Hush, baby," murmured Ava, walking around and bouncing the baby in an effort to soothe her.

"I hate arguing with you, Ava."

"Then don't."

"I didn't start it."

She gasped out aloud and glared at him. "You don't even know how you come across. Well, let me tell you." She jabbed a finger at him, and he knew she was madder than mad. "You're mad at me because I've been out all day and you're mad because for once you were left with the baby and I can tell you're not too happy about it."

He opened his mouth and stared at her with narrowed eyes. "That's not true. It was unexpected, but I coped."

"You *coped*?" She raised her eyebrow. "You *coped*? I

cope every single day, Nico. I make it work with the baby and the store, and now this...this...this lousy crib problem which is the last thing I need. I could be staring at a potential lawsuit, don't you get it? And that's *one* customer. Who knows how many other children might get hurt because of me? What if a child dies? I'll carry that with me forever."

He wiped a hand over his face. His wife wouldn't be in this mess if she'd listened to him, if she'd taken time off to enjoy motherhood. He'd given her a privileged life and she had no real reason to work, but it would be the wrong thing to say to her now.

"I'm thinking of going to Denver next week. Connor says it will look much better if I'm proactive."

Connor? His insides flared. "When did you speak to him?"

"Earlier today."

"You had a long lunch that turned into dinner almost, with Dino and Leo and—"

Her blue eyes widened in amazement. "Andrea," she said slowly. "It was only me and Andrea." She stopped rocking the baby. "What's the matter with you?"

Nothing was the matter with him.

"You having all these meetings with Ines," she said in a tone that put him on high alert, "I'm supposed to be okay with that?"

"Ines?" He stared at her dumbfounded. "You're... worried...about...about her?" The shock of her words hit him like a ton of bricks. He stepped towards her. "Ava, darling, don't be so ridic—"

She stepped back. "Don't *darling* me. I'm not worried about Ines. I'm being a total jackass like you."

Elisabetta started to whimper.

"I'm sorry." He felt like a real douchebag. She walked away. "Where are you going?"

"To feed her."

"But I just fed her."

"I *need* to feed her." She walked into the nursery and sat down, opening her shirt and putting the baby to her breast. Elisabetta guzzled away contentedly and Ava closed her eyes, as if feeling relieved.

"I forgot," he said, softly. "You hadn't fed her all day. It must be getting uncomfor—"

"Just go, Nico." She didn't even open her eyes. "Just let me be."

CHAPTER EIGHTEEN

She felt his kiss first. Soft, and quick and her eyelids flew open. Nico's face hovered over hers for a few seconds before he stepped away.

"What was that for?" she asked, feeling confused as she lifted herself up on her elbows and saw that he was sharply dressed and suited.

"Because I'm still crazy about you even though we seem to argue most of the time."

She watched him put on his jacket, quietly admiring the way his shirt hugged his back. Then she sat up, wanting to talk, wanting to dissolve this coldness between them. "You haven't told me anything about your hotel," she said.

"You weren't in the mood for talking last night."

"That's not fair," she shot back. "You weren't exactly being an angel yourself."

Nico straightened up his tie and gave her a look which had her heart melting. They never used to have many disagreements before and, on the rare occasions when they had, the making up part was the best; rolling around in bed for hours. The way things were now, the making up part never happened, and that was as much her fault as Nico's.

"I was trying to be honest with you, Ava. It seemed odd to me that Dino makes the mistake and you're the one who has to go abroad to fix everything."

"Not again," she said, hating that each time they talked it turned into bickering. "Sometimes what I want more is your support."

"I don't like the idea of you and Elisabetta going all the way there."

"I'm going, and I don't know how much more I can explain to you my reason for going."

He winced, pursing his lips together, and she could see he was forcing himself to stay quiet.

She tried to turn his attention to something else. "Is the hotel still opening on time?"

"What do you care?" His voice was level but his tone seemed off. "You're going to Denver."

"I'm not going for the entire month," she protested, growing irritated by his petulance. "I *need* to go. I wish you could understand. I can get everything done quickly and be back within a few weeks."

She didn't expect it to take more time than that, at least she'd have started the ball rolling with CPSC. She had no real idea how long incidents such as these dragged on. "You're not opening until the end of February and I will be back in time."

She was trying to make everyone happy and was trying to take into consideration what mattered to him which was why it hurt so much when he couldn't do the same for her.

"You've already made up your mind, Ava. So go."

She *was* going but she didn't want to leave knowing that things between them were sour because of it. She counted to ten quickly, hoping that she could prevent another bad start to their day. "You're looking very smart today," she told him. Whenever he wore a white shirt with a dark suit, it made him seem ten times more handsome than he already was; something about the contrast of the dark and light fabric against his olive complexion. She wasn't sure what emotion was more dominant, the urge to run up to him and throw her arms around him or her desire to be totally pissed off at him for the rest of the day.

"I'll be back late." He grabbed his cell phone and slid it into his jacket pocket. "I'm going to Ravenna today. I already mentioned it to you."

With Ines. Of course she remembered. "The photo shoot," she said, her words dying to a whisper. No wonder he had taken so much time getting dressed. No wonder he looked so drop-your-panties gorgeous this morning. He left, walking out of their bedroom without so much as a backward glance at her.

She wasn't jealous or worried about Ines, and knew she had no real reason to be, but she was still envious that he was driving her to Ravenna and back, that they'd have the whole day together while she was stuck at home. And because they'd parted on not-so-great terms, she felt justified in wallowing in her self-pity for a little while longer.

She sank back against her pillows and glanced at the alarm clock, making up her mind to lie in bed until Elisabetta's cries woke her. She needed this quiet time to decide how she was going to plan the next few crucial weeks.

Going away now might not be such a bad thing after all. To put some distance between her and Nico might help put their relationship back together again.

"**Y**ou're going to Denver at a time like this?" Elsa stopped spreading marmalade on her toast.

"Yes, absolutely I am, and at a time like what, Mom?" Ava wondered if her mother and Nico were in cahoots together. Did neither of them take her business seriously?

"You know things aren't going too well for Nico and that he's under a lot of pressure."

"So am I, Mom!" Why could no-one see that? She'd only just explained the crib problem to her mom but Elsa couldn't understand why Ava was the one who had to fly to the US to deal with things and not Dino. "I'm not having an easy time of it either."

"You need to see something," her mother said and scurried out of the kitchen and returned a few seconds later. "This was lying in the living room yesterday." She placed the paper on the table for her to see. "He doesn't know I've seen it. But I'm sure this isn't helping the situation. Poor Nico."

Ava leaned against the worktop and read the article slowly.

'The Cazale Midas touch dies with Edmondo Cazale'

Reading further, it mentioned the delays of the Cazale Ravenna opening and taunted Nico by saying that he wasn't cut out for the grown-up world of business. "No wonder he was in a bad mood last night," murmured Ava.

"He wasn't in a bad mood," said Elsa, "I don't think Elisabetta gave him much time to worry about what the papers had to say. At least, he wasn't in a bad mood until you got home and then the two of you fell out again. I could hear you. Do you need to go to Denver, honey? Can't it wait?"

"Don't you think I would wait if I could?"

Elsa sighed. "Sometimes, honey, I'm not so sure. It seems that each time you reach a tough point, you want to run away."

Ava couldn't believe her ears. "I'm not running away, Mom." It was difficult, trying to remain calm when her mother had obviously not understood where she was coming from. "I wasn't planning on going to Denver yet but I have no option. Why can't you see things from my point of view?" Her mom always seemed to have plenty of support where Nico was concerned.

"I'm trying to understand, it's just that I was thinking of staying in Verona for a few more months," her mother confessed.

"You were?" This was news to Ava. She didn't think that Verona had much to keep her mom's interest here. Not now that Edmondo had gone. But maybe being here was the thing that had helped her to deal with his loss. Ava threw her hands up in the air, feeling helpless. "I'm not suggesting that you return with us and you're more than welcome to stay here if you want. I'll be back in a few weeks' time."

"But how will you cope with the baby alone?"

"Like most women do," Ava replied wearily. "I've looked after Elisabetta long enough now and I'm sure I can do the same during a transatlantic flight over the pond."

"I'll have to come back with you," Elsa insisted, speaking to herself, and not looking too happy about it either.

"You don't have to do—"

"I'm coming."

There was no use in trying to change mom's mind. Ava scratched her cheek. "I didn't know you'd grown so fond of Verona," she said. *Now that Edmondo was no longer around.* Or was there another reason her mother seemed so taken by Italy?

"I can't explain it." Elsa cut through her toast diagonally. "I feel grounded here. I feel more at peace."

"If it helps, I'm only planning to go for three weeks," Ava told her.

"I'll come back with you."

"I'll book the tickets."

CHAPTER NINETEEN

Nico walked into the Casa Adriana early with the hope of getting some work done before he left for Ravenna with Ines.

She had a stylist and photographer booked so that she could take more pictures of the new hotel for a media package she was putting together. But as soon as he walked into the lobby his eyes caught sight of yesterday's paper which was lying on the couch. He should have thrown it away yesterday. He walked over, gritting his teeth together and read it again:

'The Cazale Midas touch dies with Edmondo Cazale

"Nico?"

He looked up in irritation, only to find Demetrio hovering nearby. "Demetrio." Nico acknowledged his new colleague briefly before turning his attention back to the paper.

"Aren't you going to Ravenna today?"

Nico squared his shoulders. "That's right."

"Ines has got some cool design concepts for the media kit." His colleague was as eager to make small talk as Nico was to avoid it.

"Yes."

"I'm going to grab a coffee. Can I get you one?"

"No. If you don't mind, Demetrio, I'm waiting for Ines and I'd rather just catch up on the news while I have a chance. If you need me for anything, perhaps we can discuss it tomorrow?"

The man looked slightly taken aback by Nico's answer but recovered enough to say, "Sure, don't mind me." Demetrio's mouth set in a hard line as he walked away quickly and Nico turned his attention once more to the offending article. He'd already read it a few times, and each time it seemed to dig the heel into him even harder. Whoever wrote this piece had obviously wanted to twist the knife deeper. But it was the last line that kicked him in the guts and left him winded.

'Cazale Junior would have better success if he returned to drink and gambling, and left the running of the business to his beautiful and talented wife, Ava Ramirez. The American beauty seems to have been a great catch for Cazale Junior. Possessing both beauty and brains, this stunner runs her own hugely successful online store for children.'

He folded the paper and threw it onto the sofas, only to turn around and see Gina rushing through the double doors of the entrance.

"You're early," he commented, wondering why most of his team were here so early.

"I left work early yesterday," Gina replied. "And I remembered that one of our guests had changed their booking." She looked worried. "I hope it's not too late."

"Too late for what?"

"They wanted to arrive this afternoon, instead of tomorrow."

"I'm sure it will be fine." Nico was once again impressed

by Gina's dedication and loyalty. "That's the only reason you've come in early? You could have asked anyone on reception to take care of it."

"Perhaps." Gina hovered in the lobby and was obviously anxious to get to her office.

Nico glanced at his watch. It was half past seven and he'd told Ines they would be leaving at eight-thirty. He'd hoped to get some work done prior to that, but maybe it was an opportunity to talk to Gina—so that he could find out exactly what was going on with her.

"I need to get going," she said, and started to walk towards her office. He followed. "Aren't you and Ines going to Ravenna today?" she asked.

"In an hour's time."

She walked into her office and turned to him. "Was there something you wanted to see me about?"

"Not particularly. I thought it would be a good time to catch up on things, if you've got a few moments." Seeing Gina, he was suddenly consumed by a deep-seated desire to offload what was bothering him. Gina knew him almost as well as Ava. "Besides, Ines isn't here yet," he said, hovering around the door as she shrugged out of her coat and hung it up on the coat stand.

Gina stared at him. "Did you want to come in?"

He did.

She sat down and stared at him as he paced around the room with one hand in the pocket of his pants, and the other one rubbing his forehead.

"Ava is going to Denver next week," he said, finally. "She's had a problem with one of her product lines and she's worried about getting hit with a lawsuit."

Gina's mouth opened, fish-like. "A lawsuit?"

"It's happened all of a sudden and she's leaving next week."

"She must be worried sick. I mean, a lawsuit." Gina paused in silence. "It could prove costly."

"That's the last damn thing I need."

"How's Ava handling the news?"

He stopped pacing around. "As well as can be expected. She's anxious to get out there and do what she can. A young baby has been injured and I think that's really shaken her."

"What products are we talking about?"

"Cribs."

Gina raised an eyebrow. "Cribs?" She looked shocked. "This is terrible, Nico. All babies use cribs, from newborns to toddlers. I can understand why she's rushing off."

"I wish she wasn't. Elisabetta is only two months old and I can't see how Ava going there is going to fix anything."

Gina frowned. "She's doing what she needs to do to protect her business, Nico. You'd do the same."

He sat down in the chair, feeling uneasy. "You might think I'm being selfish and that I'm thinking about myself, but I'm worried about her going all that way with Elisabetta. I already have enough on my plate and the thought of her and Elisabetta being out there and dealing with all of this—"

"She'll be fine, Nico. You're worrying for no reason. This is Ava. She can handle the baby and the business. She obviously knows what she's doing, and with your support she'll get through this."

He blinked a few times. Maybe he should have been more understanding. He'd been so annoyed to hear that she'd already made up her mind to go that he hadn't stopped to think of how she was feeling.

"If you're so worried you could always go out there with

her," Gina continued. "The Cazale Ravenna is almost ready, isn't it? It won't need your attention as much."

"Go out there?" *How could he when he had so many things to do here?* "The spa is almost ready but the safety people are dragging their heels. All of this has gone on for too long. I can't leave everything and fly to Denver. I can't. The papers are already waiting for me to fail grandly."

"You saw the paper?" Gina's face sank into the palm of her hand. "I thought I'd thrown all our copies away."

"What for?" he answered, glancing down at his wedding ring. "Maybe they have a point."

"Nico!" Gina scowled at him. "What sort of attitude is that."

"It's how I feel."

"You sound defeated and that's not like you."

"I *feel* defeated."

"You mustn't believe the media."

"The blasted media." He slammed his hand on the armrest.

"What do they know?" Gina was doing her best to cheer him up, but it didn't help.

"We'll get through this," he said, feeling bolstered by her belief. Just as he and Ava would get through this difficult patch. "What's going on with you?" he asked, eager to get to the bottom of whatever it was. Clearly there was something. "Is there anything I need to know?"

Gina shook her head, and kept her lips tightly closed together.

"Demetrio?" he asked.

"What about him?"

"How's his upgrade project coming along?"

"He's ordering the equipment."

Nico nodded. "If truth be told, Gina you seem a little distracted." *A little off.* "How is your mother?"

"She's back to her usual self." Gina picked up her pen again and rolled it around in her hands. "Everything's fine here, Nico. You don't need to worry."

CHAPTER TWENTY

It seemed that no sooner had she made up her mind to go to Denver, than the day of her departure was upon them.

A clipped voice announced the boarding times for a flight to Venezuela over the airport speakerphone. And still they waited. The call for Ava's flight hadn't yet been announced and she was eager to get going so that she could settle Elisabetta. Ava glanced at Nico who sat beside her on the uncomfortable plastic chairs in the departure lounge. He held his daughter in his arms and a piece of her heart tore because she could see right through his false, steel-edged expression. He wasn't saying much but she could tell that he was sad to see them go.

"She'll sleep most of the way there," he said, taking Ava's hand.

"I hope so." She had tiny balls of cotton ready to insert into her baby's ears once they were seated in the plane. This past week she'd packed and gotten together everything she would need for the trip but it had been difficult to focus because she'd heard from the parents of the child who had fallen. They were threatening to sue. The fear of losing her business paralyzed her and made her even more eager to get to the US.

Ava had plans, once she'd arrived in Denver, to meet with a representative from the CPSC as well as the lawyer that Connor had recommended. Kim and Rona had managed to get in touch with a lot of the customers who had purchased the problematic cribs, but they were still hunting down the remaining people.

"Take care of her," Nico said, letting go of Ava's hand and stroking his daughter's face. It surprised her, his sudden gentleness. Luckily Elisabetta was fast asleep—even amid the clattering of the noise all around them. Verona airport was small and not that busy, but the noise was louder than what Elisabetta was used to.

"You know I will." She wasn't for one moment looking forward to the long flight ahead of her.

Nico had been different during the last few days and if he was sad to see her go, he hadn't done or said anything to stop her from going. She laid her hand against his cheek; she had sensed that something was going on with the hotel, but he hadn't been very forthcoming when she'd asked him and so she'd let the matter drop.

"Send me pictures of her every day."

"I will," she promised, wanting to put his mind at rest. "She's not going to change that much in three weeks, Nico."

"She changes every day," he insisted bending down and kissing his sleeping princess on the forehead. Princess—that was his name for her and Ava knew exactly how Elisabetta would be treated as she grew older. She'd have to make sure he didn't spoil her too much.

"Say hi to Carlos and Rona for me."

"I will." At least her sister and brother—in-law would get a chance to see their new niece. It would be interesting to see how Tori reacted to the new addition. "I'll be back before you know it."

He nodded, saying nothing.

"Please understand why I have to go. I have to track down all the cribs and deal with the angry parents. It's better for me to be there than Dino."

"Of course I understand, I might not like it, but I know why you're going. I hope the powers that be see how forthcoming you're being." He had an intense look in his eyes. "I'm behind you all the way, Ava, even though it might not seem like it."

He was trying. She could tell. "Let me know how it goes with the safety inspection."

"Okay."

"I'm going to be back in time for the opening."

"Okay."

"I will be," she cried, a little annoyed by his monosyllabic responses. Another announcement cruised over the speakerphone and they both cocked their heads listening to the flight number.

"Did you hear that?" said Elsa, appearing out of nowhere with a stack of magazines in her hand. "That's us. I got you something to read," she said, sifting through the bundle of magazines.

"You keep it for now, Mom," said Ava, not hopeful that she would have any time to read a magazine during the flight and if by some miracle Elisabetta slept, she'd probably end up sleeping too. Why waste the opportunity?

"We should get going," Elsa stuffed the magazines into her handbag. Ava and Nico got up slowly at the same time and turned to one another. She saw the way he hugged Elisabetta tight, and she leaned in and kissed him. A kiss that was short but ran deep, that sent shivers along her back not because of passion, but because it was a temporary letting go, and there were still so many things left unsaid and unfixed between them.

"Honey, we're going to be late."

"We have time, Mom," Ava insisted, as she watched Nico smother his daughter's face with kisses. He reluctantly handed the sleeping baby to Ava but the sudden movement from his warm hold to her arms must have jolted Elisabetta for she stirred. Anxious for her baby not to wake up and raise hell, Ava rocked her. The last thing she wanted was to leave Nico with a memory of his daughter in tears.

"Lay her in the stroller," Elsa whispered.

"I'm going to hold her." She turned to Nico. "Don't worry about her." She needed to alleviate his tension. "She'll wake up soon and then I'll feed her. She'll be fine."

He put his arms around them and kissed her. "Take care of yourself," he told her, and she suddenly felt tearful, the suddenness of their departure making her feel lost. "Don't go working your crazy hours," she chastised.

He gave a shake of his head, then narrowed his eyes. "You too. Don't go overboard." Then, he pressed his lips together as if unsure. Hesitant. "I love you, don't ever forget that."

"Never," she said, but she doubted he heard because it was barely a whisper. She stepped away, and their hands, still joined, slowly peeled apart. She placed her hand across the baby's chest and tipped her forward slightly so that Nico could see her face. And then she was suddenly blinded by the flash of a camera, and another and another. It was enough to rouse Elisabetta. And when another announcement sounded over the speakerphone at the same time, it was too late to hope that she would remain asleep. Her lower lip trembled, and her eyes slowly fluttered open. She whimpered at first, but only for a few moments, until the whimpering turned into an almighty cry.

"We'd better go," said Elsa, pushing the empty stroller along. Ava waved at Nico, then turned and walked away quickly with Elisabetta howling in her arms, and the blinding flashes of a camera following them.

"Get lost!" he yelled, his lips flattening into a sneer. Nico shot a threatening glance at the lone photographer who'd taken the intrusive shots.

Trust this son of a bitch to ruin a tender moment.

In the distance he could hear his daughter's cries and he spun around to take one final look as Ava slowly disappeared out of sight. For a few moments he stood there, collecting himself and then he turned to go. But another flash of white light blinded him for a few seconds. The smug grin on the photographer's face taunted him. "Thanks, man," he said and to add insult to injury, he stuck his thumb up.

The rage Nico had tried to suppress now bubbled up and he couldn't help it when his fist met with the man's camera, knocking it onto the floor. "You're welcome, *man*," replied Nico. He was suddenly seized by the desire to stamp his foot all over it, but the thought of Ava suddenly reappearing and seeing this stopped him cold. Instead he walked away, with the man's shouts and curses trailing behind him.

Onlookers flocked to the scene. Some of them might even have recognized him, others might have caught the tail end of the fracas. He fully expected this garbage to make the papers tomorrow.

As usual there was nothing major to report, but he had no doubt that the papers would conjure up something out of nothing. And for that reason along, he hoped the camera was smashed to pieces.

CHAPTER TWENTY-ONE

"Why's she always crying?" asked Rona, tottering about in her skin-tight jeans as she cleared the table. Ava picked up the jug of water and followed her sister in the kitchen.

She'd been here three days and still she felt a twinge of jealousy whenever she stared at Rona's super slim figure. Today her sister flaunted it in her painted on tight jeans and boobs that defied gravity. In that moment Ava decided that she would get back to her daily runs once she returned to Verona.

Running?

Who was she kidding? She could barely crawl out of bed in the mornings. With Elisabetta still getting up twice during the night, there was no way that Ava could spring out of bed in the morning and as time wore on, she felt herself get more and more sluggish.

"She's unsettled," said Ava, returning to the living room to take the baby from her mom.

"You girls want a hand clearing up?" Elsa asked.

Ava shook her head. "We're almost done." She skillfully side-stepped Tori who sat on the floor looking up at her. Her niece clapped her hands together. "Me, baby me," she wailed.

"You want the baby?" Ava asked. Elisabetta seemed to be nothing more than an object of curiosity for the toddler, and Tori treated her as if she were a doll. Ava had to watch her like a hawk.

"Thanks for having us over," she said to Carlos and Rona. Her brother-in-law was an amazing cook and it was hardly surprising given that his family owned a string of restaurants. Not only was he a good cook but Carlos was good all around. He worked crazy shifts in the family restaurants, and then came home and did more than his fair share with Tori and cooked and helped around the house. Ava suspected her sister still had no idea how lucky she was. If only Nico did a fraction of these things. The comparison flashed in her mind quickly and left her feeling guilty. She knew that Nico had a lot on his shoulders but a little more support from him would have helped.

The best thing about coming to her sister's was that Rona had all the toys a child could ever want. There was plenty to keep Elisabetta occupied, unlike in her own apartment.

Ava had borrowed the travel cot from her sister and the small baby bouncer but she had no toys apart from the small bag she'd packed for the trip over. True, her daughter was still too young to appreciate many of them but the new sounds and flashing lights, as well as Tori's squeals and peals of laughter kept her enthralled.

Her own apartment was a child free zone and it was another thing Ava needed to think about. She'd have to let go of the lease on her apartment especially since they now had the new warehouse. Prior to that her apartment had been used to store products and this had been the main reason she'd held onto it for so long.

Now her home was in Verona. She could always stay with her mom whenever she returned to Denver. Thinking about it, it felt odd being back in her old apartment with her baby daughter. It was strange to think this had been her home before she'd met Nico. It now looked small and shabby compared to the beautiful home she now lived in.

"Hey, Lisabetta," Ava murmured, trying to soothe her. She was soon going to be three months old and Ava had slowly started to wean her off the breast. Being over here meant she could no longer feed her daughter on demand and she had a busy schedule ahead of her.

"Here." Carlos wiped his wet hands with a towel and held his arms out. "Give her to me." He gently took the baby from her. Ava watched entranced as her daughter quieted in his arms.

"He's got a way with babies," murmured Elsa, sitting down on the couch and taking every mega block that Tori was handing her one by one. "She doesn't seem scared of him at all."

"I wonder if she's mistaking you for Nico?" asked Ava. "Though I can't see how." She was surprised at her daughter's sudden silence. Carlos had a closely shaved goatee beard, and Nico was clean-shaven, most of the time, when he didn't spend too many late nights pouring over his work.

"I'm just good with babies," said Carlos smugly.

"He's had to be." Elsa coughed lightly, just out of Rona's earshot. Ava grinned. "Nico would be amazed," she said.

"He should have come along," Carlos replied, making funny faces at Elisabetta. "She has his nose."

"And his dark hair," added Rona.

"And his forehead," said Elsa.

"Thank goodness she has my eyes," murmured Ava, sinking into the sofa. "I hate to think I carried her for nine months and she has nothing of mine to show for it."

"Time to have another one. Maybe the second one will look more like you," said Rona, collapsing beside Ava. "I'm exhausted."

"Why?" Carlos had a twinkle in his eye. "I did all the cooking."

But Ava was still thinking of her sister's comment. "I can't imagine having two babies to deal with."

Elsa patted her on the knee. "Not now but perhaps later ... but don't leave it too late."

Ava couldn't see when the time would be right to have baby number two. "It's not going to happen for a while," she insisted. "Nico has his mind set on opening new hotels, at least three more, that was the latest announcement, and I still want to branch out into Europe."

Elsa turned to her daughter, shaking her head in amazement. "Why? Why are you both so intent on racing ahead that you're forgetting to stand still and appreciate what you have now?"

"We do appreciate everything!"

"Baby steps, Ava," her mother cautioned. "That's what the pair of you should be taking. You can't work all your life in order to build a better life because life happens regardless of the plans you make."

"You don't understand, Mom," Ava began, then stopped. There was no point in trying to explain all over again.

"See how much your granddaughter missed you?" Rona asked her mom. With Grandma's help, Tori had finished building a tower and she clapped excitedly when she added the last brick at the top.

"Only my granddaughter?" her mother asked her. "*You* didn't miss me?"

"Yeah, we did," Rona replied, "But we weren't sure whether you were ever coming back."

"Mom wasn't ready to come back yet," Ava added.

"No?" asked Carlos.

"You're not thinking of moving there are you?" Rona asked, her face a picture of shock. "Me and Carlos we're looking to have number two soon and we're going to need your help."

"What if I decide *I* need mom's help?" Ava asked, always mindful of her sister's plans to dictate her mom's timetable.

"You said you weren't looking to have number two yet!" Rona cried. "Besides, you can afford to pay for help."

"That's not the point," declared Ava, mildly annoyed.

"I'm getting used to traveling between the two countries," Elsa replied. "I quite like moving around."

"What do you mean?" Rona cried. "You're not having a mid-life crisis are you, Mom?"

"No, honey. But that's only because I passed the mid-life stage more than a decade ago."

"Are you thinking of moving to Italy, Elsa?" Carlos asked, even more intrigued. Elisabetta reached out and tried to touch his beard.

"Mom has a nice life in Italy," said Ava, speaking up for her mom. The moment she said it, it occurred to her that it was true. It didn't matter what Elsa did, where she went, at least she was out and about doing things, which was more than she did here in Denver.

Ava remembered how, after Edmondo's death, her mother hadn't wanted to do much. The fact that she was keeping busy, even by visiting nurseries with Salvatore, was surely a good sign.

"I like it," Elsa replied and said no more.

"A cup of coffee would be good," said Carlos. "Why don't you make it, babe?" he asked his wife. Rona looked pained to have been asked to do something and Carlos paid her no attention as she got off the sofa reluctantly.

CHAPTER TWENTY-TWO

"I'm going to leave soon," said Nico, discreetly checking his messages on his cell phone before slipping the device back into his pocket.

"You can't leave yet," Pelosa told him. "You might as well make the most of it now that you're here."

Nico had come to Ravenna today with his lawyer and his father's good friend, Corso Pelosa, in order to show him around the almost finished hotel complex. This evening the Chamber of Commerce here had put on a local business event and Ines had suggested that it would be a good idea for him to attend. She had extolled the importance of networking with the local businesses and to build up local awareness of the soon-to-be opened hotel.

Tonight, Nico felt that he'd done as much networking as he could stomach. Next time, he would leave this to Ines.

He loosened the collar to his shirt in irritation, silently annoyed by Pelosa's suggestion to stay on. He'd had a twelve-hour day and there were still things he needed to do when he got back home. He shrugged as he looked around the room teeming with suited men and women. "I have a lot of paperwork to go through."

Pelosa patted him on the back. "But now that you're here, try to enjoy it, eh?" That was the problem, he couldn't enjoy it. Not when yet another day had ticked by and there was still no notice from the safety department. Things were beginning to run late again. His men had finished the work but there was still no date for the next inspection and they were already into the second week of February.

"It's good to show your face at events like this, Nico. Your father always attended. How do you think he built up a network of good business friends?"

Nico was about to pull his phone out again to check but was wary that Pelosa was watching him.

"What news are you expecting?" Pelosa asked. "This is the third time you've checked your phone since we arrived."

"The safety inspection for the new hotel, the officials are dragging their heels and we're still waiting for a date."

"Patience, my boy."

That's what Edmondo would have said. His father would probably also have told him to get the whole building rewired from the start and then he wouldn't have been in the mess he was now in. But Nico had been in too much of a hurry. He hadn't done anything wrong or illegal—he'd listened to the advice of the architects and construction managers. It had made sense to do so. But if he'd ensured that everything was new, the wiring and all, then this might not have happened.

Or would it have?

Would Vieri have found another way to hamper his progress?

"Talking of patience..." Nico looked up and Pelosa cleared his throat. "You opening that new hotel will create employment and new business opportunities here. It's a good thing and it will stand you in good stead." Pelosa leaned closer. "It will help mitigate the effects of those less appealing stories that the press has printed about you." The old man eyed him carefully. "It's time you stopped breaking photographers' equipment, Nico."

Nico He colored at the elderly gentleman's suggestion and wondered why Pelosa had taken all day to bring this up. "He woke Elisabetta up. We were trying to keep her asleep so that she wouldn't be difficult to handle on the plane, and this son of a bitch appears out of nowhere and starts snapping away. He didn't seem to care that the bright flash had woken up my daughter. I got angry."

The old man placed a comforting hand on Nico's shoulder, much like Edmondo would have done. "They're baiting you, Nico. Don't fall for it. I keep an eye on what the press say about you, not only because it's my job but because I care. They're playing dirty. They're trying to drag you down."

"It feels as if I'm already on the floor," Nico muttered.

"You're not. The Cazales are never on the floor for too long."

The tension in Nico's neck relaxed a little and he smiled, reassured by the man's words. For as long as Nico could remember, Corso Pelosa had guided Edmondo through a maze of business legalities and problems and offered much simple advice along the way. He now appeared to be doing the same for Nico and he was grateful for it.

He looked around at the small groups of suited people who were no doubt making small talk, making business deals and arranging their next meetings.

Being at the Town Hall on a Monday evening wasn't where he wanted to be but his home wasn't any more appealing. It was empty, and he missed his girls. He never thought he'd see the day when he would miss Elisabetta's cries and squeals but he missed them more now than ever. Their going away only reminded him even more of what it was he'd lost and how lucky he was to have such a full life.

He glanced at his watch again, determined to make a move when another smartly dressed man approached them. It was only after a few moments that it sunk in and Nico realized who it was.

Armando Vieri.

"Corso Pelosa?" The tall and lanky man offered his leathery hand to Pelosa.

"I don't think we've met," Pelosa replied, shaking hands firmly as Nico looked on, a quiet rage building in his muscles.

"The pleasure is mine. Mr. Pelosa. I've heard good things about you from my business acquaintances." The man turned and fixed Nico with his lackluster eyes. "And you must be?"

Nico was temporarily stunned into silence—not because he knew for sure that the man knew exactly who he was, but because he couldn't imagine Silvia allowing a man like Vieri near her, let alone into her bed. His skin crawled to see Vieri's wiry hair and age spotted skin so close. His leathery lips crinkled into a smile and Nico inwardly recoiled.

What did Silvia see in him?

"Nico Cazale," said Nico, smoothly, and pressed the man's hand harder than was necessary.

"Of course." The man flashed Nico an insincere, plastic smile. "Armando Vieri. I feel as if we've met before. Have we?"

"I don't think I've had the pleasure," replied Nico.

"Perhaps I'm confusing you with your father."

Nico shrugged but said nothing.

"Are you in the same business?" Vieri asked.

"Yes."

"Ah! You're the man behind the new hotel. The...the..."

He clicked his fingers as if doing so would magically recall the name to him. "The...the new wellness center."

"Spa center," Nico corrected.

"You're from Verona?"

"Yes."

Vieri's head bobbed up and down. "My girlfriend is from Verona."

Nico nodded but remained quiet. There was much he wanted to say but something told him that quiet dignity would prevail, even as the blood raced around his body, making his muscles shake. He glanced at Pelosa and was rewarded by a reassuring smile.

"She hated it," Vieri continued. "The small town mentality. The wagging tongues, the gossip."

"Perhaps she wanted to get away from her past," Nico offered.

Vieri frowned at him as if he had no idea what Nico was talking about. "Perhaps she wanted to move onto better things." He looked around, as if he'd found and located someone in that brief second. "Excuse me, Gentlemen," and he rushed away.

"You handled that well." Pelosa looked immensely proud.

"Do you think so?" Nico wasn't convinced. "What I wanted to do was to wipe that smile off his face."

"You can't prove he had anything to do with your hotel inspection."

"I can't prove it but my gut tells me otherwise, and that's good enough for me."

"You can't go after him," Pelosa warned. "Your father was a man who conducted business with respect and he commanded respect. That's the type of man I see you as, Nico."

"It's not so easy following in my father's footsteps,"

murmured Nico softly, wiping his hand across his face. He watched Vieri slither among the people in the room and he wondered at the type of networking the man did and the influence he had on account of his role as a politician.

Nico wasn't cut out for mingling with such men—men who wielded power and made deals over a glass of sherry. This had never really been Edmondo's world either; his father had much preferred the company of down-to-earth men, humble men, who knew their roots and never forgot them, men who never trod over others in their quest to achieve more. From some things he'd read about Vieri, it appeared that the man liked liquor and fast women and glitzy late night clubs. As sly and as manipulative as Silvia was, her being with a man like Vieri did not make any sense.

"Your father was always going to be a hard act to follow, but you're cut from the same material. Just be who you are and do as you're doing."

Nico's expression softened as Pelosa's words fell on his ears. "I plan to," he assured his friend. "I can only control what's in my hands." He made a wry face. These days it felt as if there wasn't much in his control especially with regards to the safety inspection and the men who seemed to be dragging their feet over it.

But it only made him more determined to turn the Cazale Ravenna into one of the most desired places to visit in Italy.

CHAPTER TWENTY-THREE

Ava had been here a week and they had made good progress but there were still over a hundred cribs which hadn't been recalled.

Each day that passed with the faulty cribs out there made Ava shudder at the thought of another child being injured. She couldn't rest easy until every one of them had been called back into the warehouse, but it was slow going. Parents weren't always easy to track down, and even when she or the others left their return phone number, they didn't always call back.

While Kim and Rona concentrated on this, she'd been busy getting together all the information required by the CPSC. Her contact at this agency seemed to be pleased with the way Ava had handled things.

She worked at the warehouse every day and left Elisabetta in the care of her mom. Elsa would come over to her apartment early each morning. It was ideal because it meant she didn't have to wake the baby up and drag her across town to her mom's place. But despite being aware that it wasn't an ideal situation for her mom, there was nothing she could do.

Her goal was to resolve this mess without it hitting her bottom line. She prayed that the dreaded 'L' word wouldn't become a reality, for a lawsuit could cripple her, and her end goal was to resolve everything satisfactorily and to return to Verona in time for Nico's hotel opening.

In the afternoons she tried to go home for a few hours so that she could spend time with Elisabetta before she rushing back to the warehouse. Her days were long and she was constantly exhausted by the time she returned home late in the evenings.

Tomorrow she had plans to visit the parents of the child who had been injured. Luckily for her they lived no more than a two-hour drive away.

She leaned back in her chair and squeezed the back of her neck when the buzzer to the warehouse door sounded. She didn't look up, thinking it was another routine delivery that Rona had gone to see to but the sound of Connor's voice jolted her.

Connor?

"There you are." He strode towards her desk in the open plan office area and seemed completely oblivious to the look of disgust on Rona's face as she hovered behind him.

"Hi," Ava said, unable to hide her utter shock at seeing him again. She wasn't sure whether to get up and give him some sort of welcome. They hadn't seen one another for months, and in that time she'd gotten married and had a baby. There was more than a lifetime's worth of distance between her and this man whom she'd once been destined to marry.

"I'm going home," Rona announced, ignoring Connor completely. "I'll see you tomorrow."

"I'm going to make a move as well," said Kim, turning her computer off.

"Bye, girls." Ava leaned back and folded her arms, wishing

she could go home but she had a few hours' worth of work to do.

Connor looked all around. "It was high time you bought this place."

"I couldn't continue using your garage and my apartment for storage." She attempted a laugh, but it died a quick death. In the silence that followed Ava tried to think of something to say to break the awkward quietness. She considered broaching the subject of the money he owed her—something she still felt guilty for not telling Nico about.

"You look well," he commented, finally.

"Thanks." She sat back in her seat, noting that he'd put on some weight and that his hair seemed a little thinner.

"Are you winning?" he asked, in typical lawyer-speak.

"We're getting there. We're hunting down the sold cribs and getting them returned here. Shania's good," she said, referring to the lawyer he'd recommended to her, an expert in the field. "She thinks I'm doing all the right things."

"No sign of lawsuits yet?"

"Not yet." And hopefully never. She checked the mail, as well as emails and comments on her website religiously, keeping a careful eye out for negative feedback and potential murmurings of lawsuits. "I'm planning to visit the injured boy's parents tomorrow." It was something she hadn't mentioned to Nico because she sensed he wouldn't be happy about her going, and judging from the look on his face, Connor's reaction seemed to be the same.

"I don't think that's a good idea," Connor advised.

She folded her arms. "I disagree."

"If I were your lawyer, I wouldn't recommend you do that," Connor insisted, leaning on the edge of Rona's desk.

"I believe it's the right thing. As a mother, I feel it's something I need to do."

"But you don't know this woman, Ava and you're going in cold. She's not a friend, she's not someone you bonded with over an antenatal class."

Ava frowned. The words *antenatal class* seemed odd coming from Connor's mouth. "It's a conflict of interest, Ava. You could be seen to be buying the customer off."

"They haven't sued me yet. I'm going because as a new mother, I feel for this woman and her child."

"I still say you're making a mistake."

He hadn't yet made any mention about Elisabetta and she wanted to see if talk about a baby might yet prompt him to do so.

"Congratulations," he said, finally. "You have a daughter now."

"It's taken you long enough to acknowledge her," she muttered.

"You know how it is." He loosened his tie. "I've been meaning to come over and see you but things are so busy for me lately."

She stared at him.

"Did you get my Christmas card?" he asked.

"Yes."

"I wasn't sure if I should send it. Rona told me about the baby and Nico's accident and..." He shrugged and looked down, as if he was about to say something. "It's not easy for me."

"What's not easy?" Things hadn't been easy for her when he'd shattered her dreams, either. She was most interested to hear what he had to say.

"This time last year...do you remember?"

This time last year? She looked at the calendar on her desk.

Holy crap. Of course. That's when it had all happened.

This time last year she'd been broken. Her wedding plans had crashed to the ground. Connor had dumped her and she'd canceled everything. This time last year she'd been getting ready to go to Verona. It was right that she had forgotten. Who would want to remember that? Her life now was so busy, so full and moving along in the right direction—most of the time—that she no longer lived her life as if the past were still a part of it.

Nico had erased all memory of Connor and having Elisabetta now meant that she focused on the present more than ever before. "It's not something I waste any time over," she told him, not caring whether things were easy for him or not.

"There are times when I think about it," he said softly, staring at the floor. "About how it could have—"

Something inside her snapped. "Please don't. You need to get over it, Connor."

"Here." He moved off the table and stepped towards her, before fishing out a piece of paper from his folder. "The money I owe you. I didn't mean for it to take so long. I'm sorry."

"Thanks." She was genuinely surprised. A wave of relief rolled over her at the thought that she didn't have to ask him for it.

"It's not all of it."

She looked up sharply.

"It's $8K. I wanted to give it to you while I could. I should have the rest of the money soon."

She'd already reconciled herself to not seeing the other $2K. "Well, okay," she said, "Thanks."

"I'd like to come over and see your daughter." He looked away and shrugged. "If that's okay with you." His flat voice tugged at the part of her that was still able to show some pity for him. She couldn't turn him away.

"Sure it's okay. She's with my mom during the day. Maybe one evening you can come over when I'm home. I have two more weeks left here, though."

"I'd like that." He looked more relaxed than he'd been since he'd arrived.

CHAPTER TWENTY-FOUR

The bastards had dragged it out just as he'd feared. Nico gripped his cell phone so hard it was a surprise it didn't shatter.

"The first week of March?"

The bastards.

He'd been counting on his hotel to be open by then, not for the safety inspection to take place then. The marketing plan had been working towards that date, the advertising packages had been planned with that date in mind. Even the launch party.

Shit.

He'd have to get Ines on the case immediately and hope she could reschedule everything.

"I don't understand," raged Bruno. "I put in for a date at the start of January. They had plenty of time to schedu—"

"It was never going to happen when we wanted it to," said Nico, his voice flat, and dull. "You were right, Bruno." His project manager had warned him to put in some contingency, but he'd refused. He'd been so hell bent on making that date that he'd been blind to all advice. Yet now, surprisingly, his whole body was calm. Calm or numb, same difference.

"Are you coming over?" Bruno asked.

"What for?"

"So that we can contest this."

"Will it make any difference?"

Bruno snorted. "Are you feeling alright, Nico?"

"I've never felt better."

"You understood what I said, didn't you? The safety inspection," repeated Bruno. "It's not going to take place until the first week of March."

"I heard you just fine the first time."

"Aren't you even angry?"

Nico sniffed loudly. "I'm not letting myself get angry." Because if he did then Vieri, or whoever it was that was behind this, would win.

He had to think of the long game, not the short game. It was a few weeks away, less than a month. It could have been worse. It was bad, but hell, it could have been a lot, lot worse. And when they came to inspect it, they wouldn't find anything else, because he'd gotten some independent safety experts to give the hotel an internal inspection for his own peace of mind.

He was more than ready for them. The shell infinity pools were fine, as were the indoor treatment rooms, the salt room, the outdoor treatment areas and the garden showers. They had all been safety checked.

Come at me again, Vieri.

There would be no way he could prove this, nor would he want to try. His father had always conducted his business fairly, unlike other unscrupulous businessmen, Vincenzo Azzarone being the main one that came to mind. Silvia's father had used underhanded ways to make his family's fortune. It didn't surprise Nico that his daughter might have followed in her father's footsteps. Pelosa might not believe him, but Nico knew that Vieri and Silvia were behind this. What beef could that woman still have with him?

No. He wasn't going to get annoyed. In fact, he'd surprised himself with how unaffected he was. Thinking about it, they were looking at a delay of a few extra weeks. It meant that the hotel wouldn't open until mid to end March. Of course it would siphon even more money out of him but what could he do?

What exactly did Vieri want from him? To prove a point? To be an asshole because he could?

Because Silvia had put him up to it?

Nico had no proof and he wasn't going to waste any time or money on trying to get some. He decided to do nothing but bide his time.

"What are we going to do now?" Bruno asked.

"Sit tight," Nico ordered.

He broke the news to his management team, and then spent the next two hours going through the revised marketing and advertising plans with Ines. He left her to deal with the postponement of the launch party.

Once that was over, he did something he rarely did, something he hadn't done since the time he'd had to look after Elisabetta. He went home early. But coming home to an empty home only made him even more despondent.

He sat in his plush living-room with its heavy, velvet embossed curtains, his feet sinking into the thick, wool carpets and his body resting against the sumptuous deep sofas, and he still felt lost. This place offered no comfort. It offered no comfort because it wasn't a home, not without his wife and daughter.

The silence crashed around his ears. He didn't like it and

couldn't get used to it. At night he would often sit in the glider, thinking and remembering. Back in his bedroom he would look at the empty crib and remember the noises Elisabetta made and the way in which she kicked her arms and legs around when she was excited and happy. Sometimes he'd turn on the crib mobile.

He even missed her wailing.

There had been many times in the past when he had longed for silence. Now that he had it, he detested it. Sitting in the glider, all he could do was think of Elisabetta and how soft and delicate she was in his arms, how she would look up at him with those shiny eyes, and how the touch of her itsy-bitsy fingers felt around his fingers.

All of a sudden he was overcome by a profound feeling of sadness. A lump of regret rolled in his throat as he recalled the number of times he'd been irritated and annoyed by her crying. He rubbed his thumb across his brow, closing his eyes and trying with all his might to recall the sound of her voice. And the sound of Ava's voice crashed over him. In his mind's eye he saw her face and he suddenly longed to hold her and to have her in his arms at night.

It was coming up to midnight but it would be a perfect time to call Denver. Ava hadn't picked up when he'd tried earlier and he'd called her once more but, just like before, her cell phone went to voicemail. Irritated, he called the warehouse. Like most times, it was Kim who answered. Sometimes he wondered whether Rona still worked there.

"She's not here," Kim told him.

"I can't get a hold of her on her cell either. Where is she?"

"She's gone to visit a customer but I expect she'll be back around six o'clock if you want to try then."

"What customer?" Ava hadn't mentioned a thing when they'd spoken last night.

"Uh—" Kim paused, and he heard the hesitation. "Didn't she tell you?"

His heart started to race and worry pinched his sides. "Tell me what?" The moment he said it he already had an uneasy feeling he knew exactly where she'd gone.

"She's uh—she's gone to check in on the family whose baby got hurt."

"She's gone alone?" Even visions of Connor accompanying her would have put his mind at rest.

"Uh-yeah."

"Didn't Connor go with her?"

"Connor? No," Kim made a pffft noise as if the suggestion was ludicrous. "Ava left the baby with her mom."

Nico breathed easier. At least she'd been sensible about something. He didn't like the idea of Ava going to a stranger's house and apologizing for something that wasn't her fault. A part of him wished that Connor had gone with her because the idea of his wife venturing into an unknown person's house didn't sit right with him.

What the hell had she been thinking visiting the parents of an injured baby?

No way were they going to welcome her with open arms. Instantly, his mind conjured up horrific scenes of imprisonment in a dark basement and he began to fear the worst.

"She should be back in a few hours' time," said Kim. "I'll let her know you called, if she calls in."

"Why isn't she answering her cell phone?" Nico demanded. Here he was sitting in Verona, waiting and hoping against hope for this hotel to open—waiting for something that was out of his control, and his wife was halfway across the world trying to save her business. Where was Dino Massari?

The one whose goddamn factory made the cribs? Why wasn't he out there doing something?

"Aaah," said Kim, as if she'd understood the reason for his call. "I was on a call to her a few moments ago. She was parked outside the house and getting ready to go in. Her battery was running low and she'd put her phone on vibrate."

Nico's face contorted. For all he knew she could be going to the home of a deranged new mother and her psychotic husband.

He didn't like this.

He didn't like this one bit.

CHAPTER TWENTY-FIVE

T he woman peered at her suspiciously through the six-inch crack of an open door. "Hi," said Ava, taking a deep breath. "I'm Ava. Ava Cazale. We spoke on the phone yesterday? You must be Gwen?"

The woman's expression hardened. "You're early."

By five minutes. She stared back helplessly and heard TV commercials playing in the background. She wondered if the woman wanted her to come back in five minutes' time.

"Come in." The woman opened the door wider.

Ava forced a smile. Her stomach quivered as she followed Gwen Harding inside. She glanced around the room quickly. It was clean and well-kept and the layout and size of it reminded her of her own apartment.

"I didn't expect you to show up," she said, fixing Ava with a not-too-welcome stare.

"But we spoke yesterday," Ava countered. She had distinctly told the woman she would be coming today. An uneasiness shrouded her as she stood around, not entirely sure what to do next. She stared at the small pile of children's toys that lay on the floor, not sure whether she should sit down or not.

"Yeah, we spoke." The woman crossed her arms. "But I didn't expect you to show up." Ava stared into the woman's cold and unsmiling face, hoping for that tight mouth of hers to soften. But it did not.

What now?

Maybe it had been a huge mistake coming here. The crib mix-up hadn't been her fault but in the eyes of this pissed off mother, Ava was the one to blame. She should have listened to Nico, and her mother and Connor, and Kim and Rona. Maybe she should have heeded the advice of all those people instead of stubbornly following her gut instinct.

An uneasy silence made the already stretched out moment seem longer and more awkward. They hovered inside the living room, standing face-to-face like boxing opponents sizing one another up. Ava briefly considered the option of leaving but decided to give it one more try. "Look, Gwen, may I call you Gwen?" The woman's face remained hard, and she offered only a quick blink, as if signifying a 'yes'. It gave Ava the strength to continue. "I understand how you feel—"

"No, you don't."

Ava swallowed.

"It didn't happen to you. So you can't know."

Ava swallowed again. The way this woman carried on was as if her child had broken a bone. He'd had a bump on the head, minor injuries, nothing long lasting. She wasn't trying to excuse what had happened, but she hadn't expected the woman to be this pissed.

"You're right," said Ava, trying again. "I can't know. I don't know, because it didn't happen to me. I wanted to visit because I'm a mother, too, and I feel really bad about what happened to your son."

The woman folded her arms even tighter across her chest. "It's been tough on us all, him especially," she said, "being so young and all." Her words made Ava feel even more guilty. "I unders—," she stopped herself in time. "I'm *sorry* that this happened to your son."

"Sorry isn't going to pay the hospital bills. I hope he hasn't suffered any long-term brain damage."

Brain damage?

Ava blinked. "He had a bump on the head."

"A nasty bump on the head. You shoulda seen it. The size of a golf ball. You'd feel real bad if you'd heard how much he cried. How he hollered when he fell off and landed on that hard wooden floor. You shoulda seen the bruising along his arm."

Ava lowered her head, imagining the very scene the woman had painted, but with Elisabetta. If she were in this woman's shoes how would she feel? And yet the baby had only fallen. No broken or fractured arm. "Did he suffer a concussion?"

"He was crying, and he was drowsy, and he just wasn't himself. They kept him in overnight for observation. Think about it, a baby so young. He can't tell us what hurts or how he feels."

"Of course not," Ava agreed. Seeing your child hurt had to be one of the hardest things for a parent to bear. No wonder Gwen Harding looked like she wanted to rip Ava to shreds. "I expect it was unbearable for you all. I feel terrible, and I wish there was something I could do."

Don't talk about the lawsuit. Don't be seen to making a bribe. Connor's last words to her, when she'd told him she wasn't going to change her mind. "I wish him a speedy recovery." Although, by now, she expected the baby to be fully recovered.

"Is that why you're here?" The woman asked her as they still faced one another.

"What do you mean?" Then the penny dropped. "I'm not trying to buy you off, if that's what you think."

The woman's eyes narrowed. "I don't want you thinking you can come over here and be all nice to me and hope we won't sue, because we are. You can't get away with this—"

Ava shook her head. "That's not why I'm here." She had to be careful with the words she used. "I don't make the cribs. I only sell them, and I didn't know there was a problem until it was too late. It's the truth, and I don't blame you for not believing me." But as she spoke, she noticed that the woman's gaze fell to the large diamond on Ava's engagement ring, and then her watch, and then the bag she carried. She was scoping Ava out.

Instinctively, Ava folded her arms, hiding her watch and ring. She had been undecided about what to wear for this visit and in the end had chosen a pair of trousers with a jacket and blouse. She had wanted to look smart and professional but here, in this woman's home, she looked too business-like.

Flashy.

Polished.

Made of money.

Maybe sticking to her maternity clothes might have been more appropriate.

The woman said nothing. She didn't need to, her hard face and disbelieving expression told Ava all she needed to know. "Look, Gwen," she said in a last-ditch effort to reach out. "The moment I found out, my team and I started to recall all the cribs sold with this particular problem. I got on a plane and I'm here, and it might seem odd to you—it sure feels odd to me now to be standing here in your home—but I'm a new mom myself. I feel for you, even though I'm not in your shoes."

"You have a baby?"

Ava nodded. "She's almost three months old."

"You flew here? Where're you from?"

"Oh, no, I drove here from Denver but I don't live in the US anymore. I've moved to Italy."

The woman's eyes opened wide. "You came all that way to see me?"

Ava nodded. "I came all that way because I needed to fix this before another baby got hurt."

The woman blinked a few times as if she was considering what Ava had told her. "Denver's quite a distance away."

Ava nodded.

"You want some iced tea, or something?"

"A glass of water would be good, thank you."

The woman disappeared only to return again with some water. "Thank you." Ava took the wet glass that was offered to her. Then, the sound of a baby crying suddenly broke the awkward tension in the air.

"Perry's up. I'll go and get him."

The woman reappeared a few moments later holding her son in her arms. He had a head of mussed up blond curls and he was chubby and adorable, even more so when he rubbed his eyes. Seeing him made Ava instantly long for Elisabetta. "Hello, Perry," she said, softly. "How are you?"

The child blinked at her then moved closer to his mother. "He needs his milk, don't you little buddy?" Gwen gently rubbed noses with him. She disappeared into the small kitchenette and Ava followed. Gwen seemed to struggle to balance the baby on her hip while she made up his milk.

"I can hold him, if you want," offered Ava.

After a moment's hesitation, Gwen handed her baby over and much to Ava's surprise, he came to her easily. She couldn't help but grin back at him. He looked fine. Just fine. Just as she'd expected him to.

And that was when she understood it. Did his mother think taken Ava's visit here to mean that she was checking out the baby, as if she didn't quite believe her? It would explain her coldness, and her exaggeration of the boy's fall. The woman was suspicious of her and it didn't matter that Ava had explained the real reason for her visit. The woman had already made up her mind about Ava long before she'd even turned up.

"I'll take him now," she said. They returned to the living room and sat down. Ava took the couch opposite and watched the baby grab his bottle and start drinking noisily. A part of her felt as if this had been a wasted journey and she wasn't sure what she had intended to achieve or what she should do next.

It was time to go back home to her baby.

Nico had been right. This journey had been pointless. Connor had been worried that her visit might be construed as her trying to buy them off but the truth was that hadn't been the motivation behind it. It wasn't in her nature to bribe anyone.

"I can arrange for a new crib to be sent out to you, if you would like," she offered.

"A new crib?" Gwen looked at her as if she'd said something offensive.

"The correct one, this time. But you probably won't ever want to buy anything from me again—and that's fine, too," she said quickly.

"We don't mostly buy things online," said the mother. "Everything we need we get from Wal-Mart."

"Wal-Mart is good."

"But see, this time my folks wanted to give us something for his birth so they offered to buy us the crib. My dad insisted on helping us out and my sister told me about your site. She's always on the internet. I don't know where she finds the time."

"Has anyone arranged to have the crib shipped back?" Ava asked. "We would obviously refund you in full."

"My husband told me to keep it here for proof."

"For proof?" But just as she asked the question, the answer dawned upon her. *Proof. For the lawsuit.* "I see," Ava replied quietly as the baby guzzled his milk. It made her think of Elisabetta and she wondered how her mom was doing looking after her. She didn't intend for today to be yet another long working day. She had a few hours of work to do at the warehouse before she went home. "I should go," she said, springing into action and getting up. "I'll see myself out." She waved a hand towards Gwen, as if to stop her from getting up. "Thank you for your time."

"I appreciate you coming." The woman's unexpected words raised a smile on Ava's lips. As she approached the door, she heard the sound of a key turning in the lock, and then the door opened. A stocky man wearing builder's overalls with a safety helmet in his hands, stepped in.

"Who are you?" he asked, suspicion layered thick in his voice. He stopped in his tracks with the door still ajar. Gwen came up behind her still with the baby in her arms. "She's the lady we got the crib from."

"That's *your* store?" The man gave Ava a menacing stare and closed the door.

"I was leaving." Ava felt uneasy with the way he was looking at her.

"What do you want?" he barked.

"Nothing." She clutched her bag to her stomach, a weak form of protection. "I came to see your baby."

"What for?" He took a step towards her, forcing her to take a step back. "Is that 'cos you think we're lying?"

"Donny." Gwen's voice had a warning tone to it.

"Did she get you to sign something?" he asked his wife. Gwen shook her head. He turned to Ava. "Isn't it wrong for you to show up on our doorstep like this?"

"I never meant to cause any offence." She should never have come here. "I admit it was for purely selfish reasons. I have a young child myself and I felt sick when I heard what had happened. I didn't come here to buy you off or to silence you. I came here as a mother and because I feel bad for what happened to your baby."

"We're going to sue you," he snarled. "We're going to expose you."

Ava blinked at him in surprise. "Expose me?" Now it was her turn to get angry. "Expose me for what?"

"Selling them things when you shouldn't have been."

"There is nothing to expose." She struggled to keep her voice steady. "But you're welcome to do what you feel you must." It wouldn't do her any good to lose her temper now, and her fear still lurked somewhere beneath the thin veneer of anger. "I don't make the cribs, I only sell them and I sold them in good faith. We never meant for any of this to happen. You're right, I didn't have to come here. Perhaps I should have listened to everyone and not come here. But I didn't listen and I dragged my three-month-old daughter all the way from Italy just so I could try to fix this problem quickly. I didn't have to come and see you, and I haven't offered you any money, or bribed you or advised you on what to do. I am sorry that this happened but this was a genuine mistake. You need to do what you feel is in your best interests and I have to do what's right for me, and coming here today, to meet with you—even if it was for my own selfish reasons—was something I felt compelled to do. That's all I have to say. And now I must get back to my baby."

She glanced at Gwen who now held the baby to her shoulder, and the knowing looks exchanged between husband and wife didn't go unnoticed by her. "Excuse me," she said, managing to raise her voice only slightly as she edged towards the door. The man stepped away and it was with some relief that Ava opened the door and stepped out. Gwen came up behind her. "His bark is worse than his bite, but we only want what's right for us."

Ava nodded. "Thank you for seeing me," she said, then left. She couldn't wait to reach the safety of her car and once she was inside she breathed out slowly, her body sinking into the soft leather seats as she exhaled loudly.

It wasn't until this moment that she realized how tightly wound up she'd been. After a few moments, she took out her cell phone and saw the missed call from Nico. A feeling of relief washed over her, calming her frayed nerves as she pictured his face before her and wished he was here beside her. She called him quickly, desperate to hear his voice.

"Are you alright?" It was the first thing he said.

No. Was the first thing that came to her mind but Nico sounded worried and so she replied, "Yes. Why?"

"You went to see them, didn't you?"

Kim or Rona must have told him. "I did." She closed her eyes and braced herself for his telling off.

"I wish you'd have listened to me, Ava." She went quiet, hearing his words, her senses still reeling from meeting with the Hardings. Nico berating her did nothing to ease her mind and she half-wished she'd called Kim instead. "Ava?" he asked when she fell silent.

"I'm listening." She didn't have it in her to fight, not when the outcome clearly pointed to him being right. There had been no point wasting a day coming here. Even seeing the baby who was now completely recovered had upset her, because it made her miss her own daughter.

She'd left Elisabetta for this?

"Say something."

"You're right." There. She hoped that made him feel better.

"What's wrong?"

What's wrong? She'd called her husband because she missed him and all he did was have a go at her. "It's a long drive back. I should go."

"What is it, Ava?"

She sat in the silence, contemplating what had happened back there. "You were right. I shouldn't have come here."

His voice turned anxious. "Did they say something? Did they do something?"

"No." What were they going to do? "It's nothing," she said, knowing he would jump to conclusions. "They didn't *do* anything, but they weren't exactly happy to see me. I know you already told me this and I'd rather you didn't rub my face in it." Silence filled the air like a slowly inflating hot air balloon until finally she said, "My phone will probably die soon. I should go."

She thought she heard him let out a disappointed grunt. "Drive safely. I don't want you thinking of what happened back there. I'll call you later."

"Okay," she said, and hung up, without even asking him how his day had been. As an afterthought, she called Kim to quickly get an update on the crib recall.

"We tracked some more down," Kim told her.

"Excellent," said Ava. Good news in an otherwise crappy

day. "Anything else?" She had changed her mind about returning to the warehouse and now she looked forward to going home to be with her daughter.

"Are you coming back here?" Kim asked and the way she said it told her that she needed to.

"No." Her body tensed, bracing itself for the news that was sure to follow. "I wasn't going to. Why?"

"In that case you'll want to know—" said Kim, being uncharacteristically vague.

"Know what?"

"Another parent called this morning to report that their baby had been injured. The mom said the baby fell out and fractured her shoulder."

"A fractured shoulder?" gasped Ava. "How old was the baby?"

"Thirteen months only."

"I can't see how that would happen." Ava tried to imagine a baby just over a year old, falling out with enough force, from such a short height and fracturing a shoulder. "What else did the mom say?"

"It was difficult to make out. She was being hysterical. She just yelled down the phone and kept saying it was our fault."

"How's the baby?"

"The mom said it could have been really bad—"

And at that moment, Ava's phone battery died completely.

She slumped back in her seat and all of a sudden it stopped; her breath, her movement, her thoughts. She'd read about the dangers of drop-side cribs and of the fatalities when tiny bodies became entrapped, and her insides melted to a mush. She had never in a million years envisaged being in a situation where she had indirectly caused this to happen.

For the first time ever the store was too much for her. The

pressure was getting to her and the constant juggling of it as she thought of Elisabetta at home with Grandma—all of these things together now slowly crept out from the hidden corners of her mind.

She didn't need this.

Nico had been right. Why was she killing herself, spreading herself too thin, trying to make everything and everyone happy, except for herself?

Lately, the worry over her business hung over her like a guillotine. What would it be like not to have any more Gwen Hardings to deal with? No more reports of injuries. No more irate parents yelling at her.

What would it be like to be a lady of leisure?

If she sold the store, she would never have to deal with things like this again. She started the engine and drove away, still thinking about the idea.

CHAPTER TWENTY-SIX

Why the hell was he signing this off? Nico stared at the invoices he'd just scribbled his name onto; they were for the software and hardware Demetrio needed.

Gina could have done this. Why hadn't she? There was something not quite right between the two of them and he would get to the bottom of it in time. For now, he trusted Gina and knew she would come to him if she had a problem.

For now, company dynamics were the least of his worries.

He pushed the paperwork away and browsed through his email inbox once more.

There was nothing.

Nothing from Ava, at least.

There had been a time once when the two of them had sent one another emails hot enough to make him lose focus for the day. But now there was nothing new from her except a photo of Tori sitting next to a sleeping Elisabetta. Ava had sent this a few days ago and he'd stared at it a million times already because this days'-old picture was the most recent one he had of his daughter.

He felt for Ava, now that he had some idea of what it was

like to look after a baby. It couldn't be easy even with Elsa helping during the day, and from what he understood, Elsa returned to her own place in the evening. He knew that working long hours and having business worries to contend could eat away at a person, like starving maggots burrowing through, and he wished he could be there for his wife to help alleviate the stress. The more he thought about it the more guilty he felt and he felt terrible for the way he'd spoken to her earlier after she'd visited that family, but he'd been worried about her.

Couldn't she see that?

He knew how nasty people could get and he wanted to protect her. He'd waited up until 2am just so that he could call her again but when he did she'd been busy with Elisabetta. At least, that had been her explanation for not being able to talk to him. He didn't blame her. Maybe she was still mad at him. Their disagreements were becoming the norm, even despite the physical distance between them. He didn't like it. He didn't like it one bit.

Something had to change.

He pushed away from his chair and walked over to where his father's photo hung. He could imagine Edmondo giving him advice that was sometimes harsh and sometimes not what he wanted to hear but always exactly what he needed.

What now, Papa? What would you do now?

Of course there was no answer and, frustrated, he walked over to the window and looked out at the gardens. Seeing the dirty gray clouds in the dishwater-colored sky only made him feel more despondent. Verona was best enjoyed in the summer when the landscape was green and lush like a velvet carpet spread out all around. Not now.

A walk would help clear his head. Sitting in here with his

own miserable thoughts circling around would only plunge him further into misery.

He walked out into the Casa Adriana gardens, breathing in the cool fresh air of the February morning. As he walked past the pergola he noted that the table and chairs inside it had waterproof covers on.

Had Elsa done that?

Usually it would have been his father. With his hands deep in his pockets, feeling the slight chill on his back, Nico followed the pathway, observing the mostly evergreen shrubs and trees. The flowers were no longer in bloom but the gardens were green and alive and beautiful even on a day as miserable as this. In the distance he saw Salvatore and, puzzled by the man's appearance, he walked over to him.

The wizened old man with deep wrinkles and an unsmiling face, nodded at him.

"Salvatore," said Nico. "I didn't expect to see you back until next month." The gardens didn't need much upkeep during the winter months and yet the more he thought about it, he could have sworn he'd seen Salvatore here more often than not.

"It still needs looking after," Salvatore replied. "Not so much, but..." He stood with his shoulders hunched together. "The gardens are big. There is a lot to do."

Nico nodded. He had a landscaping company that took care of most of it but Salvatore had always done a few odd jobs every now and then, while Edmondo had been alive. His father had kept a close eye on the gardens himself but after his death Nico had asked Salvatore to do more days. He hadn't wanted to let his father's beloved gardens languish, not even for one day.

Salvatore rubbed his grimy hands together then placed a dirty hand on his hip. "You don't want me to work here?"

"What?" Nico shook his head quickly. "No, no. *No.* That's not why I'm asking." Then after a while, "You're doing a good job, Salvatore." He thought better of asking him about his working hours and days. They stood quietly for a few silent moments while Nico tried to think of something to say but the old man beat him to it. "How is your baby?"

"Elisabetta?" Saying her name made Nico smile. "She's...." And then he wondered, because he didn't know how she was. He *assumed* she was fine, and growing and developing, and coming up with more funny faces and interesting new mannerisms and sounds. Her hair might be a little longer, her face might have changed slightly again. But in all honesty, he didn't know. He wasn't there to see. The thought cut through him like a hot, slippery knife, sharp and painful. "She isn't here," he said, finally.

Thousands of miles separated them.

Salvatore's heavily lined face crinkled some more. "Not here?"

"She's in America, with her mother."

"She's gone to America, eh? Your wife?" The way he said it Nico wondered if the gardener knew something he didn't.

"On business," Nico explained. "She's gone on business."

Salvatore nodded. "And her mother?"

"Her mother?" Nico's brows pinched together. "You mean Elsa? Yes, she's gone back as well."

"They are coming back soon?"

Nico was taken aback by Salvatore's interest in his family. "Ava and the baby will be back soon."

"And Elsa?"

Nico nodded slowly, at last understanding the intent behind the questions. A smile forced the corners of his lips to curl up slightly. "I don't know. She will stay there for the summer, I think."

The gardener nodded "You are sad alone, Si?"

"Si."

The gardener opened his mouth to say something but the beeping sound of Nico's phone interrupted them. "Excuse me." He stepped away to take the call.

It was time to get back to work.

CHAPTER TWENTY-SEVEN

Ava had been out all day and had spent another long day with the woman from the CPSC.

And this after arriving at work early in order to deal with more documentation and paperwork and coordinating the recalls, as well as having a three-way call with Dino and Andrea. She'd told them about the latest turn of events with the second child who had been injured.

She hadn't even told Nico yet.

Guilt sped through her like a shot of adrenaline. She used to tell him everything, once. They used to talk all the time; share words, jokes, moments, feelings and good and bad days. She tried to bury the guilt with a nod. He'd called yesterday and she'd been too busy to speak to him for long.

Sometimes she wondered if she should have stayed at her mom's place the whole time she'd been in Denver. She hadn't fully appreciated until now how much of a help it had been to have Nico, her mom and Helena around. Having a second pair of hands to help with the baby was a godsend.

It was approaching seven by the time she returned to the warehouse to pick up the new catalogs which had arrived from new suppliers. She wanted to look through these at home later this evening.

"What are you doing here?" Kim asked her as soon as she stepped inside.

"I could ask you the same," Ava threw back as she combed through the piles of paperwork, all marked as 'URGENT' with Post-It notes plastered on. "Shouldn't you be at home with Danny?"

"He's got a playdate with a friend but I'm going to pick him up soon. What's your excuse? Don't you have a baby to go home to?"

"I do." Ava powered on her computer. She sat down, tilting her head forward while she waited for her computer screen to come to life. But she had a few things to take care of first. As desperate as she was to get home—as much for her mom's sake than anything else—Ava knew that these things would fall to the wayside if she went home first. "Any more calls from the Dawson mom?" This was the name they'd given to the mother of the second child who'd suffered the shoulder injury.

"No," replied Kim.

"Do we have any more detail on the fractured shoulder?"

Kim shook her head. "I'm sure we'll hear from her soon. I'm going home." Kim headed towards the door. "And you should be too." She paused to put her woolly hat on. "You do know that it's Valentine's Day today."

Was it?

Ava smiled at Kim weakly. "It is?"

"Not that you can do anything about it, what with Nico being over there and you being over here."

Ava tapped the sharp lead end of the pencil against her notepad, leaving miniature gray-black marks on the lined white paper. It was a day she preferred to forget. "Do you have anything planned?" As far as she was aware, Kim was still single.

Kim smiled. "All I want is a nice evening in with my little boy." She waved and disappeared.

Valentine's Day. It conjured up images of toys and over-glittered cards and teddy bears clutching cheap red satin love hearts. It wasn't something that she chose to celebrate because it was the date of her other wedding. The one to Connor.

And yet this was her first Valentine's with Nico. There was no point thinking too much about it since they were continents apart.

If anything the real date, the start of *their* romance, that was the date that counted. It had been the day when Nico had come to find her in Venice, the first day he'd given her the bracelet, the same day they'd first made love. That had been the start of their romance, and it was the start of so many other special times, so many beautiful days and memories she had made with this man.

She smiled thinking about him.

It was strange how things tended to be so fraught between them when they were together and now that they were apart, she longed to be with him. Like the day he'd come to the airport to see her off. It had made her sad to be leaving him all alone and that look in his eyes had stayed with her the entire flight. She felt like that now, sitting here in Denver, alone in the huge warehouse while Nico was probably at home, alone in that rambling huge mansion of his.

What were they doing?

***

She arrived home later than she'd hoped and her mom looked exhausted. Waves of guilt washed over her.

"Sorry, Mom," she said just as Elisabetta's cries screeched out from the bedroom.

"I can't settle her." Elsa sighed loudly. "I've tried, but she might be overtired. She didn't sleep well earlier."

This only made Ava feel even more guilty. "I was trying to be as fast as I could but I had so many things to sort out. It seems to be never-ending."

"It's okay, honey." But Elsa's words didn't ring true. Her mom looked beat. It came as no surprise, after all she'd looked after Elisabetta every day, except for weekends, since they'd arrived here. It wasn't fair to anyone, not her baby and not her mom.

Ava rushed into her bedroom and her heart clenched at the sight of Elisabetta with tears streaming down her cheeks. Picking her up and holding her tightly, she wiped her tears away and smothered her with kisses. The baby calmed down and her crying trailed away. But when Ava touched Elisabetta's forehead, she found it to be warmer than usual. She wondered if she was coming down with a something. Her daughter's tiny hand skimmed over her jaw and Ava clasped her tiny hand and kissed it.

How could she run an international business with a young baby who needed her? Maybe it was time to throw in the towel?

Perhaps Nico was right. She *could* be a better mother by being at home. She didn't need to work and Elisabetta needed her the most now. She could always concentrate on her business later, when the children no longer needed her.

She walked out into the kitchen where Elsa was putting the baby's bottles into the sterilizing unit. "Leave that, Mom," she said, feeling guilty. "I can finish it off later."

"It won't take me long," Elsa insisted, continuing regardless.

"Sorry."

"Stop apologizing, Ava." Elsa turned around with an empty bottle in her hand. "You're in a tight corner, I can see that. Let me help. That's what moms are for."

"I'll try to work shorter days."

"Don't do that on account of me. I know you have a job to do and you don't have much time to do it in. Don't you worry about me. I can manage. How do you think I managed to raise you girls by myself? Admittedly, I don't have as much energy as I used to but she's not running around yet." She wiped her hands. "That's when the real trouble will start. You'll have to hire help then." She dissolved into baby talk as she spoke to Elisabetta. "She has a slight temperature," Elsa noted. "She didn't have one earlier."

"I'll give her some Tylenol."

"Good idea. It might help her to sleep. Maybe that's why she was so restless earlier. You try to get some rest, too," she said, putting her coat on. "If you don't mind, honey, I'm going to leave."

"Say bye-bye to Grandma." Ava took Elisabetta's arm and gently waved it at her mom.

"Go easy on your mommy," said Elsa, kissing her granddaughter on the nose.

"'Night, Mom," said Ava, seeing her mom to the door. The sound of the door closing made Elisabetta erupt into a fresh round of tears.

Not again.

Ava paced around the living room and hoped that tonight wouldn't become one of *those* nights. She wanted to get changed, and eat, and unwind, maybe take a long, hot soak in her bathtub.

It wasn't going to happen.

Maybe a feeding was the thing that her baby had missed

the most. She'd started weaning her off the breast now and had resorted to giving her the night feeding only. Laying the baby on the couch, she slipped off her jacket and undid her blouse. Then she eased onto the couch and sat back, closing her eyes while Elisabetta took to her breast. It seemed to help, and the baby guzzled away hungrily.

After a short while, Elisabetta fell asleep and Ava placed her in the crib, only remembering then that she'd forgotten to give her Tylenol.

But she was able to eat in peace, and shower, and was about to get into bed when Nico's text came through. Wary of disturbing the baby, Ava walked out of the bedroom and called him back.

"Hey you," he said, softly.

"Hey," she replied back.

There was silence for a few moments.

"You sound tired," Nico said. "Bad day?"

"Where should I start?"

"Tell me."

And she proceeded to tell him about the second reported injury. He sounded notably shocked. "How is the child now?"

"I don't know. We haven't heard anything more and I've called many times but I only get the answering machine. I've left messages but nobody has called back. It's all very strange."

Nico frowned. "I feel bad for you. All of this is out of your control and I know you're working so hard to put things right, it doesn't seem fair that this should happen to you. I was starting to believe that things were going well—you sounded busy, and the recalls were happening."

"I thought we were over the worst of it but it seems not. I dread each time the phone rings because it could be another parent with more bad news."

"How are you doing?" he asked, his voice low and soft. "I

wish I was there with you. I wish I could make it all better for you." He'd caught her at a low point and she couldn't keep her guard up anymore. Nor could she convince him that she was still this super woman who could run her business and raise a child. How could she when she no longer believed it herself?

Maybe if she didn't have these potential lawsuits hanging over her head, or the threat that her business could go bankrupt, or the worry of other customers or having to deal with hysterical women screaming at her down the phone—maybe if she didn't have any of these things to contend with then, maybe then, she *could* do it all. But right now, she was beat.

"I'm not sure how I feel." She hugged her knees as she sat back on the sofa. "I've been questioning a lot of things."

"Like what?"

She struggled to vocalize her feelings.

"Ava?" When he spoke to her like that, as if he was really listening, as if there was no Bruno or Ines or spa hotel matters on his mind, when he was all hers and wanted to know how she was, when he sounded as if he really cared, when he was all of these things, then he was the old Nico and she missed him more than ever. "Tell me."

She bit her lip. "I feel...odd." She'd reached a turning point today. It was all catching up with her and seeing her mother looking so worn out earlier, and with Elisabetta not being well, and with everything going on at work, well, today she'd turned into a mess of emotions and she hated being without him.

"This never seems to be a good day for you," he said.

"This?"

"Valentine's Day."

"Ugh." She wrinkled her nose in a shiver of disgust. "Who

cares about Valentine's Day?" She paused a while, reflecting on her decision. "I think this is it," she said, slowly.

"This is what?"

"Maybe you're right. I'm taking too much on and maybe I should sell the store and be done with it."

"You can't be serious."

"I *am* serious," she said, yawning.

"What's brought this on?"

"Nothing, and everything. Being here and dealing with all of this and my mom looking exhausted, and Elisabetta not being well."

"What's wrong?" Nico sounded anxious.

"She has a slight temperature and my mom said she was difficult to settle earlier on."

"What is it? A fever? Is she teething or—"

Ava laughed. "She's not teething yet, at least I don't think so, according to my trusted baby book they usually start teething around six months."

"But it can be as young as three months."

"Really?"

"Anywhere from three to twelve months. Is she drooling a lot? Does she have swollen and bulging gums? Is she rubbing her face or trying to chew anything she can get her hands on?"

Ava snorted in surprise. "Do you have your own baby book?"

"A man's got to read something, especially when he's sitting at home missing his two favorite girls."

The image of Nico sitting at his desk in his study reading a baby book made Ava giggle.

"But seriously," he continued, "is she doing those things?"

The guilt resurfaced and trebled. "I'm not sure," she replied in a flat voice. She wasn't sure because she wasn't around during the day to see. "I might not go in tomorrow if she's still unwell." And then she remembered. "Damn it. I need to go in tomorrow. I have a meeting with the CPSC."

"Can't you postpone it?"

"I'll have to do something. I'll see how she is in the morning." She yawned again.

"Go to sleep. Maybe your tiredness is forcing you to make these decisions about your store. We'll talk about it more later, but I want you to go to bed."

She'd expected a victory dance, or something along the lines of 'I told you so.' Nico's suggestion to talk later about her decision to sell didn't make sense. "I will go to bed, but first, tell me. How are things with you?" He'd hardly said a word about the spa hotel and it was due to open soon. "You don't have long to go before it opens."

"Not long, no."

"I'll be back by then," she reminded him.

"Yes, you will be, now go to sleep!"

"I will."

"And Ava?"

"Hmmmm?" Another yawn.

"I wish I was there to help."

"I wish you were, too."

CHAPTER TWENTY-EIGHT

He'd made up his mind as soon as he'd put the phone down. Now, five days later, Nico was packed and ready to leave for Denver. He was going to surprise his wife.

Talking to Ava had left him feeling concerned. It wasn't only that she sounded worn out, or that he could hear the tension in her voice, or that the thought of her dealing with all that stress alone—while Andrea and Dino were taking it easy —made him angry. What worried him was that Ava had reached such a low point that she was considering giving up her business. This didn't sound like the woman he knew, and his decision to go had been easy. The Cazale Ravenna lost out when it came to his wife.

"She has no idea you're coming?" Gina asked.

"None. It will be a complete surprise to her." At least he hoped the surprise wouldn't backfire on him.

"How long are you planning to stay there?"

"A week, maybe."

"Maybe?"

Nico looked up. Something in Gina's voice sounded different. "Is that a problem?"

"No."

"We intend to be back on time because she still thinks the Cazale Ravenna is opening at the end of February."

"You haven't told her yet?"

"No." He hadn't seen the point of telling Ava about the delay. He'd tell her when he saw her.

She'd told him she felt guilty for leaving Elisabetta with Elsa. There would be no need for that guilt once he got there. He'd look after their baby while Ava got on with her work. For a change, their roles would reverse, and right now, Nico was happy to let matters be.

But Gina didn't seem so enthused. He'd been expecting her to be her usual happy and supportive self. He'd expected her to reassure him by telling him that she would take care of things in his absence. Instead she didn't offer any such assurances and the more he thought about it, the more it dawned upon him that she'd been rather quiet during the management meeting. It was almost as if Demetrio had been in charge. Gina had sat back, hardly saying a word.

"Do you want to tell me what's going on?" Nico asked.

"Going on?"

"Something's up with you, Gina. Something you're not happy about. Is it the work?"

A flush crept up her face. "No." A false laugh. "Why would you think that?"

"Gina." Nico leaned forward. "You and I go back a long time. Don't do this. Don't pretend." He could see the conflict across her face. The flicker of a changing expression. After a few seconds, she said, "I was hoping to take some time off."

"Time off?"

"Yes."

Of course she needed time off, she'd been working crazy hours over many months. He'd been too busy worrying about his problems to properly acknowledge how much he'd pushed onto Gina. He'd intended to do something about it, give her a pay raise and time of in lieu—but what had he done? Nothing. She'd covered the hotel when he'd gone on his honeymoon and she'd done the same after his accident. It had been remiss of him not to compensate her earlier, either in the form of a bonus, or time off, or both.

He wondered when she wanted to take the time off. In his own mind he was hoping it wouldn't be soon, not until after the Cazale Ravenna had opened, but it would be unfair of him to deny her. "How long did you want off?"

"I was hoping for a month."

His mouth fell open. *A month?*

And before he could catch his breath and question her, she added, "Or two."

Two months?

How would he ever cope?

"Two months," he said slowly, as if he'd been handed a prison sentence. It pained him to smile and yet this was the only answer he could give her, because he didn't want her to fall sick or, even worse, leave.

"I know it's a long time," Gina said, obviously seeing that he hadn't taken the news well. "And I've been meaning to talk to you about it for a long time."

Maybe that was why she'd seemed distracted lately. "I owe you that much time off in lieu," he said quickly, eager to cover up his shock. "Two months should be fine. We'll find a way to cope now that there's the four of us." But all the same he wondered if it was too much for her, the pressure, the responsibility. "Is the work getting to be too much?"

"No," she said, quickly. "No, Nico. The work I can handle."

Something else?

"I've got personal matters to take care of."

Personal matters? He waited for enlightenment. "Is there anything I can do to—"

"No," she replied. "There isn't."

"I'm sorry. I should have made it my priority. You've worked hard ever since the wedding and before it. It was remiss of me to not take this up with you sooner."

"It's not that, Nico," she insisted. But the phone rang then and he was momentarily torn between letting it ring and continuing their conversation, and dealing with *this*. The shock of Gina's two-month break had hit him hard. He grabbed the phone receiver roughly. "Yes?"

"Silvia Azzarone for you," said the receptionist.

What the hell? "Tell her I'm busy." He slammed the phone down and turned to Gina. "If you ever want to discuss anything, with me or Ava, you know where to find us."

"I know." Gina got up. "Don't worry. I'll wait until you get back from Denver, and for the hotel to open. I'd never leave you in the lurch, Nico. You've been good to me."

Have I?

He doubted that there was much truth was in that.

CHAPTER TWENTY-NINE

"Yes!" shrieked Rona, jumping up from her desk. "Another one down!"

"Cribs?" asked Ava, dubiously. She never could tell with Rona.

Her sister nodded.

"How many does that leave now?" Ava asked, feeling a sense of apprehension. She wondered if they were down to single figures yet.

"Another nineteen," her sister replied. "Don't worry, we're getting there."

Ava sucked her lips in, thinking. She had less than a week left and she was determined for all the problematic cribs to be recalled before she returned to Verona. The last thing she wanted was to hear of bad news when she was back home. In Verona she would be too far away to be able to make a difference.

"We're getting there," said Kim, walking in with a tray of hot drinks. "I'd say we've done very well." She handed Ava her mug of hot chocolate.

"You sure have," Ava replied, even though she didn't feel

she could completely rest until all were in. "You girls have done a great job." She turned to her sister. "Have you arranged for it to be—"

"Yes," said Rona, and rolled her eyes. "I know the drill. The customer wanted a refund. They're not interested in buying a replacement crib from us, or for that matter, anything else."

Ava winced. It hadn't been the first customer who had reacted in this way. She didn't blame them. She'd have done the same if she'd been in the customer's shoes. "How many of the new cribs have we sold?" Andrea had sourced a new supplier and both she and Leo had both heavily researched the history of the manufacturer. The cribs were a good alternative to the d'Este ones. But she sensed that Andrea wasn't fully on board with her decision to stop selling d'Este cribs—especially since it wasn't the cribs themselves that were faulty. It was easy enough for the correct fixed-side cribs to be sent out—but Ava was in no mood to give Dino more business just yet. He needed to prove himself and lose that arrogant manner of his.

"Not many," replied Kim, sitting down. She tapped on her keyboard a few times. "Seventeen," she announced. "But it's early days yet. We only put the new products up a few days ago. Give it some time."

Depending on her decision, she might not need to give it any time. It would be the new owner's problem—if she decided to sell her business. Ava doodled away on her notepad, trying to figure out what to do.

"Hey," said Kim. "Ava?" She looked up. "Did you hear me? I said we sold seventeen of the new cribs."

"I heard you," she said, hastily scribbling over her scribble. "It's not looking great." The d'Este cribs had sold like tickets to the Superbowl. It had taken one advertisement and a newsletter. The new alternative cribs from the new supplier weren't selling anywhere near as well.

"I sent you a link to that article on a mommy blog." Kim took a sip from her mug. "Have you had a chance to read it?"

Ava nodded. "Unfortunately, yes." Yet another blog talking about the crib problem. But this particular article seemed to focus more on Nico's wealth and her own story—as a woman from Denver who'd gone to Italy and found love. It was hardly an informative and factual piece.

"I'm not sure it's bad publicity," said Kim.

"Isn't bad publicity good?" Rona asked.

"No," Ava replied, she held her warm cup in both hands, savoring the heat from it. "I think bad publicity is bad publicity."

The idea to sell out was looking more appealing by the day. When she'd left Elisabetta this morning, she had paused to think what it might be like to stay at home and look after her all day without any of these business headaches swallowing up her time. Articles like the one that Kim had mentioned seemed to be a sign of the way in which her decision should go. But at the same time, she also had to think of what the consequences of her selling the company might mean to Rona and Kim.

Her sister now worked at the warehouse five days a week instead of working from home a few days and a few days in the office. It was something that Ava had enforced after she'd bought the warehouse. But whether she worked at home or in the office, Ava knew that her sister benefited from being employed. She could work from home under urgent circumstances, if Tori was sick, or if Carlos worked a double shift.

It was the same for Kim. The woman had been a virtual assistant, providing remote support when the store had been a sideline for Ava, but as it had grown in the past year, she'd recruited Kim full-time. She was a single mom and thankful for the opportunity, but more than that, Kim treated her work as if she owned it. She always went over and above what was expected of her. Nico had noted her work ethic and had often suggested to Ava that Kim could cope with more responsibility. That was back in the day when Ava had had plans to expand and to open a sister store in Europe, a plan she had put on hold as her pregnancy had progressed.

Those dreams now seemed fragments of the past.

Now she had other priorities.

She could sell the business at a good enough profit. Sales had been phenomenal the past year and if she sold for a multiple of earnings, she would do well out of the sale.

"Bad publicity doesn't have to last long," said Kim, "We'll wow them again soon enough. We'll find some more amazing products to sell." She settled back in her chair and began typing away. Nothing seemed to dampen her spirits though it was obviously easier being an employee than a boss.

"You always sound so positive," Ava remarked.

Kim turned her head, taking her focus away from her work. "I love this job. I love our company. So what if we've hit a bad patch," she said, as if it were nothing major. "All businesses have them. It's unfortunate ours resulted in young children getting hurt but it's not something we did on purpose. We learn from it and move one, and we should be thankful that nothing worse has happened."

Ava marveled at her ability to be so positive. She'd felt that way once—formidable, dauntless and unstoppable.

Once.

"Have the Hardings filed a lawsuit?" Rona asked.

"Not yet." She'd been looking out for it, ready to give to her attorney to deal with but as yet there was nothing.

"Anything from the Dawson woman?"

Ava shook her head. Surprisingly, that one had gone quiet.

"Are you going to visit them?" Rona asked. "I'll come with you if you want support." Trust her sister to look for any excuse to get a day out of the office.

Ava hadn't even considered the option of visiting this family, not after her experience with the Hardings. It had turned quiet from both families and they hadn't heard anything further from either set of parents. "They've threatened but I can't do anything unless they file a lawsuit."

"Let's hope we hear nothing further from them. I dread the day we get hit with a lawsuit," said Kim.

But the fact that things had suddenly gone quiet made Ava even more anxious and her insides knotted at the thought of a lawsuit landing on her lap. "Why are *you* dreading it?" she asked Kim. This wasn't *her* headache.

Kim put down her cup. "I'd hate for anyone to sue us. I couldn't bear the thought of our business going bankrupt. Think of all that hard work you've put in."

"*We've* put in," Ava corrected her. "I couldn't run this company alone, not without you two helping me." Expanding the team was the reason she'd been able to do so much, as well as getting married and having a baby.

"Next stop is our European operations," said Kim, referring to the ideas that Ava had shared with her last year. Ava stared down at the drink in her hands and watched grains of undissolved chocolate powder float around the surface of her half-empty drink. She looked up and her nervous eyes met Kim's questioning stare. "We're still going ahead with that plan, aren't we?"

"I'm not sure," Ava replied, looking away. "I haven't had

time to think about it." She didn't relish the thought of ending Kim's dream job.

"How about we have a meeting tonight?" Kim asked, excitement bubbling up in her eyes. Ava groaned at the idea of a meeting. She was already meeting'd out. But Kim seemed to have mistaken her silence for contemplation. "Now that you're here, we should use this time to decide on future plans for the business. You know, expansion and growing the product line and all that other stuff that we can't talk about properly in emails."

"Do we have any more of those chocolate chip cookies?" Rona asked, getting up from her chair. "I need some mid-morning chocolate." She disappeared into the small kitchenette area.

"I haven't had time to think about any of that," confessed Ava. Her trip here had been purely an emergency one and she hadn't even considered the idea of using it for anything else.

Kim made a face. "You're worried about the Hardings, aren't you?"

Ava shook her head. "It's not that."

"We could get take-out at your place and take turns looking after Elisabetta, if that's what you're worried about." She looked at Ava, cocking her head and when Ava didn't say anything, she said, "Are you—are you having second thoughts about the business?"

Ava could picture it now—Kim's heartbreak when she owned up to her new game plan. A coward's way out. She'd leave Kim with no option but to return to her previous role as a VA. The woman was far too hard-working and business-minded to be a virtual assistant. Far too loyal and ambitious. She'd never be able to run her own business, not without an injection of money, not as a single mother supporting a young son. She pictured Kim and Danny struggling to get by. Ava shuddered at the thought of it. How could she do that to her? The hope in Kim's eyes burned too brightly for Ava to pour water over it and extinguish her dream.

"I'm not sure about a lot of things right now," she said, excelling at vagueness once more. "But it has crossed my mind."

"No," Kim said it as if Ava had been thinking of committing a murder. "You can't." She shook her head, her eyes wide and that hope extinguished. "You've built something successful, Ava. You've—we've come too far to give up now. It would be a mistake."

Ava sat back and placed her hands on the back of her shoulders, just below her neck. For some reason it felt slightly reassuring. "Lately, it all seems so difficult. I thought I loved it, but it's taken so much out of me."

"It's called running your own business." Kim got up and walked over to her desk. "Nobody said it would be easy. If it were, everyone would be doing it. It takes a lot of guts and balls and hard work."

"There must be easier ways of earning a living."

"There is but I can't see you answering to a boss."

Ava sighed loudly. Being married to someone like Nico meant that she never needed to work again. Before she could answer, Kim said, "The image of you sitting in the front row at the Milan fashion shows, dripping in designer clothes doesn't really fit, either. It's not you, Ava. You'd be bored." Kim wasn't going to stop until she'd prised the idea out of her head. "Trust me," said Kim. "I've worked with all sorts of entrepreneurs before, from stay-at-home-moms running their business from their kitchens to a couple of guys running an international business from their basement. It's not easy. You've come a long way. I don't think you fully appreciate how much you've achieved. So many small businesses fail before they get to the end of their first year."

Ava closed her eyes, not ready for more conflicting advice. "I don't know. Right now, I can't focus on things clearly."

Kim shrugged. "Don't have a knee-jerk reaction. You've had a lousy day and nightmare parents to deal with but don't let that rush you into making a decision that might affect the rest of your life."

Rona cruised back in with a brown paper bag. "Cookie, anyone?"

CHAPTER THIRTY

S he looked haggard. Sunken eyes, thinner lips.

Nico was tempted to ask her what was wrong, but more than that, he wanted to know why Silvia was here.

"I called the other day but your receptionist wouldn't put me through."

"I was busy and I'm busy now, Silvia," Nico said, his jaw tightening. He had an evening flight to Denver and a to-do list as long as a row of Cypress trees. But even if he had nothing to do, watching paint dry would be preferable to talking to Silvia. "What do you want?"

She ran her hands through her straggly hair. It wasn't platinum blond anymore but dull, as if it had been trodden on with half-muddy boots. "I wanted to see you."

"What for?"

She shuffled in the chair, toying with the handbag she wore over one shoulder and which now lay on her lap. "Just." She shrugged, and even her shrug was half-hearted. Unsure. Not all there. Typical.

"I thought you didn't live around here anymore?"

"I move around." She looked away.

"I ran into your boyfriend a few weeks ago."

"You did?" She chewed her fingernail, something he'd never seen her do before. In fact, this wasn't the Silvia he was accustomed to. Gone was the veneer of sophistication layered thick over a self-obsessed mannequin. The Silvia before him was a shadow of her former self.

"He's... Nico opened his mouth and couldn't find a way to back out easily. "He's not what I expected." *He's not your type.*

"Yeah...he's..." Silvia played with the clasp of her designer handbag. "He's mature. He's very cultured, very knowledgeable about things. He's *different*." She coughed lightly. "Anyway, I wanted to see how you were."

"Why? Were you worried about me?"

"Should I be?"

"I've been in a car accident," he said, even though he suspected that she already knew. It had been in the papers and wherever she lived, he had a feeling she'd have known. "I was driving back from Ravenna in the rain. I'd just found out that my hotel safety inspection had failed." He scrutinized her face for her reaction, trying to see beneath the surface, trying to look for signs of guilt, or something, anything.

"I read about that." Her face was a picture of innocence. "It sounded bad. That's why I was worried about you."

"I'm better now and I'm really busy so—"

"What happened to the Cazale Ravenna?"

Her question aroused suspicion in him and he wondered if she had come on a spy mission for Vieri. "Did he send you here?" Nico got up from his chair and folded his arms. He wanted Silvia out and hoped this would help to shift her.

"No." The cry was a little too indignant, a little too loud. "I came because I ... I was passing by like I told you. I wanted to see how you were. I know it's not like in the old days between us."

"It's not and it never will be. I'm fine. The hotel hasn't opened yet due to all manner of bureaucratic bullshit. You wouldn't happen to know anything about that would you?"

Her cheeks colored and she shook her head. "It wasn't me, if that's what you think. It wasn't my idea."

"What wasn't?"

"You don't understand, Nico. Armando—he can be controlling. If he gets something in his head he won't stop."

"Controlling?" His thoughts immediately turned to Silvia's daughter. "How's Alessa?"

"She's a girlie girl. Happy at school. She didn't like it when we moved but we're back now. I mean, we kind of, you know, we're back and forth."

"That can't be good for her. She needs to be settled."

Silvia's laugh was short. "You always wanted what was best for her. I loved that about you the most, how much you cared about her."

"She's a sweet girl."

"Those were the good days, Nico. Don't you remember?"

"Stop." He snapped. "Stop living in the past. Stop walking back into my life. Stop doing whatever it is that you're doing, if it concerns me...just stop."

"I didn't mean for any of it to happen. It was Vieri. He likes to pull people down."

The way she was going around in circles was driving him insane. He almost felt pity for her, until he remembered and his bullshit detector kicked in. It wasn't making sense. She wasn't making sense. She looked off-center. Muddled. Not a woman who wanted revenge, he sensed, but a woman who was riddled with remorse.

"What is it?" he asked, irritated by her riddles. "Say what you want to say and be done with it."

"I didn't think he would take it this far."

It was the closest he would ever come to an admission that she'd had something to do with it. "Do you know something, Silvia?"

She stared at him with longing.

"I was mistaken in thinking there was something decent about you buried deep down inside, something that could be salvaged," said Nico. "Many times I hoped there was something, but no. There isn't."

Her lips wavered. "I'm...I'm trying not to live in the past, I wish I hadn't messed up so much back when we were together."

He bent down, so that his head was level with hers and looked directly into her eyes. "You can start now. You can make amends now."

Her eyes widened as she sat forward, looking eager. "How?"

"By walking out of here and staying away from me and my family." His words were harsh because he wanted her out, because her toxicity was in danger of taking over his mood— on a day when he was flying off to Denver to be with Ava. He couldn't hold back.

"You really mean that?"

"I really mean that," he growled, and watched the light in her eyes go out. Maybe she finally understood, maybe all he'd needed to do was to be this brash in the first place. She had no excuse for doing what she had done, however she'd convinced Vieri, and it amazed him, her propensity to scheme and interfere and to inveigle the politician into doing the dirty.

Nico's nostrils flared as he looked at her, trying to conceal his disgust. He couldn't believe that he'd once been intimate with her, that he'd allowed himself to become involved with someone so messed up, that he'd been so blind to everything she was.

He saw her clearly now for what she was; a walking pillar of malice and everything about her, everything she ever did or said, left him stone cold. He saw a trail of misery in her future and prayed for poor, innocent Alessa. That little girl did not deserve this. "You've taken up too much of my time." He walked over to his door and held it wide open. "Tell Alessa I said 'hello'."

It was undignified and cruel the way he had thrown her out but it was nothing less than she deserved.

CHAPTER THIRTY-ONE

Whenever she was down, talking to Andrea always helped. Besides, she didn't want to pour out her troubles to Nico especially since they were so far apart. Ava knew he would worry about her. Andrea, on the other hand, cared, but would still sleep at night.

"We're down to nineteen cribs," said Ava.

"That's great news!" cried Andrea. "You've managed to get so much done in such a short space of time. I don't know how you did it all, and with a baby in tow."

"My mom took care of Elisabetta. I couldn't have managed alone." She'd told Andrea everything, about the visit to the Hardings, the shoulder injury reported by the Dawson woman and her recent plan, still tenuous, still not fully formed, of selling the store.

"Dino and I know how much it has helped you being out there."

"I told Nico it made sense for me to be here. He wasn't happy about it but, its done now. I go home in a few days!" She was looking forward to it. "Besides, it was always my intention to come out here regularly to keep an eye on the warehouse but, who knows, maybe I won't need to fly back at all now, not if I sell?"

"I can't believe you're thinking about it," said Andrea. "You and I met because of your store!"

"That's right, we did," Ava agreed, taking a walk back down Memory Lane.

"If you're serious..." Andrea hesitated. "If you're serious about selling the store...then..."

"Then?"

"Dino might be interested. He's been amazed at your sales volume."

"Dino's interested in my store?"

"Not your store, exactly. But he's considered setting up something similar in the US. They have no presence there at the moment, and his company only sells to Italy and Europe. He's often talked about how well you're doing." Ava wasn't sure how she felt about someone like Dino taking over her store. After a few seconds of thinking about it, she decided she didn't like that idea at all.

"You and Dino have been talking about me?" she asked in a husky voice. "Did these discussions happen to take place over dinner?"

Andrea's cheeks turned rose pink. "It was purely business, I promise."

"Did Leo happen to be present at these 'business' meetings?"

"No." Andrea laughed. "One of us had to stay behind and keep an eye on the stock. With two units it gets slightly tricky having to go in and out of the each all the time. It's annoying. We need to find something quickly."

Ava smiled and decided to wait until she returned To Verona before getting the low down from her super secretive friend. She wouldn't have much success prying anything out of her over the phone.

"Let's catch up next week," Andrea suggested. "You'll want to spend the weekend settling back home and catching up with Nico."

The closer it got towards the end of the week, the more Ava found herself getting excited about going home.

Verona was home. And so was Nico.

Maybe they'd needed the time apart in order to appreciate that being together meant so much more.

CHAPTER THIRTY-TWO

"What time does she normally get back?" asked Nico, kissing the top of Elisabetta's head again.

He'd landed in Denver a few hours ago and his little girl had gone to him easily, as if she'd known exactly who he was. Never again would he go so long without seeing them.

"She'll be here soon," said Elsa, smiling. "She didn't say she was working late today and she's been trying hard to get home on time lately." She glanced over her shoulder at him. "I'm sure it feels like a long wait already."

Nico tickled Elisabetta's cheek. "It's been painful, being without them for three weeks, but ever since I landed, time just seems to have stopped."

Elsa chuckled. "You should take a nap. Hasn't the jetlag kicked in yet?"

"I can't sleep." Then to Elisabetta, he said, "We don't want to sleep, do we? Not now when mommy's going to come. You can't wait, can you? Me neither." He kissed her on the nose, his voice rising in pitch as he talked to his daughter.

In the three weeks since that he hadn't seen her, his little princess had grown. It saddened him to know that he had missed out on time that he would never get back.

Elisabetta gurgled happily, and all he could do was kiss her again, this time on her cheeks, first one then the other, before blowing a raspberry on her forehead. Blowing raspberries made his little girl squeal. Her chubby cheeks filled out like little meatballs and she let out another beautiful, bubbly little sound—a cross between a squeal and a giggle. Encouraged, Nico did it again and she squealed again, bursting out into infectious little giggles.

"You're going to surprise her, for sure," said Elsa. "I can't say it's been easy keeping this from her. Why don't you extend your trip a little longer, Nico? The two of you can spend another week out here. It might be the thing you need."

"We could both do with a break," he agreed. "I'll see what Ava says." His other concern was Gina and he was being especially cautious now. Otherwise he would have, as he had done in the past, extended his trip without giving it too much thought, always knowing that Gina was there to keep the hotels running in his absence. But a few more days would give him and Ava a week in Denver together. And it wasn't as if they had to rush back for a hotel opening. "When will you next visit Verona?"

"Why, with you, when you both return."

He looked at Elsa in surprise. "You're coming back with us?"

"Is that a problem?"

"No," he said, "You being in Verona is never a problem. But I was under the impression that you were going to spend a few months here. I even told Salvatore you weren't coming back yet."

"Has that old fool been interfering in my business again?"

"No," said Nico, not sure why he was getting defensive.

"He was asking about Ava and the baby and I'd mentioned that you'd all gone—"

The sudden sound of a car pulling up in the driveway stopped him.

"She's back!" cried Elsa, and she walked over to the window to peer out from behind the curtains. Nico followed suit. A tingly feeling danced in the base of his stomach and he wasn't sure if Ava would be mad at him or happy to see him. Before he had a chance to ponder too deeply, the door opened and she stepped in.

He didn't even get a chance to hide.

"Nico?" The word escaped her mouth like a fast breath. She laughed, a happy laugh, a surprised laugh and then in the next moment she lunged towards him and before he knew it he had his free arm around her and was kissing her on the lips. For a few seconds they were a mixture of kisses, and hugs, until the baby, probably overwhelmed and caught in the middle, started to cry.

"Lisabetta," said Ava, taking the baby from him and soothing her with kisses. "Sssshhhhh, Mommy's home." His daughter buried her face in Ava's chest, her tiny hands clutching Ava's hair and blouse as Ava looked up at him with shiny eyes. "I had no idea you were coming!"

It was the best kind of welcome to see her face light up like that.

"I wanted to surprise you." He took her bag and helped her out of her coat.

"I'm so happy you're here," she exclaimed, "and after the day I've had..."

"Maybe now you'll take things easy." Elsa started putting on her coat. She turned to Nico. "I am so glad you're here and I hope you have better luck convincing my daughter to take things easy. Lord knows I've tried and failed."

Ava rolled her eyes at her mother. "I've been better this week. I've been only doing a few hours at the warehouse."

"You were better," said Elsa, doing up her coat. "And Elisabetta having that cold helped you be better." Elsa winked at her daughter. "I expect you'll both want to catch up."

Yes, thought Nico. He'd missed his wife, and there was a lot of catching up to do.

"Goodnight." Elsa kissed them all and left.

"What kind of day have you had?" He grabbed Ava's hand. She made a face in answer.

"I don't want to talk about it." But this was exactly where they'd gone wrong before. They'd both been too busy, and their busy-ness had pushed them away. He'd come here for a reason and putting the magic back into his marriage had been one of them. "We'll talk about it later," he said. "Give her to me." He held his arms out for the baby, "and you unwind. I'll feed her and put her to sleep, and then you and I can talk."

Ava looked at him in confusion for a few seconds, her mouth hanging open but he noticed that she didn't even try to say 'no'.

"Okay." She handed the baby back to him. "I'll go and—" But he snaked his free arm around her waist, pulled her closer and kissed her, not giving her a chance to reply. This time the kiss was a little longer, a little deeper and when he moved away she had that surprised look in her eyes. "I've missed you," he whispered, a need to have her, to make love to her, to lie beside her, awakening within him. He had every intention of making it up to her.

Elisabetta was asleep and they'd eaten dinner and were lying on the couch talking and catching up on one another's lives.

Ava had told him about everything that had been going on with her and he'd told her about Gina wanting to take time off, and the safety inspection being delayed again, and about Silvia's visit.

They lay together, him on his back with her snuggled up against his chest. It was just like in the old days, except that the sofa wasn't as wide and they were bunched up close together. On the surface of it their bodies were still, but deep down, where blood rushed and muscles softened, and heartbeats raced, their bodies started to vibrate, slowly dancing to a sultry tune. Nico loved the way she was all squashed up next to him, and he liked the feel of her warm body, soft and pliant.

"I'm surprised she had the guts to come and see you," Ava murmured, her fingers snaking along his chest slowly and seductively.

"It was more like she needed to confess."

She lifted her head. "You said she was being very vague."

"She didn't outright say 'Vieri did this to you' but it was enough for me to read between the lines. It's more what she didn't say." It had been more the way she looked, as if she was afraid of saying too much. "I don't want to waste any more time talking about her or that asshole she's dating."

"You're more worried about Gina, aren't you?" Ava asked, dropping small kisses along his breastbone, making his stomach flip.

"I can manage without her for a few months." What he couldn't envisage was the Casa Adriana without Gina being there at all. She was as firmly ingrained and a part of that place as the checked marble flooring of the lobby.

But right now, he didn't want to talk about work. He wanted to make love to his wife and yet he wanted to let her lead, and she was doing just fine as far as that went. "I'm so happy that you came," she murmured. He could hear it in her voice, could see it in her eyes, how happy she was. Jumping on that plane and listening to his gut had been the best decision he'd made and lying here on the couch with Ava in his arms made all the problems on his shoulders temporarily vanish away.

"Aren't you worried about the delay? It will be nearly a month later than you had hoped for." She lifted her head and rested her chin on his chest.

"I'm more worried about you." He entwined his fingers in her hair.

"You don't have to worry about me, Nico." She slowly started to do undo his shirt buttons and his breath hitched when her fingers raked over his naked chest. The temptress— she had no idea what she was doing to him.

"I can and I do worry about you," he murmured, his voice low because all he wanted to do was to show her how much he had missed her. "It's my prerogative, as your husband." She stared up at him with her large blue eyes, listening. "I don't want to make the same mistake my father made." His father had spent most of his life building his business that he barely had any time to spend with his family. Nico saw it all clearly now; the time he'd lost could never be snatched back and this was made painfully obvious in the three weeks he'd gone without seeing Elisabetta's new smiles and mannerisms.

"And there's me thinking you only came because you were afraid I'd go and visit that other family."

He winced. It had been a factor—but it hadn't been the only reason. "I didn't like the idea of you turning up on the doorstep of people whose child had been hurt by something they bought from you. What made you think you were safe going to see them?"

"You were right all along," she said, lying back down with

her cheek against his chest. "I was crazy silly to do that but I have no intention of doing something so stupid again."

"And now you're talking about selling out, and I don't see that making you happy." When she didn't say anything, he pressed her further. "Is that what you really want to do?" She shrugged, still silent as she lay on his chest. "Ava?"

"Isn't that what you want?" she asked.

"I want you to be happy. Running your business makes you happy but I don't want to see you killing yourself, running yourself to the ground—rushing everywhere and struggling to do everything, sitting at your desk feeding Elisabetta and checking your emails at 2am. I just want you to slow down. I'm scared you'll make yourself ill. But I also know that you love what you do, or at least, you used to love it."

"I love it when I don't have lawsuits and other problems to deal with."

"You were this ambitious and strong-minded woman I met and fell in love with, and you're still the same now except that we have a baby and you're still trying to carry on the way you did before. You can't. Something has to give."

"That's why I'm considering selling out."

"You don't have to sell. Just get more help. Give Kim more responsibility, take on more help at home. Work when you're at work and play when you're at home, play with me," he begged.

She dropped a kiss on his lips and he deepened it, because she was impossible to resist. "We'll get through this together, Ava." He needed her to know how much he was going to be there for her. He took her hand. "I came here because I missed you and Elisabetta. Because I didn't want to make the same mistake my father did. Because when you told me you were thinking of bailing out on your business I knew something was wrong. Because I've been a jerk lately, and because I love you and I'm no longer putting you second. I never intentionally put you second, but the papers and the media, and the pressure, the cost of not opening ... I couldn't find the time to fit you in and I'm sorry." She rolled on top of him and he wrapped his arms around her waist. "I came here because I miss my wife, and because she won't make love with me anymore." She licked her lips and smiled when he said it. "I miss those nights with her."

She stared down at him with dark eyes and he knew what that look meant. His hands slipped down to her blouse, his fingers working quickly to unbutton it. They kissed for longer, their mouths and bodies melting into each other. It had been too long.

She hoisted herself up a little to make it easy for him as he fumbled and felt his way around her clothing. "Nico," she murmured, and he hoped this wasn't an *I'm-not-ready-yet* announcement. It didn't seem to be, the way her fingers trailed along his chest. Hope grew as sharply as his excitement. Nothing was going to get in the way today. Not leaky breasts or other excuses. He stroked her hair, his fingers itching to stroke her skin, to trail along her collarbone and slip lower. "I've missed you," he whispered, his voice hoarse, his skin prickly with anticipation. He tugged off her blouse and stared at her hungrily. She wasn't wearing a maternity bra today and he was desperate to strip her down but he was also wary of letting the pace be something she controlled even if it killed him to slow down.

"Nico," she said, in a voice that promised much. "It's been too long..." And then she licked her lips and bent down and licked his lower lip, slowly, teasing, dragging out the moment, making time slow down while his insides shuddered and jolted and waited for release.

Damn right it had been too long. Months of no sex made

him feel like a virgin at a bachelor party. He couldn't wait, not when she looked at him like that, her scorching gaze sending shockwaves through his body, it took all his restraint to hold back, to keep up the pretense that he had this under control.

He could no more control this than he could the twitch between his legs, or his heavy breathing. He could no longer hold back, and his mouth sunk to her neck. In the next moment they were a chorus of strangled noises, soft mewls and moans with hands and fingers flying everywhere, each trying to remove the other's clothing. Hungry lips teased and sucked, and tongues sought and thrashed. In seconds he was down to his boxers and she wore only her bra and panties.

He didn't wait for her to take off his boxers. He fumbled, pulling them down as fast as he could while still lying down, and then he watched as she pulled her panties down, and then at last removed her bra.

A hungry growl escaped his lips. He lay back as she slowly and silkily slid onto him, burying him deep within her. He uttered her name, unable to hold back as her warmth and wetness turned him delirious. She moaned softly as she bent down to kiss him, their lips joined, tongues deep and wet and probing as she found her rhythm. They breathed like one, fast and ragged and all he could see were her eyes, wet and moist, her mouth half-open. He put his mouth to her breast and sucked hard, heard her moan as she writhed above him, dissolving into pleasure, into him, into them.

It was fast and out of control, as if it were their first time together, and in a strange way, it almost was.

CHAPTER THIRTY-THREE

The best thing about Nico appearing out of the blue was that everything was spontaneous—having sex, having meals, working, everything. They ditched the daily timetable and were at last able to reconnect, get back on track, make up for lost time, as much as it was possible to.

Having lots of sex while the baby napped was a great way to do that. Ava slowed down, spent a few hours at work instead of the whole day and Kim and Rona understood. Nico had a chance to be a stay-at-home dad and look after his daughter.

It was better for Elsa too. They hadn't seen her much since Nico had arrived and Ava was glad that her mother could spend time with her neighbor and spend her day as she pleased.

Ava would start work early in the morning and be back in time for lunch. They'd spend the rest of the day together, eating out, going for walks, visiting the park, but most of all, being together. Most of the time they liked being back in Ava's apartment and preferred to spend the evenings with only the two of them and Elisabetta. It had been hard to turn down dinners with the family and they'd had dinner at Elsa's once when she'd insisted on having her whole family together.

Apart from that, and Nico going out with Carlos once, they had managed to keep their time just for themselves. She had even managed to postpone Connor, who had texted a few times, expressing his desire to see the baby.

Having this time with Nico was precious because she knew all too well that once they returned to Italy, she would have to fight for his attention because she'd be competing with his chain of hotels. He said he would make more time for her and Elisabetta, and she believed him, but she knew that despite his best intentions, there would be many moments when business decisions were crucial and required his all. At times like that she would have to take a back seat.

Because the hotel wasn't opening yet, there was no need to rush back but Nico seemed mindful of not being away too long. They were due to fly back together on the first day of March.

The days melted away, and before long they were at the end of their time in Denver. It was late afternoon and they were still in bed, holding hands, their bodies loose and well spent, feeling lazy and contented. Elisabetta's travel crib moved around a lot more, from the bedroom where it was during the night, to the living room during the day. There was only so much sex they could have in the living room.

"I wish Carlos didn't have dinner planned for tonight," she said, sighing.

"He's been wanting to have everyone over all week. We have to go today."

"I like that the two of you get on," she said. "Sometimes I think you two get on better than Rona and I do."

Nico chuckled. "Carlos is easy to get along with. He

always made me feel welcome." Her brother-in-law was good like that.

"We should pack," she said, as he propped himself up on his elbow and his hand skated along her belly.

"We could do something else."

She snickered. "We've been doing something else all afternoon. What time is it?" She reached over to pick up her cell phone just as Nico bent down and left a trail of kisses along her shoulder. "Time for more fun," he murmured, his hand dipping lower, his fingers probing. "You want me again," he said, and when he moved closer she felt the jab of his excitement along her hip.

"This whole week has been like another honeymoon," she mewled, arching her back as his fingers worked their magic. The beep of a text message coming through temporarily interrupted her and she reached out to check her cell phone but Nico grabbed her forearm, entwining his hands in hers and holding her captive. "It's only ten minutes since you last checked," he whispered, blowing on her wet nipple before he bent down and sucked it again.

"It might be..." Rona or Kim or something to do with the cribs, but the thought was soon lost as electric sparks skimmed across her skin. Each time he flicked his tongue over her breast, her insides fluttered.

Nico shifted himself on top of her and stared down at her with hungry eyes. "Nothing you can do about it right now," he told her, and thrust into her, the friction and feel of him made her body rumble, leaving her senses intoxicated. She opened her mouth and moaned, because it felt so good, and when his mouth claimed hers and he buried himself inside her, it felt even better.

'**I**'*ll be passing by around 7. Hope you are in. Would like to see the baby before you leave.*'

The shock of the text message had just about worn off by the time Nico came out of the shower. Ava broke the news to him. It was a message from Connor.

"He's coming *now?*" he growled.

"At seven." They had half an hour. At least she was showered and dressed and ready.

Nico scowled. "Why's he coming?" His voice was peppered with irritation as he pulled on a casual shirt. His hair was still damp and beads of water rested against his neck.

"He wants to see Elisabetta." She took his towel and dried his neck. "I've been putting him off, because we had better things to do," she said, kissing him again, trying to cheer him up. "Be nice to him." She was aware of Nico's feelings toward Connor. He dismissed her comments with a wave of his hand. "I don't want to be late getting to Carlos' place."

"I doubt he'll stay for long." Especially now that Nico was here. She had just finished putting on a pair of clean tights and a new top on Elisabetta when the doorbell rang. She picked up the baby and walked towards the door.

"I thought he was coming at seven."

She shrugged and lowered her voice. "What do you expect me to do? Turn him away?"

"I prefer that option," said Nico. "Give her to me." He took Elisabetta.

"Be nice."

"I'll try."

She opened the door to a nervous looking Connor. "Hi, Connor. Come in."

"Sorry for the short notice and for being early." Connor walked in and looked around. "But we're going away tonight, and I didn't want to miss you in case you left before we got back."

She found the over-explanation forced and caught the subtle emphasis on 'we' but didn't press him on it.

"This brings back memories," mused Connor as he followed her into the small living room. Ava's muscles tensed on seeing Nico standing there like a wolf guarding his pack.

"Nico?" Connor couldn't hide his surprise.

"Connor," said Nico. The two men faced one another for a few awkward moments until Ava raised an eyebrow at Nico, prompting him to step forward and offer Connor his hand. They shook hands briefly.

"Congratulations." Connor eyed Elisabetta as if she were an untouchable porcelain doll. "Hello Elisabeth," he said, peering at her as if he didn't want to risk touching her.

"Elisabetta," Nico corrected, speaking with an over pronounced Italian accent.

"Right." Connor smiled at the baby then turned to Ava. "She's beautiful. She's the spitting image of you with those eyes."

"She's an Italian princess." Nico hugged his daughter closer to his chest as a few more seconds awkwardly ticked by.

"Would you like to hold her?" Ava asked, more to make small talk than anything else. If Nico hadn't been here she had a feeling that things might have moved more smoothly but having her former lover and her husband in the same room didn't bode well.

"No, no," Connor insisted, shaking his head as if she'd asked him to hold a burning log. "I'm not good with babies. Though I suppose ..."

She waited for him to finish his sentence but he didn't. "Sit down." She hoped that he might relax a little. He seemed to be very edgy. They all sat down in the small living room. "Can I get you a drink?" she offered.

"No, thank you." Connor looked uncomfortable. "This is for," he paused, before saying her name. "For Elisabetta." He handed Ava a small box.

"That's very sweet of you." Ava opened the box. "Awww," she gushed, pulling out a fluffy little donkey and a comforter. "How cute! Look Lisabetta." She waved the fluffy donkey before Elisabetta's eyes.

"Is there an age limit on that?" Nico asked, and immediately looked at the label. "Not suitable for children under 12 months. Would you look at that?"

Ava threw him a stony stare. "Thank you," she said to Connor. "It's very thoughtful of you. She'll be able to play with it when she's a little older."

"I had no idea you were here," Connor said to Nico.

"I missed my wife."

Connor cleared his throat. "Actually, Ava, if you don't mind, I'll have a can of soda."

Ava disappeared into the kitchen and when she returned, Nico was securing Elisabetta into the baby bouncer. The baby gurgled and waved her hands excitedly when he turned the music on.

"She seems happy," Connor commented. "I expected her to be crying and whiny, but she seems kind of calm. That's good to know."

"They can be a lot of work." Nico placed his arm protectively around Ava's shoulder and pulled her closer towards him. "I underestimated how tiring and full on they can be. Ava's been amazing, dealing with everything."

Connor glanced up at them and for a moment, as he took them both in, his smile slowly disappeared.

"I'm married to a superwoman," declared Nico, "And I

didn't even know it." Ava shuffled uncomfortably. Nico was laying the love on strong, and she knew that most of it was to piss Connor off.

"We're having a baby," said Connor, matter-of-factly, dropping the bombshell.

Ava sat up. "Who's having a baby?"

"Meredith and I."

"Congratulations." Nico sounded rather enthused about this latest announcement.

Meredith. The name didn't sound familiar. Connor cleared his throat again and his cheeks turned a deeper shade of pink. "She worked in that law firm and...she was the one I met at the conference..."

Ava frowned. "Have I met her?" She wondered why he was telling her this.

"No," said Connor, "She was the one ..."

Ava looked at him, puzzled. It sounded as if he was about to make a confession.

"The one I met at the law seminar ... in Connecticut."

The impact of his words shot through her like a bullet from the past.

"The one you cheated on me with?" she asked, her voice sounding edgy, and shrill. She tried to calm herself down. "Why are you telling me this?" She was astounded by his thoughtlessness in raking up that episode from her past. It was something she wanted to forget' a past that had no future in her life.

"She—uh, she left her husband."

Oh boy, it just kept getting better.

Ava sat forward, moving away from Nico's protective arm and looked at Connor as if he'd gone mad. "I don't need to know the details. I don't need to know anything at all." *Because I don't care.* But he'd raked up that pain from the past, from that moment in her life. He'd brought it all back to the present. Why did people do that?

"I want to ..." He cleared his throat. "I want to own up to what I did. Meredith thinks it would be good for me to have closure."

Ava fought to stifle her gasp of astonishment. "Closure?" she cried, needing to make sure she'd heard right. He could take Meredith's advice and choke on it for all she cared. "I had closure the moment I met Nico. You were already out of my head before the plane landed in Verona."

It wasn't that she felt any feelings for this man, or that she was sad, but Connor bringing up that time now stirred up old memories. She felt Nico's hand closing over her arm, hugging her tighter.

"I need closure," said Connor. Ava looked at him wondering what she'd missed. The man had never been in touch with his feelings before. This confession, so unnecessary, especially in front of Nico, puzzled her. Was it because he was becoming a parent, or because he was in love? What was it?

"She left her husband?" Nico asked, his voice casual.

From the sounds of it Connor and this woman both deserved one another.

"You told me that babies weren't in your career plan," Ava challenged, quoting his exact words from that dump-text he'd cowardly sent her.

"People change."

She gritted her teeth together, unable to hit back with a suitable answer. People *did* change, and sometimes they grew a spine too.

"When's the baby due?" Nico asked.

"August."

"That's the time of our first anniversary," commented

Nico, his warm hand reminding her of how lucky she was to be sitting here with this man who was now a part of her life, instead of that man opposite her.

Connor would have made her life miserable.

"A year," she gazed into Nico's shining eyes, feeling his love for her reflected back.

"We'll go back to Venice?" he suggested. She thought back to that moment when he'd come looking for her in Venice, when he'd given her the bracelet, when it had all started, the point at which they were fated to be together. "Venice," she whispered, her collection of happy memories from that time making her heart sing. Elisabetta had been conceived there, and perhaps by the time of their first anniversary it would be time to make baby number two.

She snuggled closer to him, resting her head against the hollow of his neck and forgetting, or not caring—she wasn't sure which it was—that Connor was still here.

She glanced at the man she was once going to marry. Thank goodness fate had intervened. She'd been heartbroken when he'd left her but connecting all the dots looking back on her life, she could see that ultimately it was for the better. Nico was her soulmate, and it was their destiny to have found one another. "I hope you'll be happy, Connor. It sounds like a new start for you."

He didn't say anything, except nodded. "And this," he said, pulling out an envelope from his jacket pocket. "This is the rest of it. I'm sorry it's taken me so long to pay it all back." She froze, staring at him in disbelief. Her heart pounded hard and slow and her stomach filled with tiny fissures of ice. He wasn't to know that she'd never told Nico about the money. It wasn't his fault but at this very moment she hated him all the same.

A spell of silence fell over her, and she couldn't think of

what to say or how to respond. She wasn't sure what Nico would make of it. She wasn't sure how to explain it, any of it—the money and the unintended deceit.

"You told me you'd pay her back within the month and that was five months ago." Nico's voice was barbed, his tone acidic. She spun around.

He knew?

"I'm sorry. I—I tried my best," stammered Connor, standing up. "I've paid back the entire $10k now what with the $8K I gave you a few weeks ago." He turned to address her but she only wanted to burrow deep into the undersides of the sofa cushions, like a biscuit crumb, small and insignificant and out of sight.

"You should be disgusted with yourself." Nico's face darkened like thunder.

"I'm sorry," Connor repeated and she could tell by his tight expression that he was anxious to leave. "I'm sorry for a lot of things." Somehow she sensed that this was it—the final goodbye, that they wouldn't see much of him anymore, that he would soon become wrapped up in his new family and there was no need for her to ever run into him again. In a way, she hoped so. Their paths would probably never cross again once she returned to Verona.

"When's the wedding?" Nico asked, standing up and pulling her up with him.

"We haven't talked about a wedding, yet."

"Weddings aren't your strong suit, are they?" Nico shot back.

"Nico." Ava silenced him with a harsh stare.

"Goodbye." Connor held out his hand for her to shake. It seemed an odd gesture, but nothing else would be fitting. She shook hands with him and he waved pathetically at Elisabetta, who was busy trying to grab the plastic hanging mirror on the baby bouncer.

Ava walked him to the door. "Goodbye, Connor, and good luck."

"You too."

Her heart thumped like a wild galloping horse as she returned. Nico had taken Elisabetta out of the rocker and held her in his arms. With her insides feeling hollow she waited for the explosion but all he said was, "We'd better leave. Carlos will be waiting."

She eyed the envelope still lying on the table. "How did you know?"

"Not from you, that's for sure."

"I tried to tell you."

"Tried?"

"I did try but you always hated it when I mentioned his name."

"Maybe you didn't try hard enough."

"That's not true."

He turned his back on her and picked up Elisabetta's coat, ignoring her as if he didn't want to discuss the matter further.

"How long have you known?" She wished he would erupt and get angry. She preferred that to his cool and collected manner.

"I've known since the last time I was here."

That long ago?

She stepped back in surprise and watched as Nico balanced Elisabetta on his lap, gently threading her arms, one by one, into the sleeves of her fluffy cream coat. "It's ironic when I look back on it now, how angry you were with me for not telling you the truth about the warehouse fire. I did it to protect you, I did it so that you wouldn't worry and stress over it on our honeymoon.

And all you could do when you found out was get mad at me. So much for your 'no secrets and lies'. And yet you thought nothing of keeping a $10K loan to your ex a secret from me."

"I didn't lie about the money." It was a weak attempt at recovering herself.

"You didn't lie about it, you just didn't tell me and that's almost as bad as lying to me—especially when it concerns your ex-lover."

She hated him using that word. Tossing it at her like a grenade. "I'm sorry, Nico." But he wasn't listening to her.

CHAPTER THIRTY-FOUR

"Thanks. That was quite a feast you put on," said Nico, taking the opened bottle of beer from Carlos.

"Don't mention it, buddy. We hardly ever get to see you guys. It was a pleasure."

The two men had come outside onto the porch for a breather. They held their bottles up. "To life with the Ramirez women," said Nico, referring to Ava's maiden name.

"We couldn't live without them."

The two men clinked their bottles together.

"No," said Nico, slowly, he couldn't live without Ava. They had eaten a huge dinner and it had turned hot and stuffy inside. The slight chill outside cooled his skin. Lights from the surrounding houses on the quiet street glittered like golden sequins in the velvet night and Nico was almost content. His belly was full. All hell was breaking out indoors with Elsa and her daughters sitting in the living room talking and Tori playing.

He knew Ava would keep a close eye on her niece because Tori got over excited when Elisabetta was around and treated her like one of her play dolls, prodding her and examining her. She most probably would have tried to lift her if Ava hadn't been around.

"You seem kind of quiet tonight," observed Carlos. "Everything alright with you, buddy?"

Nico sucked in a breath. He and Ava weren't good at hiding their iciness. The truth was, it hit harder than he thought it would—this whole business about her lending money to Connor. It wasn't even the money so much. His wife was the type of person who would help anybody, which was why he didn't put it past that slime ball of her ex to ask someone like her for money. But she was also a shrewd businesswoman, even with that heart of gold and he knew she would have claimed it back at some point. What hurt the most was that she'd hidden the whole transaction from him. Her defense when he'd questioned her had been weak and flimsy. It wasn't true that she'd *tried* to tell him. How many chances had he given her to come clean?

"'Course, if you'd rather not say..."

"It's..." He shook his head then put the bottle to his lips. There was no use in involving Carlos in any of this. He took a big gulp and thought about it some more. Maybe he needed to get it out of his system. "Beachcroft turned up at the apartment before we left."

"Connor?"

Nico nodded.

"What the hell for?"

"He said he wanted to see Elisabetta."

"Ava's been here all this time and he only thought to come now? Did he know you were here?"

Nico shook his head. "He looked surprised when he saw me, so I guess not. I don't think it was because of Elisabetta. He came because he had news to share, or offload, depending on how you look at it."

Carlos raised a thick bushy eyebrow. "What kind of news?"

"He's having a baby, apparently. With the woman he cheated on Ava with."

Carlos shiny brown eyes opened wide and his hand clutching the beer bottle hovered in mid-air. "Are you kiddin' me?"

"You know about that?" Nico asked, surprised.

"Well, not because Ava told me...but, you know how tight sisters are."

Nico shrugged.

"Of course, I don't know who he cheated on her with. All I knew was that the sleaze ball ditched her a couple of weeks before the wedding. Are you sure it's the same woman?" Carlos asked.

"That's what it sounded like. She's leaving her husband, too."

Carlos slapped his hand across the back of his neck. "Well, I'll be damned. That no good sonofabitch."

"Ava said they deserved one another."

"They sure as hell do." Carlos turned and pointed at him with the bottle. "Is that why you're mad at her?"

"I'm not mad at her," Nico proclaimed.

"No?" Carlos sounded as if he obviously thought otherwise.

"Why would I be mad at her about that? It sounds to me as if she was the one who was wronged."

"Then what *are* you mad at her about? The two of you didn't even speak to one another over dinner."

"She loaned him some money a few months' ago."

"She did?"

"It was last year, some time. He needed $10K."

Carlos spluttered on his mouthful of his beer. "$10K? But he's a lawyer! Why's he short of money?"

"No idea," said Nico, draining his bottle dry. "The man's an asshole."

"He is," replied Carlos.

"I've never liked him."

"Me neither."

Silence fell as the two men bonded in their unified contempt towards Ava's ex. "So..." Carlos' brow crinkled into tiny creases. "You're mad at her because she gave him the money?" More silence. "Shouldn't you be mad at him for asking her in the first place?"

"That too," drawled Nico. "I hate the man. You know I hate the man, right?"

Carlos nodded.

"But I'm mad at her for not telling me."

"She gave him $10k and never told you?"

"That's right. But I knew about it because Connor mentioned it to me last year. Do you remember when I came over to find a warehouse and you helped me to move stuff out of his garage?"

Carlos nodded. "You knew then?"

"I knew then and I've been waiting for her to tell me ever since and she never did and today he comes over and gives her a check in front of me and that's how it all came out."

"And you're mad at her for what?"

Nico looked at Carlos in confusion. "She could have told me. She made a big enough deal about me keeping the warehouse fire from her. We've had all week together. I can't see how she didn't find the right moment to tell me. And then I find out that he gave her $8K a couple of weeks ago. How could she not have told me?"

Carlos wiped his hand across his brow and shook his

head. "I don't know, buddy." The two men grew silent and after a while Nico started again. "You can't have secrets, not with your ex. She shouldn't even have been in touch with him." He paused, remembering Silvia. "It all seems like one big mess with one thing after another. Things haven't been that easy for us lately."

"You've had a lot going on," Carlos agreed. "You both need to cut yourselves some slack. A baby, and all those business headaches you've both got going on. It's a wonder you're not strangling one another."

"You could say we've tried, metaphorically, although Ava's too sophisticated to want to strangle me," chuckled Nico. "And my anger is more of the deadly but quiet kind."

Carlos laughed. "I'm planning on being with Rona for the rest of my life but living with someone forever has got to be one of the hardest things."

Nico nodded in agreement. "I never expected it to be this hard. I thought being married protected you against that."

Carlos snorted. "I'm still trying to figure it out, buddy." His face became more serious. "Marriage is the hardest thing. Don't get me wrong," he said, shaking his head. "I love that woman to death and I'd do anything for her, but she drives me insane on more than four days of the week." Nico stifled a laugh. He knew what Rona could be like. "But I can't imagine my life without her," continued Carlos. "I love her. I love her despite her crazy, illogical reasoning and her belief that the world spins around her."

"And I love Ava because she makes me a better me." Nico winced. "My problem is I end up taking my business frustrations out on her. I can be a miserable little shit to live with."

"Sometimes it's better to get it out of our systems. Women have coffee mornings specifically designed for this, did you know that? They sit in groups with their friends in a coffee shop talking about all sorts of things. Dude, they sit around dissecting and analyzing a problem like it's some kind of lab rat."

"I believe it's called 'gossip'."

"Whatever." Carlos shrugged. "But see, we're not like that. We keep it all in and I'm not sure that's a good way of handling it."

"Hmmmm." Nico agreed.

Carlos glanced over his shoulder before edging closer to Nico. "This goes nowhere but you recall that time in Verona when I got into a fight in the parking lot at your hotel?"

He did remember, just like he vaguely recalled how tense things were between Carlos and Rona around the time of his wedding. "Was that around the time Tori went missing?"

"Yeah." Carlos coughed. "She had a flirtation back in Verona."

"I figured."

"You knew?"

Nico nodded, giving it up reluctantly. "Not because Rona told me...but, well, sisters being tight and all that. I don't think we'll have any secrets between us—it sounds to me as if Rona tells you everything, and Ava tells me everything."

"Doesn't surprise me," said Carlos. "See, this's what I mean. They like to talk. But as for that episode—nothing happened. Nothing like *that*." He seemed resolute in his belief. "She maybe had dinner with him a few times, might even have kissed him a couple of times."

"And you're okay with that?" Nico didn't understand how Carlos could stand there so calmly. If it were him he'd want to gouge the man's heart out. "She kissed a man and you didn't mind?"

"I did mind, once I found out and I was—to use your

expression—a miserable little shit to live with. I gave her the silent treatment." Carlos lifted his bottle but it was empty. "I took her for granted. It's no excuse, but it was kind of my fault too. I was working way too hard, all those nights at the restaurant. All she wanted was for me to notice her, to let her know I was there for her, to let her see that I still found her attractive. I guess," he paused, "I guess it went way deeper than that though, I guess she needed to know that she mattered. But we worked through it and we've been tight ever since. Sometimes, it takes a shock, it takes for something to happen for you to see that you already have the world at your fingertips."

Amen, thought Nico. He already knew that.

"Now she wants another baby."

Nico smiled widely. "Another baby?" Tori was eighteen months old now and the timing seemed about right. But Carlos didn't seem to share in the excitement. "You don't look so keen."

"Oh, just-uh, you know, the cost of it and all that. I don't mind working hard for my family, but I guess I need some time to get used to the idea. Rona won't want to work once we get pregnant."

"Ava will always have a job for her, I'm sure." That was, if she still had the store. He decided not to add to Carlos' worries by mentioning that Ava was thinking of selling the business.

"Rona's not the type to manage two children and work, not even doing part-time hours. She's not Ava," said Carlos, smiling. "But we'll see how it all works out. It will work out, 'cos it has to, right?"

Nico couldn't help but agree. He liked Carlos' outlook on life and the fact that this huge bear of a man didn't let anything frazzle him too much. That he took everything in his stride, unlike Nico, who seemed to get wound up over the smallest of things. He liked Carlos a lot, and more than anything, he liked that he and this man were more than friends—they were part of the same family.

"Another beer?" Carlos asked, turning towards the door.

"Are you going back in?" Nico asked.

"Hell, no!" Carlos cried. "I'm getting our beers and coming back out."

"Good idea." Nico grinned to himself. They'd be returning to Verona tomorrow, and it would be a while before he got to trade advice with someone who understood him so well.

CHAPTER THIRTY-FIVE

"That's wonderful news." Ava felt a sense of joy as she sat back in her chair.

A second baby for the Hardings. Baby news was always happy news.

"I told my husband I don't have the energy to sue. All that time and effort, and money and stress. We're happy our son is okay." Gwen Harding's words were sweet music to Ava's ears. The news couldn't have come at a better time for her especially since they'd received notice from the Dawson's attorney that a lawsuit had been filed against them for injuries caused to their daughter.

They'd arrived back in Italy a week ago and today she'd come to the hotel in order to organize her office which had been neglected ever since she'd had Elisabetta. She wanted to rearrange the furniture and create more space. It felt like starting over.

"I'm very happy for you, Gwen," said Ava. At first when she'd answered the call, the sound of an American voice and mention of the word 'crib' had her worried. But Gwen Harding's announcement that they would no longer be pursuing a lawsuit was news worth celebrating—even in light of what was happening with the Dawsons. But she didn't want to think about the ramifications of a lawsuit now.

"It's a summer baby, so I have some time to get things ready and at least the morning sickness is over."

"That's good to hear," said Ava. She'd been lucky and hadn't suffered too much with morning sickness. She cleared her throat. "Would it help if I made arrangements for the crib to be shipped back?" she asked, seeing as they no longer needed it for proof. "Or if you like, I'd be happy to have a brand new one sent out—the proper fixed side ones that we normally sell—but I understand if you'd rather not buy from my store again."

"I'll need to take another look online."

It surprised her that someone who had been as cold as Gwen Harding would even consider shopping on her site again.

"Sure," said Ava. "And..." she paused, "I'd like to offer you a credit note to the value of three thousand dollars." She'd pulled the first figure that came to her head. "You can purchase anything from the store up to that value. I feel it would only be right, given what has happened."

"Does that include shipping?"

Huh? "No," said Ava. "Don't worry about the shipping. The shipping's on me. You take a look online and email me a list of the things you like and I'll take care of everything here."

"That's mighty kind of you."

"You're very welcome," said Ava, unable to stop the smile spreading from cheek to cheek.

She hung up and examined the trio of photos she'd placed on her desk in readiness for her return. There was one of her and Nico on their wedding day, one of the two of them with

Elisabetta when she was a few days old, and one of Elisabetta alone. Ava was still smiling when Nico entered.

"Guess who's having a second baby?" she asked, getting up because she couldn't hide her excitement.

"Rona?"

"Rona? Pffft," she snorted as she walked over to him and grabbed him by the waist. "My sister can barely manage one baby, how do you think she's going to manage two?"

"*Us?*" Nico asked, making a wild guess but she could tell by the way he said it that he didn't really mean it.

"Not possible," she said. "I'm being careful."

"Don't be too careful," he murmured, lowering his lips to the hollow in her neck and planting a soft kiss there. It was the type of kiss that had the potential to make her toes curl. "I want to make more babies with you."

"I want to have more babies with you." Her mind started to get dizzy from the feel of his lips on her skin. "But we have a plan, remember?" He lifted his head and surveyed her with interest. "I'm returning to work after Easter, I'm still interviewing for nannies—"

"None of them were any good?"

She shook her head. "I didn't get the right vibe from them." She'd interviewed two this morning and she didn't feel comfortable about leaving Elisabetta with either of them. "It might take a while to find the right person."

"And if you don't find anyone soon, I'll look after her." He was making an effort to be supportive and she liked it. And for some reason, she liked to think it wasn't just because Dino was interested in her business. The more she relaxed, and the more she and Nico talked, the more he supported her and helped with the baby, and the more she was able to finally feel secure. To not feel as if she had to do it all. He helped her to discover again what she loved about running her online store.

"How can you look after Elisabetta? You're so busy as it is."

"And you're not? The hotel will be open in a few weeks and after Easter everything should be starting to settle down."

It was true. The safety inspection had taken place last week and they had the go-ahead to open. It was all systems go again; the advertising, the media blitz and the launch party. "Let's see what happens by then," she said. "I've got a few more nannies to interview next week. Now," she said, her squeezing his waist. "Are you ready?"

"Ready?" Nico stared at her blankly.

"We have a lunch date, and you've forgotten already." She'd decided that since both of their schedules were hectic, going out to lunch at least once a week would help them to take time out, away from home and away from their offices. "My mom's happy to have Elisabetta while we go."

"She was in the gardens earlier," Nico told her.

"Poor Salvatore."

"Do you think—"

"Do I think what?" asked Ava, moving over to her desk to grab her bag.

"That's the reason she came back?"

"You mean because she's so obsessed by the gardens?" Ava shrugged. She was suddenly reminded of one of the reasons she'd come in today. "I need a new printer, to be placed over there, and also a scanner." She turned around. "I think an L-shaped desk might be better for me, what do you think?"

"Nice," said Nico. "Why do I get the feeling that before long, this office is going to be too small for you?"

"I also need a warehouse."

His right eyebrow shifted north.

"But not yet," she said quickly. "In time. When we open

in Europe. Now, let's go to lunch. The Hardings aren't pursuing things further and I have a good reason to celebrate. I'm in the mood for an indulgent lunch and it's been a while since I had a glass of champagne."

"I thought you didn't like me to wine and dine you."

"That was when we were dating." Ava looped her arm through his. "I didn't need for you to impress me back then but it's nice to be offered that occasionally."

"I can do that."

"Also, that Harding woman didn't have much of a case, it sounds like. I offered to send her some things for free."

Nico's eyes opened wide. "For free?"

"I was relieved she wasn't going to sue. I told her she could have anything she wanted up to $3000."

"But $3000?" He almost choked.

Ava recalled her visit to the family. "For all I know, she might not even be pregnant."

"She might not be." He kissed her on her nose. "She might want all your free stuff so that she can sell it on eBay."

Ava blinked rapidly a few times.

"What are you going to do? Fly out there to check?" Nico grinned at her. "Send her the stuff and forget about it." He made a move to leave. "Give me ten minutes. Gina wanted to see me about something."

"I'll see what other new office furniture I need."

Nico knocked on the door to Gina's office and walked in. She looked nervous and he had an uneasy thought that he wasn't going to like whatever it was she wanted to see him about.

"You wanted to take some time off," he said, pre-empting the conversation as he sat across the desk from her.

And that was when he saw it. A white envelope addressed to him in her handwriting, lying on the desk. "What's this?" But a sinking feeling in his chest prepared him.

How had he not seen this coming?

"It's my resignation letter, Nico."

Of course it was. He narrowed his eyes and stared at the white envelope in disbelief. "So you want to leave?" The question hung in the air like a decaying cobweb.

"It's been a difficult decision to make."

"I was under the impression that you wanted time off. Could that still be an option?" he asked, his voice hopeful.

"I don't think so, Nico." He saw from the way her mouth set that this was as difficult for Gina as it was for him to take it in.

"But why? What can I do to make you stay?"

"You can't do anything."

"Where are you going?"

"It's—"

"Complicated," he said. "I know. You said that last time. But what's the reason behind it? I need to know so that I fix it or help or do what I can."

But if she already had a job lined up then it was too late. He had increased her salary when he'd promoted her, but she'd also been due another promotion for all her hard work as well as a bonus of some sort. He'd been too swamped to take care of such matters.

Gina looked up at him with puppy dog eyes. "My decision to leave is not a reflection on you or the Cazale hotels or the Casa Adriana. It's my personal circumstances."

Personal circumstances. He couldn't really help with that and it seemed that she'd already made up her mind.

"I want to refuse this," he said, wishing she'd spoken to him first, before she'd made her mind up. It was clear from the stoic expression on her face that she had, that her decision was final. It would be wrong of him to try to make her change her mind even if that would be the right thing to do for him and for the hotel. For the first time, Nico had to do the right thing by Gina. "This is a sad day," he said, feeling miserable.

"I'm sorry, Nico."

"I'm sorry, too. I've placed far too much stress on you. Given you way too much responsibility and I should have known better. I should have looked after you better."

"Nico." Gina's mouth twisted. "It's many things. Other things. It's nothing to do with you or the hotel or the pressures."

"Demetrio? Does he have something to do with your decision?"

"He hasn't been the easiest of people to work with but he's not solely to blame."

"But you loved working here." Nico was determined to get to the bottom of this. "What did we do wrong? How could I get you to change your mind?"

Gina looked heartbroken. "You can't. Please, Nico. It's a lot more complicated than that."

"But you asked for leave, one to two months and I was happy for you to take that."

She looked away.

"The offer still stands," he said, determined to do what he could to make her stay.

"But—"

"The offer still stands. What is this? One month's notice?" Technically, as a member of management, it was three months' notice he required.

"Three months," she said.

It gave him hope.

It wasn't only because the Cazale Ravenna would be

opening soon and would no longer drain so much of his time, or that June, her proposed date of leaving, was a long time away, and anything could happen between here and now. It gave him time to try to make things up to her but unless he found out what the cause of her problems were, he couldn't really do anything to make her change her mind.

"I'm not happy to accept this, Gina, but duty makes me and in the meantime, my offer for you to take a long leave of absence still holds, if that would help."

Gina pressed her lips together. "Thank you."

He got up then and walked out to find Ava waiting in the lobby for him. He wanted to tell her, to share this bad news with her, but she looked so happy, and he didn't want to dampen her mood.

CHAPTER THIRTY-SIX

Three weeks later

"**B**eautiful!" gasped Ava.

She was spellbound as she walked around in her high heels, perhaps not the most appropriate of shoes to be wearing for the launch party at the Cazale Ravenna. She smoothed down the front of her dress, the dark red sequins of her fitted cocktail dressed shimmering as she walked.

"You are that." Nico entwined his fingers firmly around hers as they wandered around enjoying the fresh, spring day. The start of a new beginning. She dismissed his compliment easily and concentrated on this breathtaking surroundings around her.

She hadn't seen the Cazale Ravenna since that first time Nico had shown it to her when the old hotel had been up for sale. But what she saw now was a completely transformed property which bore no resemblance to its former self. And as for the new spa center, and the glass tunnel connecting the hotel to it, and the landscaped grounds and gardens—they were all so much more spectacular in real life than in the photos and video clips that Nico had shown her.

From almost ruins, he had created *this*. Her heart swelled with pride. "What I want," she said, in constant amazement as he showed her around, "is to stay here for a long weekend."

"We can do that." Nico squeezed her hand gently as they walked around. He looked so happy, so proud, and she was happy and proud for him, for all that he had achieved in getting it to this state. She hoped that it would prosper and do as well as he wanted, but only time would tell.

Selected people from the press where here, as were VIPs, influential guests, business leaders and partners, industry bodies and agents, as well as personal friends and family. They'd spent the better part of the last hour mixing with the businesspeople, until Nico had pulled her away and given her his own personal tour.

Andrea and Dino were here as were most of Nico's management team. Even the new nanny, Ingrid had been invited. Ava felt completely at ease with her but Elsa, it seemed, did not. Her mother followed the new nanny around, keeping a close eye on her as she pushed Elisabetta around in a stroller. The little girl looked like a cherub in her white cotton dress with a pink and white cashmere cardigan and soft pink baby shoes.

"Is that Bruno's girlfriend?" Ava asked, looking over at the man who stood in the far distance near the glass tunnel with a tall and elegant red head by his side.

"I have no idea. I don't even know if he's married."

"You've worked with him all this time and you don't know?" She was always surprised by how much Nico focused only on business.

"It's different for us men," said Nico. "We're don't jump at any opportunity to do lunch."

"Maybe doing lunch might be the very thing you men need."

"I could organize a 'thank you' dinner for everyone who worked on this project," he suggested.

"It might be an idea. They've done a magnificent job, Nico. Seeing this place with my own eyes, being here—it makes me want to *stay* here. I love it. I love all of it. You've brought it to life, all the things you used to tell me, the garden showers, and the outdoor treatment areas. I can't wait to have a massage in one of those."

"I can give you a massage out there if you like," he whispered into her ear. "But we'd have to do that in our bedroom, I can't be trusted to end it on a professional note."

She returned his smile. "I'm going to hold you to that massage later tonight." Her voice was so low and her words barely audible, but judging by the smile on his face, loud enough for him to understand.

He gave her a look that sent shivers scurrying all over her skin. "That's a promise."

They looked over to see Gina and Ines standing with a group of people. "I haven't seen Demetrio around," Ava commented.

"He's not here," Nico told her. "He's doing the upgrade in Rome and can't make it."

"That's a shame." She had been eager to watch the dynamics between this new hire and Gina.

"You didn't get any more information from Gina, then?" Nico asked.

"Unfortunately not." She had been to lunch recently with Andrea and Gina but hadn't managed to extract any more information from Gina about her decision to leave Nico's employment. "I didn't want to ask any pointed questions," she said. "I left it to her to bring up the subject if she felt comfortable, and she never said a thing." She knew that news of Gina's resignation had wounded Nico deeply. He'd been so used to having her around and had relied on her so much that the news of her departure had completely blind-sided him.

Ava sensed that he blamed himself for it even though she kept telling him that there had to be more to it than work pressure. She didn't agree with Nico's suspicion that there was something going on between Gina and Demetrio. She knew Gina, and she didn't think it was something as obvious as that. She couldn't see her leaving because of a romantic issue.

It had to be something deeper. Something bigger.

The order mix-up was nearly resolved. In a few more weeks' time the rest of the erroneously shipped cribs would be returned to Dino's factory. There was also a hint of potential good news in the air. Her lawyer had hinted that the Dawson's claim appeared to be frivolous and it was highly likely that it would be dismissed but until she knew this for certain, Ava couldn't rest easy.

Dino had forked out a fortune to have every crib shipped back to Italy and had offered to pay for the new replacements that were being shipped out. This had caused more heated debates between them both, especially when Dino had initially refused to pay for cribs that weren't his, but after much negotiating, and stubbornly standing her ground, with the thinly veiled threat of never selling his cribs again, he finally gave in.

As a result, the loss she had projected for her business wasn't going to be as much as she had forecast. The time and money she had spent in visiting Denver, in trying to do her best to recall the offending cribs, had served them all well, even if Dino Massari chose to conveniently forget this fact.

"Look at you!" Andrea squealed, tapping her on the shoulder from behind. They both turned to find Andrea and Dino behind them. This was the first time they'd been face-to-face since she and Nico had returned from Denver. They'd had meetings and conversations over the phone but the busy run up period to the hotel opening had been crazy and had prevented her from going to Montova to touch base with these two in person.

"Nico," said Dino, acknowledging her husband. The two men eyed one another before stiffly shaking hands. "I'm impressed. You've completely turned this place around. It's unrecognizable from the hotel it used to be. I'm not so sure about the location but when I come here I forget I'm in Ravenna."

"I take that as a compliment," said Nico. "Ravenna isn't a highly sought after travel location, but I consider this to be a trial. It's been a labor of love to get this place up and running."

"You've done well," Dino said.

"As have you," Nico remarked. "Your situation could have been far worse, could it not?"

Ava gently nudged him in the ribs hoping he wasn't going to use this evening to tell Dino exactly what he thought of him.

"We're still not in the clear," Andrea added.

"I know." Nico hugged Ava closer to him. "We'll have to wait and see what happens." She looked up and stared into his eyes, knowing that whatever the outcome, it would be alright. They'd find a way through it. According to her attorney, the Dawson child's fractured shoulder might not have been caused by a fall from the crib. Child protection had been involved with that family before. It made her heart heavy to hear of such things.

"It was lucky for you that my wife went over to take care of your business," said Nico. Dino narrowed his eyes and appeared to hesitate before replying. "Ava and I don't always see eye to eye."

"We don't," she answered sweetly.

"But," Dino replied, addressing her, "You got us out of a bind and you probably saved my business." He nodded at her appreciatively. "I have to ask," he said, turning to the spa center behind him. "That's one hell of an impressive building. How did you go about designing it?" He seemed to be saying all the right things, and she and Andrea turned to one another, moving away a little while the two men discussed business.

"Have you lost weight?" Andrea asked her, running her fingers gently around Ava's waist. "Or are you wearing Spanx?"

"Both," Ava whispered. "As soon as I stopped breast feeding, the weight fell off."

Andrea's eyebrow's lifted in surprise. "If only it were that easy."

"You don't have any extra weight to lose!" Ava exclaimed, staring at Andrea's skinny frame. She looked around. "Where's Leo?"

"Isn't he here?"

"I haven't seen him," remarked Ava. Ravenna was a bit of a drive away and she had assumed that Andrea and Leo might have come together.

Unless Andrea had come with Dino.

She examined her friend's face carefully. "Do you have something to tell me?" She noticed the glitter on Andrea's bare shoulders. It wasn't from the glitter lace of her black knee-length dress. It looked more like shimmery body lotion. She'd obviously made a great effort this evening.

"Like what?" asked Andrea.

"I don't know. You tell me."

Andrea looked even more puzzled.

"You and Dino are looking pretty cozy together. I go to Denver for a few weeks and come back to find you both looking very much together."

Andrea didn't deny anything. Nor did she confirm. "I'm saying nothing." They heard a rumble of laughter behind them and turned to find that Leo had joined the men.

"So, he did come," said Ava, softly. He looked handsome in his all-black outfit. Dark trousers, black crew neck shirt and a black blazer.

"When did you get here?" Andrea asked him as they joined the group of men.

"I've been here a while." Leo pulled out his cell phone. "I ran into some journalist friends and I have some news." He looked around conspiratorially and lowered his head, and they, sensing the secret nature of what he had to tell them, huddled around him. "I have it on good authority that tomorrow's papers are going to shock you." He paused for maximum effect. "Vieri, you know—Armando Vieri," as if Nico might have forgotten who he was.

"Go on," said Nico, impatiently.

"Caught with male prostitutes," he whispered.

"What?" Ava gasped. She was sure she'd misheard.

"Male prostitutes," repeated Leo, "Two of them." He put up two fingers as if to emphasize his point.

"It can't be true!" Andrea exclaimed.

Leo raised an eyebrow. "Can't it?"

"No wonder she looked so miserable when she came to see me," murmured Nico.

"Dishonest douchebag," muttered Ava. "Karma is a bitch but I do so love her." This would effectively finish Vieri's career in politics and humiliate him. "Poor Silvia." She felt sorry for the woman, even though there was no reason to.

"Poor Silvia?" Nico questioned.

"She might have had a hand in things, and she's not a nice person, but still ..." She sighed. "It must be heartbreaking to have a man cheat on her like that."

"With another man, you mean?"

"With anyone, and especially like that, and in the press for the entire world to see. How humiliating."

Nico kissed her forehead. "Humiliating, yes. At least I hope he's out of their lives and away from Alessa. Which reminds me." He looked around. "Where's Elisabetta?"

"Ingrid had her. My mom was hovering around them somewhere."

"I see her." Nico looked over towards the glass tunnel.

"She's keeping an eye on Ingrid," mused Ava. Her mother was sitting on a bench close to where the nanny pushed Elisabetta around in the stroller.

"She could almost be Ingrid's shadow," Nico muttered under his breath. "Excuse us, please." Holding hands, they made their way over to Elsa.

"Are you keeping an eye on Ingrid again, Mom?" Ava asked, jokingly.

"I'm watching over my granddaughter," Elsa replied.

"I hired Ingrid so that you'd be free to enjoy your vacation."

"Yes," said Nico, as they sat down on either side of her. "It's time for you to take it easy. Have you seen all of it? Both the hotel and the spa center?"

"Twice," replied Elsa. "I was almost tempted to wade into the infinity pool."

"There's nothing stopping you," Nico told her. "All of these amenities are yours to use whenever you want."

"That's very kind of you, Nico." In her hands Elsa had one of the beauty treatment brochures.

"Let me see," said Ava and she flicked through the glossy A5 sized magazine. "Ines has done an amazing job on these."

"She's worked a crazy number of hours on it," agreed Nico. "This whole launch has come alive because of her."

"Aren't you glad you handed that task over to someone else?" Ava asked. She knew how much he had on his plate, and that was before the Spa hotel had gotten underway. There would have been no way he'd have been able to come up with the sort of advertising campaign and launch party that Ines had come up with.

"Are there any treatments in here you liked, Mom?" Ava asked as she looked through the magazine.

"The Hot Stone Massage," Elsa replied, nodding. "That *does* sound interesting, if a little painful."

Nico and Ava laughed. "I don't think any of the treatments will be painful. That's not the experience I want my guests to take away with them."

"Are you looking to impress anyone in particular?" Ava asked, as she and Nico exchanged knowing smiles. They peered at Elsa.

"Impress anyone? At my age?" She snorted and looked around. "As if I would want such a thing." She patted Nico on the knee gently. "Your father would have been very proud of you, Nico."

"You always say that." His voice turned somber.

"It's true and I never want you to forget that." Nico lowered his head and rolled his lips together, as if he was trying to be brave, trying not to crumble. "In one of his last letters to me—an email—Edmondo told me that your spa hotel wouldn't open when you wanted it to. You were so determined for it to open in November, and I had told him that. But," Elsa stopped to take a breath, as if the mere remembrance of that time and that conversation had taken her back to that very moment. "But Edmondo," she continued, her voice wavering as it did when she was overcome with emotion, "he said that in your eagerness you'd probably underestimated the time it took to get things done, that you didn't account for all the things that might go wrong. He told me he felt sure that your original opening date would be postponed because projects like this always take longer." Elsa's lips trembled, and she sniffed, trying to compose herself. "He told me that I must come when it opened, and that it would be the anniversary of my first visit here. He said we would celebrate."

Ava took her mother's other hand and rubbed it gently. "And *that's* the reason you came back?"

Elsa nodded. "Don't you see? I *had* to be here." She lowered her head and let out an anguished sigh, as if it was impossible to hold back the sadness she was fighting so hard to contain.

Ava put her arms around her mother's shoulder.

"I made a promise to myself to honor his request, and that's why I came back with you both. I had to be here and I feel so happy that I did. I thought I would be sad, but I'm not as sad as I expected to be. I'm immensely proud of you, Nico, and I know your father would have been, too."

Nico bent over and kissed Elsa's hand. "Thank you. It means a lot."

Ava kissed her mother on the cheek and looked at her with admiration. Elsa was noble in the way she contained her grief, in the way she wouldn't let it consume her, in the way she kept it at bay. But her mother's eyes didn't lie. They were the windows to her suffering. It saddened Ava to think that Elsa had become emotionally attached to someone who could have been good company for her in her twilight years. But it was not to be. Yet her mother had weathered grief in her lifetime before and Ava knew that she would be fine. Her mother was tough.

It was Nico she worried about. He wanted to show her and everyone else that he was strong, that nothing troubled him, but she knew this man; she was a part of him, and he a part of her. She didn't rely on him telling her how he felt. She *felt* him. She felt his pain, his loneliness, his regret as much as if it were her own, and a part of it *was* hers.

She understood—without the need for words—his happiness and his grief. She wanted to reach over now and squeeze his hand, his knee, anything, but her mother sat between them.

There was many a time when she wondered what Edmondo would have made of Elisabetta, and how much he would have played with her. How he would have taken her out into his beloved gardens and what he would have made of the Cazale Ravenna. But they would never know now.

What she understood more acutely now than ever was that the Nico she'd fallen in love with was still here, except this was a man still in mourning. He was still grieving for his loss, and somehow she had lost sight of that along the way.

"So, you see," said Elsa, looking into the distance, "sometimes things happen the way they do because it's just the way they're meant to happen. You can try all you want to line up the bricks a certain way but if something's not going to happen, it's not going to happen."

Her mom was right.

"Where has she disappeared to now?" asked Elsa, looking around.

"Who, Ingrid? She's over there." Ava pointed to the hotel entrance.

Elsa squinted. "What's she doing there?"

"She might want to have a look at the hotel," Nico suggested.

"She's entitled to enjoy this day, too, Mom," said Ava. "And Elisabetta is asleep."

"In that case," said Elsa, getting up. "I'll take Elisabetta off her hands so that she can have a good look." She set off.

"You're going to have to tell your Mom to back off a little, if you want Ingrid to last longer than a week." Nico moved closer to her on the bench.

"She's a grandmother, she's just being overly protective. I'll work on her—either that or we'll have to find her a distraction."

"Salvatore and the lemon trees might do it." Nico slipped his arm around her waist.

"We should go and mingle," she said, not wanting to move from him.

"We should." But he didn't move. "I'm thinking of putting up a few small buildings."

"Where?"

"See that space there?" He pulled her to the side and directed her attention to the lane of cypress trees in the distance. "There."

She frowned. "For what?"

"For our painting and cooking classes."

"Painting and cooking classes?" Ava asked, in surprise. This was the first she'd heard of it.

"Look at it, Ava. It would be the perfect spot to have them there." She looked, but she couldn't see what he could. Couldn't imagine what he could, and maybe that was his strong suit.

"We could entice a whole new group of people. There is so much land here," he said, excitement infusing his words. "I could offer so much more. Ravenna doesn't seem like a spa haven. People know it for its mausoleums and basilicas decorated with mosaics but I want it to be known for something else. A haven, a place to unwind and relax and it doesn't always have to be about treatments and massages. My father liked to cook, as well as to do gardening, and your mother likes to paint."

"I wouldn't say it's a passion of hers ..." Ava stopped. "Did these ideas come from your father and my mother?"

"I got to thinking of ways in which people like to relax. Not everyone wants to put a mashed-up avocado on their face. I can give them alternatives and the more I can offer in a place like this, somewhere people wouldn't think to visit, the more it would make my hotel more desirable."

She turned to him. "Your hotel is already desirable. I don't know why you worry about the location."

"It's not Santorini, or Sicily or Amalfi. Those will come later."

"Nico." She shook her head. "You're doing it again. You remember what I told you about taking things—"

But he didn't let her finish. Instead he dropped a chaste kiss on her lips. "Slow. I know," he said. "But not so slow that I lose the excitement, and not so fast that I forget what matters the most." He kissed her hand, still entwined in his.

"I won't let you forget what matters the most," she said.

They stood a while and watched their guests, heard their laughter and chatter, saw the gardens filled with merriment. Nico would continue with his quest, only now she hoped he didn't feel the need to prove anything to anyone.

In a short space of time they had grown together, and grown stronger, in spite of their struggles. As long as they were together, it wouldn't matter where they were, which project he turned his attention to, what dramas awaited her with the store; they would grow old together. A prickle of shivers crept along her bare arms and she flinched involuntarily.

"Cold?" he asked, rubbing her arm.

"Happy."

"I didn't think it would keep on growing," he said, finally, as his lips turned up into a half-smile.

Her brows pinched together in question. "What?"

"What I feel here." He lifted her entwined hand to his heart. "For you, for Elisabetta. It makes me want to make the world a better place. I don't know if building hotels makes the world a better place. Maybe it doesn't but—"

"*You* make my world a better place, Nico."

"That's all I ever wanted to do from that first day I saw you, when you'd lost your luggage."

How did he do that? How did his words touch her heart so deeply that she wanted to cry tears of joy? She nudged closer to him. "We should get back to our guests." It was the second time she'd said this, but they hadn't quite managed it, always finding their own way and veering off.

"Elisabetta might have woken up and she'll be looking for us," he said, squeezing her hand as they walked along the stone pathway. "I want to carry her around and show her off to everyone."

His pride in what *they* had created was written all over him.

"You can show her off all you want," she said, content to play second fiddle to her daughter.

. . .

Thank you for reading BABY STEPS! I hope you've enjoyed Nico and Ava's epic love story. I have written a **bonus epilogue** which takes place over a decade later.

Click the link below to get the bonus!
https://www.lilyzante.com/newsletterhr

While BABY STEPS concludes their journey, you can still get glimpses into their lives in the spin-off series, ITALIAN SUMMER, which tells about the lives and loves of the other characters: Rona, Andrea, Gina and Elsa. All six books are now available.

IT TAKES TWO is the first book in this series, and this is Rona and Carlos' story.

When the passion and excitement fizzles from a marriage ...

Rona loves her husband very much, but something is missing; the sparkle, the fairy dust and the magic. Her days are full of dirty laundry and diapers, and Carlos is always working. When Ava asks for her help back in Verona, she leaps at the chance.

Gioberti's restaurant with its charming waiters provide a pull that she finds hard to ignore. Besides, it's just a harmless flirtation, and nothing more. Right?

IT TAKES TWO is available everywhere

I appreciate your help in spreading the word, including telling a friend, and I would be grateful if you could leave a review on your favorite book site.

You can read an excerpt from IT TAKES TWO below.

Thank you and happy reading!

Lily

EXCERPT FROM IT TAKES TWO

"Can I buy you a drink?"

Rona glanced at the tall stranger with his unkempt hair and eyes so intense that a lesser diva would have melted. She assessed him casually, appeared to consider his offer but shook her head even though she enjoyed the way he looked at her. "I'm good, thanks."

"I bet you're not that good. Not really. Not dressed like that." His gaze dropped to the deep V of her turquoise top and he licked his lips in appreciation.

"I'm old enough to buy my own drinks."

"I'm sure you're old enough to do a lot of things."

This guy wasn't shy. She held up her left hand so he could see her wedding ring.

"My husband thinks I am." She picked up the pitcher of Margarita in one hand and a pitcher of mint Mojito in the other and walked away.

"If you ever get lonely ..." He shouted after her. She sashayed back to the table where her friends were waiting; three pairs of wide-open eyes stared back at her.

"You've still got it, girlfriend," Mercedes commented as she refilled her empty glass. "What's your secret?"

"The five-two diet," said Rona. "It works, I'm telling you." She held up her cocktail glass. "May our girls' nights out never end—even when we're old and past it."

They all tapped their glasses lightly with hers.

"Amen," said Mercedes, solemnly. As a mother of two children under the age of five, these nights out were her life buoy.

"I'll get the drinks next time," said Celine, turning to give the man a good once over. At twenty-seven, she was the youngest of them all. She was still desperately trying to find 'the one' and had been single for nearly three months.

"I tried that diet, but it didn't work for me. Besides, I hate being told what I can and can't eat," lamented Jodi.

"Why would you bother trying? You'll be pregnant soon enough," said Celine, carelessly.

A silence hushed their carefree chatter.

"I'm not pregnant *yet* and we've been trying for months," complained Jodi, refilling her glass.

"I bet you're having fun trying," sniggered Celine. "I know I would if I had a man." Her smile vanished just as quickly. Rona rolled her eyes at Jodi. *Celine and her endless quest for A Man.*

"How come we had to keep rearranging tonight?" asked Jodi. Rona let out a low groan. "Ava," she reminded them.

"She kept you busy, huh?" asked Celine. "Maybe I need to get myself to Italy and get me a fine specimen of a man just like the one she has." Her friends knew Ava and they were all fully up to date with her exploits in Italy which had now resulted in a baby on the way as well as an impending wedding to one of the most eligible and handsome men in Verona. She was their icon. All, except Rona's.

"She's a slave driver," complained Rona. Her sister had returned to Denver briefly in order to resolve some of the issues with her online store. It was expanding too fast for her to keep up and now that she was going to live in Italy, she had to come up with a solution for handling her US operations.

Rona picked up her cocktail glass. It wasn't her problem now. The only problem she had was one called Kim.

The problem being that she wasn't a virtual assistant anymore.

Mercedes wanted to know. "How's it working out—this other woman and you? You said she was a pain in the butt."

"She still is a pain in the butt," Rona confirmed. She'd suffered while her mother had been in Verona. Carlos could only look after Tori one weekday, and the order numbers had exploded. Some days she'd take Tori with her and put her in the playpen in the kitchen, just so she could get some work done. Other times she'd do the unthinkable: start work at six in the morning and work until around eleven, leaving Tori with Carlos. Since he worked in this family's restaurant business, he often started work late and finished late. But during Ava's recent visit, she had employed Kim, who was once her virtual assistant, to help out with order processing, as well as dealing with customer queries.

"Now you're sharing the work?" Celine asked.

"She does a few days and I do a few days. Different days," Rona quickly added.

"It's working?"

"I don't have to see the woman," Rona smiled.

"How old is she?" asked Jodi, curious.

"Twenty-seven."

"And her son?"

"Is eight."

"No way!"

"She married?"

"Single mom."

"Wow," said Mercedes, her eyes wide with admiration. "That must be so hard. I bet she's really ambitious."

"Getting knocked up at nineteen doesn't sound too ambitious to me," retorted Rona, flicking her nails. "Anyhow, I only have to work two days a week now. It was killing me having to work every day."

"I bet," said Mercedes. She'd given up work the moment she'd had her firstborn and had no intention of returning. "By the way, your haircut suits you. It makes you look younger."

"I didn't realize I looked older before," Rona replied, running her fingers through her light brown hair. Previously long and layered it had now been stylishly cut to just below her shoulders. She couldn't resist swishing it around—just like the models did in those hair ads.

But Carlos hadn't even noticed until she'd forcefully stood in his way. "What?" he'd asked, frowning at her.

"Notice anything?"

"You look happier?" he'd commented, clueless.

"Anything else?" she'd asked, giving her head a jiggle.

"It's colored? And...it's...shorter," he cried in dismay. "Aww, baby, why did you go and do that for?" It hadn't been the response she'd been looking for.

"I loved your hair the way it was before." He'd told her.

She pushed thoughts of Carlos out of her mind and glanced over at the bar again. The tall stranger had been watching her and he raised his glass to her. She raised hers in return.

"Are you going to encourage him?" said Celine, irritated.

"I'm not encouraging him. He knows I'm married." replied Rona.

"Some men don't care," remarked Mercedes.

"Why don't you go over and start talking to him if you're so desperate to meet a guy?" Rona shifted her gaze from the stranger to her friend. Celine couldn't stomach it when any of the others, all married, got attention she thought she deserved on account of her single status.

"Nice to be noticed," sighed Jodi.

"What diet was that again?" Mercedes asked. "I can't diet to save my life. The only time I lose weight is when I stop breast feeding."

"Yeah," agreed Rona. "Apparently it's meant to fall off then. So I heard." Not that she'd breastfed Tori. Breasts, in her opinion, were for adult use and she was relieved she'd never let a baby near hers. Tori had done just fine with infant formula.

"Don says he wants another one," said Mercedes, her face contorting.

"Really?" asked Jodi, wincing.

"He wants four," said Mercedes, matter-of-factly.

"Ouch," said Rona, pulling a face. "How many do *you* want?"

"I don't mind. If he wants more, why not?"

"But do *you* want more?" asked Rona. It wasn't as though they were talking about a bag of sweets here. She couldn't imagine agreeing to another child or three just because Carlos thought it would be *nice to have*. She couldn't put her body through nine months of hell to be followed by hours of blood loss, damage to her sensitive parts and months of inconvenience afterwards. Not getting nine hours of uninterrupted sleep for months was bad enough.

"This is when sex gets scary," remarked Celine. Kids weren't in her game plan yet.

"He says he comes from a family of three, and that three is an odd number. So he wants two or four. But now that we've got two, he kinda likes the idea of having two more. It'll be even then."

"But what do you think?" asked Rona, intrigued.

"It's okay with me. The other two are going to be at school soon enough and it'll be nice having another one around the house."

"It would be nice to do *nothing* while the other two are at school," remarked Rona. She loved Tori more than she ever thought was possible, but she hadn't considered baby number two yet. She wasn't sure she ever would.

"Do you really need to have more poop to clean up?" asked Celine. "It seems that's all babies do all day long. Be little poop machines."

The bartender came up to them just then with a round of drinks identical to the ones that Rona had ordered. "Compliments of the gentleman at the bar." He looked over to Rona's admirer at the bar and then put down four cocktail glasses: two Margaritas and two Mojitos.

"The evening just got better," exclaimed Jodi, and grabbed hers.

"Thank you," said Celine and held her glass up to the guy who was watching them from the bar. She nodded her head appreciatively.

"I really shouldn't," said Mercedes. "But, heck, we might end up making more babies soon, so I might as well drink up now." She gave the man her best smile.

Only Rona could see that he'd kept his gaze on her the whole time. She picked up her glass and walked over to him.

Bam! She slammed it down. "I told you, I'm good. I can get my own drinks. Thank you, anyway."

He appeared amused by her response and grabbed her wrist as she turned to go. She raised her chin and stared at his eyes that now sparkled like diamonds. She enjoyed this thrill

—the chase, the knowledge that she still had it—the ability to turn heads. It excited her, especially knowing that it would go nowhere, but also to know that she was still desirable.

This easy flirtation warmed her insides.

"Do you mind?" she asked, breaking her arm from his firm grip.

He lifted an eyebrow. "You're a feisty little one, aren't you? I've seen you here before."

"You must get out a lot," she said sarcastically, leaning back against the stool next to him, not quite making herself at home, but not ready to go back to the girls just yet. She wanted to bask in a little sparring banter first. "Because I don't come here often."

"I know. Like I said, I've noticed you here before. I don't know if it's those hooped earrings, or," his gaze trailed down the length of her body again. "The way your clothes seem to hug that mighty fine body of yours," his lips parted as he licked them. He was handsome, in a rough cowboy sort of way. Nothing fine boned about him. Rough, and rugged. Kind of what she'd thought about Carlos when they'd first met. He'd rescued her from a fracas that her group of friends had gotten mixed up in. Carlos had dived right in and pulled her away from the fray.

"Do you often pick up married women?"

"We're just talking," he smiled. "And drinking. That's all."

"You come here alone?"

"I'm meeting some buddies of mine."

"Well, it's been nice talking to you and thank you for the drink but—"

"It's on me," he said and refused to take it back. "I promise you it hasn't been spiked. Ask this guy here," he nodded at the bartender who grinned at her as he wiped a glass.

"Nothing wrong with it I swear."

She smiled and wrapped her fingers around the ice cold rim. It made her feel good, always being the one to get noticed, especially when she was out with her friends.

Ruben had noticed her too, but she'd been alone then, in Verona. Alone and bored and often forcing a smile at Gioberti's lame jokes.

"Take it, no strings attached," the stranger insisted, and dragged her into the present, back in Denver.

"Just so we're clear: I'm not that kind of girl."

"If you say so."

She took the drink and sauntered back to the girls.

"Well?" asked Mercedes.

Rona shrugged. There was nothing to say.

"What'd he say?" asked Jodi, chewing on a cuticle.

"Not much." Rona twisted a lock of hair around her finger.

"How come you get hit on all the time and I don't?" wailed Celine. "Maybe I need to try the five-two diet."

Rona placed the cocktail glass next to her half empty one and smiled. She still had it, she thought, feeling smug with herself.

IT TAKES TWO is available everywhere

BOOKLIST

Honeymoon Series: Take a roller-coaster journey of emotional highs and lows in this story of love and loss, family and relationships. When Ava is dumped six weeks before her Valentine's Day wedding, she has no idea of the life that awaits her in Italy.

Honeymoon for One
Honeymoon for Three
Honeymoon Blues
Honeymoon Bliss
Baby Steps
Honeymoon Series (Books 1-3)

Italian Summer Series: This is a spin-off from the Honeymoon Series. These books tell the stories of the secondary characters who first appeared in the Honeymoon Series. Nico and Ava also appear in these books.

It Takes Two
All That Glitters

Fool's Gold
Roman Encounter
November Sun
New Beginnings
Italian Summer Series (Books 1-4)

The Billionaire's Love Story: This is a Cinderella story with a touch of Jerry Maguire. What happens when the billionaire with too much money meets the single mom with too much heart?

The Promise (FREE)
The Gift, Book 1
The Gift, Book 2
The Gift, Book 3
The Gift, Boxed Set (Books 1, 2 & 3)
The Offer, Book 1
The Offer, Book 2
The Offer, Book 3
The Offer, Boxed Set (Books 1, 2 & 3)
The Vow, Book 1
The Vow, Book 2
The Vow, Book 3
The Vow, Boxed Set (Books 1, 2 & 3)

Indecent Intentions: This is a spin-off from The Billionaire's Love story. This 2-book set consists of 2 standalone stories about the billionaire's playboy brother. The 2nd story is about a wealthy nightclub owner who shuns relationships.

The Bet
The Hookup

Indecent Intentions 2-Book Set

The Seven Sins: A series of seven standalone romances based on the seven sins. Emotional, and angsty romances which are loosely connected.

Underdog (FREE prequel)
The Wrath of Eli
The Problem with Lust
The Lies of Pride
The Price of Inertia
The Other Side of Greed
The Seven Sins Books 1-3

A Perfect Match Series: This is a seven book series in which the first four books feature the same couple. High-flying corporate executive Nadine has no time for romance but her life takes a turn for the better when she meets Ethan, a sexy and struggling metal sculptor five years younger. He works as an escort in order to make the rent. Books 4-6 are standalone romances based on characters from the earlier books. The main couple, Ethan and Nadine, appear in all books:

Lost in Solo (prequel)
The Proposal
Heart Sync
A Leap of Faith
A Perfect Match Series Books 1-3
Misplaced Love
Reclaiming Love
Embracing Love
A Perfect Match Series (Books 4-6)

Standalone Books:

Tomorrow Belongs to Us
Love Among the Ruins
Love Inc
An Unexpected Gift

ACKNOWLEDGMENTS

I would like to thank my wonderful group of proofreaders who help polish my manuscript and eliminate the errors, typos, weird words and phrases which often find their way into my story. These ladies give me the confidence to release each book and I am eternally grateful for their help and support:

Sherrie Brown
Marcia Chamberlain
Nancy Dormanski
April Lowe
Dena Pugh
Charlotte Rebelein
Carole Tunstall

I would also like to thank Tatiana Vila for creating my awesome covers:
www.viladesign.net

ABOUT THE AUTHOR

Lily Zante lives with her husband and three children somewhere near London, UK.

Connect with Me

I love hearing from you – so please don't be shy! Email me (lily@lilyzante.com), message me on Facebook or connect with me through these different platforms:

Instagram | Facebook | Twitter | Website

Follow me on Bookbub
Follow me on Goodreads
Follow me on TikTok
Join my FB Reader Group